E. R. WILLIAMS

Goblin Birth

The Natarin Chronicles Book One

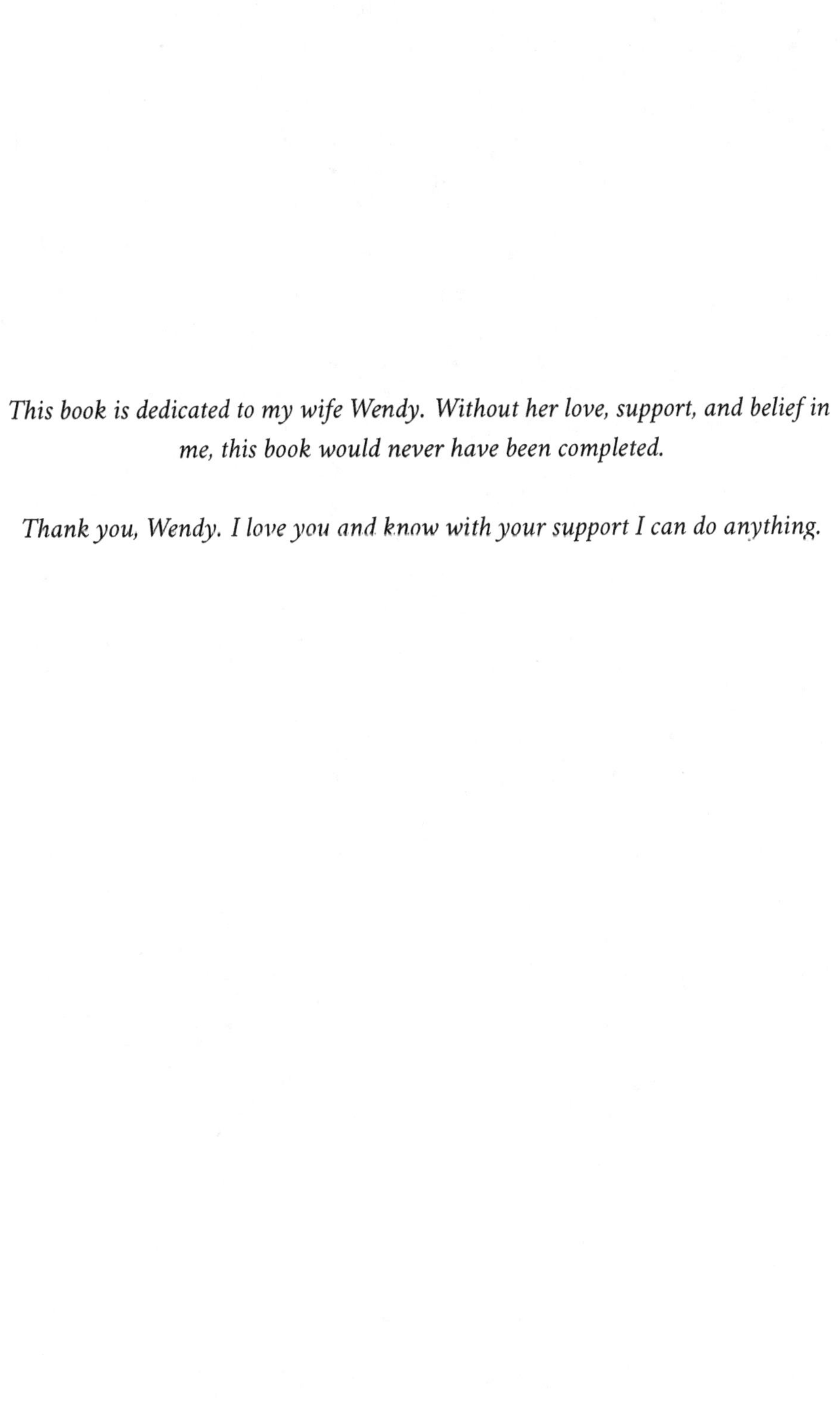

This book is dedicated to my wife Wendy. Without her love, support, and belief in me, this book would never have been completed.

Thank you, Wendy. I love you and know with your support I can do anything.

Contents

Acknowledgement

I would like to thank my beta readers for their valuable feedback. Thank you, Mark Matlock and Winston Barham.

Map of Natarin Continent

Prologue

Darmot placed a solid black stone on the altar in front of each of the dwarven chosen. He then walked to a podium that was on a raised platform in front of the main altar and began to chant. Soon a small blue light appeared on the wall in front of the participants. As the chant continued, the light started to grow until it covered the entire wall. Finally, the light shimmered, and the wall disappeared. Where the wall had been, there was now a plain of solid white light underneath a black sky. Several dark forms were moving at the edge of the light horizon. Six of the forms formed a line and began moving toward the ritual participants. Darmot continued chanting as the forms continued to advance. His chant grew louder and louder as the forms drew closer and closer. When the forms arrived at the edge of the plain, they stopped.

Darmot turned and faced the kneeling dwarves. He began backing towards the plain of light. When his heels reached the plain, he stopped, and excruciating pain shot through his body. Darmot raised his left arm and pointed at the first of the black stones on the altar. Immediately, the first of the dark forms began to enter him. The pain was incredible. Never had he experienced anything like this. His body revolted at the pain, but at the same time, he relished every moment of it. The form filled him, and he could feel it moving through and out of his outstretched finger. The form tried to draw him with it, but he willed himself to stay put. It wasn't a physical need to move, but his spirit was being called. He forced his spirit to remain in his body as the form finished exiting him. When it was gone, Darmot felt empty and alone.

But only for a moment; no sooner had the first form left him than the second entered. Now the pain increased. Darmot watched as the first form traveled across the room and entered the black stone. The stone began to glow. Purple bands of light shot from the stone to the eyes of the dwarf kneeling in front of it. The form used the beams from the stones to pass into the dwarf. The body dwarf began to change. Darmot could no longer watch; the second form was leaving him now and again calling for his spirit to follow. It took all his concentration to resist this powerful call. The second form moved from his finger into the second black stone.

The third and fourth forms tried to enter him at the same time. This pain was almost too much to bear. He almost passed out from the intensity. He refused to let a simple weakness diminish his pleasure. The fourth form backed away, and the process continued. Each form entered Darmot, passed through him, and then entered one of the stones. They moved up the purple beams of light from the stones into the waiting dwarves. By the sixth, resisting the pull of the exiting form was growing easier. He knew to expect it and would prepare himself before the call came.

Darmot had never felt such power. The forms were using him to help themselves be born. He was the hand of Duater, the Spirit of the Underworld. He felt he could do anything while possessed by the power of the white plain. When the last of the forms had left him, he reluctantly moved off the white plain and changed his chant. The wall reappeared, and the light began to diminish. When the light had gone, Darmot relaxed. He felt exhausted, and his skin was tingling. It seemed even the torchlight was painful.

He crossed to where the dwarves were kneeling. The dwarves had changed, their skin tone had gone from a light brown to a pale green, and the males had lost their beards. They stood with a slight slump forward, giving their backs a slight hump. Their arms were strong, and their hands ended in sharp claws. Fangs stuck out over their bottom lips, and their eyes glowed yellow with light from within.

Darmot noticed he had changed too. His skin had darkened and felt sensitive. The torchlight was like tiny needles sticking to him. He relished this slight pain as a reminder of the delicious agony he had just experienced.

"My children, you are given new life. This life is given to you by your lord Duater, Spirit of the Underworld. I am Darmot, his priest, your maker, and your master. You have been made to serve me. Serve me well, and you will receive rewards beyond your imagination. Fail me, and what has been made can be unmade. You will be known as goblin, which in the ancient language of this temple means raised dwarf. For you have been raised to a new level of existence by Duater through me."

Chapter 1

Leaana pulled herself out of the small pool, walking to the small fire she had made upon her arrival. The fire provided the only light this far into the cave. As she warmed and dried herself, Leanna reflected on how much she enjoyed these swims, far from the commotion of encampment life. The times she spent alone in the cave were the only moments of peace and quiet she could genuinely enjoy.

The light flared around her as she threw another log onto the fire. She squeezed water from her long hair and prepared for the task of braiding it into the traditional pattern for her position and family. Her hair was the main cause of her problems. If only she did not have the marks in her hair. The long white streak of hair that ran down the left side of her head ended in brown tips as if the spirits had dipped it in brown paint. The white streak was the birthmark that only the ones chosen by the animal spirits of her people were supposed to have. It indicated one chosen to lead the people but also one who would go through life with an animal companion with whom they shared a special bond and communion.

What was curious, though, was that the mark had always appeared only on males. Leaana's twin brother, Sagan, also bore the mark. He also had a familiar, Togan, a large white wolf. Sagan claimed to be able to smell and hear what Togan did, but Leaana was never sure she believed that. The mark made Sagan honored among her people. He was a strong hunter and truly knowledgeable in the ways of the land. He would, one day, be a good leader, she thought.

For Leanna, however, the mark had brought nothing but trouble. Being the only girl to ever have the mark made her feared by those in her encampment. Feared or pitied, she was not sure which. She had never been treated the same as the other girls. Not that she really minded much. She liked being different. Enjoyed that she had not been trained in the traditional female arts of weaving and cooking. Leaana had taught herself to cook and thought she was quite good at it, as did Sagan and Togan. However, no one seemed to know quite what to do with her. Most everyone, except Sagan, ignored her. However, Sagan took the time to find out her interests and train her privately in tracking and using a bow.

There, one of the two braids finished. Two braids because she was second born. Sagan only wore one braid because he was born four seconds earlier. The second braid is the most complex, for it must also include the brown and green ribbons that are the colors of her family. Sagan can wear the brown and green colors any way he wants. Generally, he wears them woven as a belt, but Leaana must wear them in her hair since she is female.

The warmth from the fire felt good on her bare shoulders and chest. Soon she and Sagan must go on their rites of passage into adulthood. Sagan had been preparing for the traditional trials of a familiar. These trials involved going into the wilderness and living alone with their animal guide for a full turning of the moon. The goal was to learn the ways of their animal and gain wisdom. Leaana had overheard some of the elders talking about her rites. Since she too had the marking, should they send her with Sagan just in case the spirits did choose her, or should she do more of a traditional rite for a female in the encampment? Should she do some combination of the two? No one seemed to know. If only she didn't have this blasted mark, perhaps then she could have some peace.

Leaana tied the final knot in the second braid and sighed as she realized her reprieve was almost over. She threw the last log on the fire. She would let this log burn almost completely out before going back. While it burned, she would enjoy the warmth the fire provided her bare skin and the peaceful solitude she rarely enjoyed.

As the flames danced merrily in the air, the wood began to crackle. Leaana laid on her tunic, which was spread across the stone floor to protect her from the chill. Here she could think and try to figure out her life. Sagan knew what his life would be like from the moment he was born. The mark predicted it. They were both born with the mark. For nearly a hundred turns of the four seasons, the encampment of Romin had been without a familiar. Then, she was born with the same mark, except for the brown on the tips of her white patch. Sagan's mark was the traditional solid white streak down the left side, as mentioned in the ancient writings in Mayan, the healer's hut.

The writings told the history of all the familiars that have existed since the people began to write. In fact, it was a familiar long ago that started the chronology. Every time a child was born with the mark, it had been a familiar. In every case, the mark had been the same, all white and on a male child. Never had there been a mark with a second color, and never, never, in all those turnings of the seasons, had there been a girl born with the mark. After her birth, Mayan had spent months poring over the writings to decide if Leaana's mark meant anything. In the past, when a familiar had a twin, typically only one had the mark and thus was chosen by an animal companion. There was mention of one incident, over 3,000 turnings ago, of male twins both having the mark and both receiving animal companions.

But she was a girl and had not received an animal companion. Togan had chosen Sagan very early on. The earlier the animal chooses you, traditionally, the stronger the familiar. When Sagan was only five, he was chosen by Togan. Historically, the earliest choosing was at age three, and the latest was at age thirteen. Leaana was now sixteen and still had not been chosen by an animal spirit, even though she had the mark, or, at least, almost had the mark. If only the people of Romin would treat her as if she was totally accepted, not some outcast that no one knew what to do with.

The last log was about to burn out. Leaana stood up and put on her tunic, the soft leather sliding easily over her skin, returning the warmth she had given to it by lying on it. She began to make her way back to the cave entrance with the glow of the coals supplying enough light to see the path and avoid the rocks that threatened to trip her.

Chapter 2

Sagan sniffed the air. The smell of the deer was stronger, which meant they were getting closer. The first time Sagan learned he could use his wolf familiar's sense of smell, he almost went mad. The number of odors that assaulted his nose was overwhelming. It took a long time and lots of practice to get to where he could pick out the one scent he wanted. Learning how to use this to help track an animal while hunting took even longer. Now, though, it was second nature, just like listening to a particular voice out of many in a crowded tent.

The deer was moving away. Sagan started walking in the direction the deer was heading, careful to stay downwind. He and Togan moved silently through the trees. Sagan was glad that his wolf familiar had insisted on coming along. He was also slightly annoyed that Togan had insisted they leave Sagan's horse, Karr, at home. Togan had not directly said, "Karr must stay here," the communication with his familiar didn't work quite that way. It was more of a feeling, and the quick snap from Togan's jaws when he had gone toward the grazing field for the horse sealed the deal. Karr was not welcome on this hunt for some reason.

Sniffing the air again, the deer stopped by a stream to drink. Togan sat down to wait for a moment, and Sagan glanced over to study his four-legged companion. Togan was truly a magnificent creature. Standing nearly four feet tall at the shoulders, Togan was the largest wolf that Sagan had ever seen. His all-white coat glistened where the sunlight landed on it, fading to gray in the shadows from the overhanging limbs. His head was as wide as an ax blade, with jaws powerful enough to snap a tree limb the size of

Sagan's arm. Finally, long, strong legs that could run for days without tiring completed the package of this, his closest companion.

Togan got up and moved forward again, and Sagan followed slowly, sniffing the air. The deer was still by the small stream. They could see it now, a tall stag standing in a small break in the trees by a clear blue stream. The deer was brown with a white underbelly. The antlers atop its head were massive and scarred from battles fought with other stags. Quickly, Sagan tried to count the horn points. Twenty-five? No, twenty-six. An old deer that had survived many a hunt. But not this one; Sagan took the bow from his back and selected an arrow.

Suddenly, Togan darted out of the trees and barked once, startling the stag into running for the trees. Sagan looked dumbfounded at his wolf companion. What was Togan doing? That was the perfect shot! Togan was running after the deer, now in a full sprint, pausing only momentarily to look back to Sagan as if to say, "Follow." Then, Togan disappeared into the trees after the stag.

Trying to understand what was happening, Sagan took off after Togan. Then, without realizing it, Sagan started to run faster and faster. Now he was gaining on Togan and the deer. Stunned at his new-found speed, Sagan wondered how it was possible. And then he felt it, the feeling of Togan coursing through him. Somehow, Togan was letting Sagan tap into his strength and speed. Reveling in this new-found ability, Sagan ran as hard as he could, nimbly dodging trees and bushes and easily jumping over underbrush and fallen tree branches.

Sagan quickly closed the gap separating him from his four-legged teacher and their prey. Running side by side with his wolf counterpart, Sagan was amazed at how easily they kept up with the stag. Suddenly, the deer changed direction, cutting across Sagan's path. He and Togan adjusted quickly and continued the pursuit. The deer's desperate move to elude them had only brought his pursuers closer.

Sagan could hear the stag's footsteps thundering in his ears. He could smell the fear in the animal. Never had he been so in tune with his wolf senses. He could also feel Togan, his blood lust driving them both faster.

The deer faltered and started to slow. Sagan and Togan drew even with their prey. Sagan wanted to forget about the hunt and just run with this new found speed forever. Never had he felt such power. Sagan wanted to revel in this new sensation, drink it all in. Then he felt a sense of urgency in Togan, and the desire for the kill overwhelmed him.

Sagan pulled his large hunting knife from its sheath. He plunged the knife into the stag's throat, and simultaneously, Togan closed his powerful jaws onto the opposite side of the stag's neck. Sagan pulled the knife free and slammed it in again; this time he felt it hit bone. The stag started to stumble. Leaping off the ground, Sagan threw himself onto the stag's back and thrust the knife in again and again. Togan jumped and clamped his iron-like jaws on the stag's windpipe. Overwhelmed, the enormous stag collapsed, its final breath being crushed out of it by the wolf.

Sagan jumped off the stag right before the massive creature's body would have crushed his legs. Landing on his side, Sagan rolled to his feet and looked at their prize. Togan was still clamped to the creature's throat. Sagan could taste the blood in Togan's mouth. Never had he felt his familiar's feelings so strongly. Now he was filled with a primal desire to feed. Before Sagan could stop himself, he was on all fours trying desperately to rip open the stag's throat with his teeth. Finding one of the wounds made by his knife, Sagan ripped off a mouthful of raw meat and began to chew.

The taste of the blood was salty and metallic in his mouth. Swallowing the first bite, he bent down for a second. As his mouth closed on another mouthful of raw meat, Sagan realized what he was doing. He pulled back, spitting the meat out of his mouth, and collected himself. Togan released his hold on the deer as the last of its lifeblood fell onto the ground.

Sagan stared in wonder at Togan as blood dripped down his face. The wolf looked crazed, his white fur stained in places from the blood of the kill and his muzzle drenched and dripping. Sagan suddenly realized how tired he was. He had to sleep, absolutely had to sleep. He could no longer feel Togan's strength and speed in him. Sagan looked over and noticed Togan was lying down, exhausted as well.

Sagan now understood. While Togan could share his strength and speed with him for a brief while, it would drain them both to the point of exhaustion. As with every revelation he had about the desires and teaching of his familiar, he didn't fully understand how he knew this; he just did. It was as if the animal spoke to him, but that didn't really describe the way they communicated. So today was just another valuable lesson from his furry, loving teacher.

Sagan crawled over to Togan and laid down. "Thank you, teacher, for this lesson. Now, since you are so smart, how in the world am I going to get this deer back to the Romin?"

Togan raised his head and licked Sagan's face. Sagan threw his arm over Togan, closed his eyes, and fell asleep instantly.

Chapter 3

Mayan was in the council circle of the spirits. All the leaders of the animal kingdom surrounded him. However, Sheta the bear, Roma the wolf, and Arina, the eagle, were deep in conversation about Sagan and Leaana.

Sheta, Mayan's guide in the spirit world, addressed him. "Mayan, their rites must be completed together. Sagan and Leaana must journey into adulthood together."

"But Sheta," Mayan protested, "Sagan is a familiar, and Leaana is not. Tradition dictates that he goes alone."

"Make your council of elders see that they must go together." Arina screeched. "If Leaana is to fulfill her destiny, she must journey with Togan."

"It will be difficult to convince the council," Mayan said. "Can you tell me why?"

"Mayan!" Roma snapped, growling as he spoke. "You know better than to ask. You have visited our council circle many times over the years. You know the ways. We were hesitant to intervene this much, but it was necessary. Now go back. You know what you must do."

Mayan sat straight up in bed, thrown from his sleep by the disturbing dream. The dream was still crystal clear. Indeed, Mayan knew what he must do. He must convince the council, but it would not be easy. There was no precedent for what he was going to ask, and there would not be any support. He couldn't even tell them about the vision. To do so would offend the spirits and cause hardship to Romin. He had learned that lesson the hard way years ago.

He must get up. Only two days before the rites began, there was much to do. Only two days to win this battle. He prayed that would be enough time for the sake of the encampment and for Leaana.

Chapter 4

Fataso placed the leather glove on his left hand and unlatched the cage door. Inside the cage, a large, golden brown eagle looked intently at her handler.

"Come, Aramin, my beauty!" Fataso exclaimed. "It is time for a little exercise. We start our journey for the Arctana, the Northern Elf Kingdom, tomorrow. We have been chosen by the Falconer's Guild to represent them at this year's festival."

"Shraack," Aramin cries.

"Yes, I know!" Fataso responded. "It is a tremendous honor. I would love to say that all my years of hard work and faithful service to the Guild have finally paid off. After all, I have been a guild member for two hundred years now, you know. But, alas, I know that this honor is yours. Your skill, strength, and beauty are the merits that have awarded us this honor."

"Now, I have been asked by the Guild to bring the best bird from each Falconer for the show. You, however, will be the highlight. Your majestic wingspan, beautiful golden-brown feathers, the speed with which you dive, and agility will delight and amaze our friends in the north. Now, enough of this idle chit-chat. To work!"

Fataso reached his gloved hand into the cage. Aramin lifted one large, yellow foot and gracefully stepped onto the outstretched hand. The long black talons curved gently around the tan leather glove, closing just tight enough for a secure perch but not too tight to hurt her handler. Once secure, she took her other foot off the cage perch and settled comfortably on the gloved hand. Fataso reached his right hand into a small leather pouch tied about his waist. He removed a small piece of raw meat and gave it to Aramin. Aramin closed her beak around it hungrily. While Aramin devoured her treat, Fataso placed a small black hood over the eagle's eyes so she would not be startled by the movement out of the cage and over to the practice area. The hood starkly contrasted the light golden brown of the eagle's feathers. Fataso remembered he wanted to make a new hood of a lighter color to blend in with the bird better. Perhaps he could make it during their journey north.

During the short walk to the practice area, Aramin took a moment to stretch her massive wings. Her wingspan was almost five feet. Her wings made for an impressive and intimidating sight when Aramin was in flight. The eagle could easily be seen from the back of large crowds as she performed many of her maneuvers. Seeing an eagle perform as a falconry bird was rare, as their size made the necessary sharp turns very difficult.

Aramin had proved to be an exception to this rule. While she could not turn as sharply as a falcon or hawk, she could turn much sharper than the average eagle. With a few modifications to the standard fare, and one spectacular feat designed to showcase the eagle's diving abilities, Fataso had created a show that had never failed to astound audiences, even other Falconers.

Reaching the practice area, Fataso removed the hood from Aramin's eyes and lifted his arm above his head. Instantly, Aramin took to the air, flapping her mighty wings and soaring higher with each stroke. Once she was a few hundred feet up, Aramin stretched her wings and began a smooth glide, riding the gentle breezes stirring over the open practice field. Then, after a few moments, she gracefully executed another turn, taking her back toward Fataso.

Fataso issued a quick, high-pitched whistle, signaling the show to begin. In response, Aramin began a gentle dive that took her just in front of the old elf. After soaring past Fataso, the eagle started to climb again. Reaching her original height, Aramin turned around and dove again. This time, the dive took her behind Fataso, midway down the elf's back. Again, after rushing back upwards, she quickly reached the apex of her flight.

Fataso let out two quick whistles and reached his hand into the small leather pouch, grabbing a piece of the meat stored there. Aramin began a sharp dive, and Fataso tossed the small piece of meat into the air. Changing direction slightly, Aramin caught the meat in her beak as she swooped past Fataso in a blur of golden brown. After reaching the proper distance, she watched Fataso to see what he would do next. Fataso threw another piece of meat into the air, and Aramin again dove down and caught the meat before it touched the ground. This exercise was repeated again and again. After sufficient time had passed, Fataso felt it was time to practice the next trick. He reached into the pouch again; however, this time Fataso pulled out a small stuffed squirrel with a string around its mid-section and dropped it to the ground.

As Aramin lazily drifted above the practice field, Fataso rehearsed explaining the next trick to the crowd as he took a few steps to the side. When he finished his explanation, Fataso whistled. This time, the whistle was low in pitch and not as short as the first one. Aramin instantly began searching the ground. Finding the squirrel lying in the dirt, she quickly dove for the target. With hunter instincts taking over, Aramin tucked her wings and quickly became a blur of motion. Fataso, watching closely, yanked on the small string attached to the squirrel and popped it from the ground and into the air. Aramin, screeching as she dove for her quarry, caught the squirrel as it was falling mere inches off the ground.

Fataso pulled on the string, still attached to the squirrel, to stop Aramin from escaping. Not willing to let go of her prize, Aramin was slowly pulled down within reach of Fataso. Reaching out with his gloved hand, Fataso grabbed the bird's talons. Using his other hand, he gave the bird of prey a small piece of meat from the pouch, a reward for her excellent performance. Aramin, enjoying her reward, released her hold on the squirrel and returned to her perch on the gloved hand.

"Outstanding job today, Aramin!" Fataso said. "If you perform like that at the festival, we will be the envy of everyone there. We may even get an audience at the Arctanan court."

Fataso placed the small black hood over the eagle's eyes and returned her to her cage. "Rest now," he said. "Tomorrow, we begin our journey to the north. It will be a long journey, but perhaps we will get to perform some on the way."

Chapter 5

Leaana emerged from the cave and looked up. The sky was bright, and the sun sat low on the horizon. "Oh no!" she thought. "It's almost night. Have I really been in there all afternoon? I have to get back!" Racing down the small hill, Leanna found Kada where she had left her. The horse was beautifully painted; her body was brown, the same color as the tips of Leaana's mark. She had a single white spot on her chest and a black spot above each rear leg. The horse was a magnificent sight. She picked her head up from the grass she had been nibbling to watch Leaana racing towards her.

"Sorry to do this to you in this heat, Kada, but you know how mom gets when I'm late for dinner."

Leaana quickly untied the reins from the dead tree and threw herself onto the horse's back. Digging her heels into Kada's sides, Leaana urged her mount into a fast run. In no time they crossed the small clearing that surrounded the cave entrance. Kada and Leaana raced into the trees, working frantically to dodge branches and bushes to keep the pace Leaana felt they needed to make it home. Eventually, Leaana realized she could not keep up this speed in the dense forest. She reluctantly pulled back on the reins to slow Kada. If Leaana didn't know better, she would have thought Kada had breathed a sigh of relief. Kada was now moving at a quick trot. It was still fast for this deep forest but manageable.

Leanna began to worry about not making it home on time. She remembered what happened the last time she was late. She had gotten home very late, and the family was almost finished with the evening meal when she finally made it home. She was instantly sent to bed without dinner, and her mother seemed very upset.

A short time later, Leaana was called from her room by her father, who had proceeded to spank her with the stiff leather strap he used for sharpening the family's knives. This particular memory caused her to increase Kada's pace as she reminisced.

With her back end sore and tingly, she had been made to wash the family dishes. Being left alone with her chore, Leaana thought about how severe her punishment had been. True, she was getting older, and with her increasing age, her punishments had increased in severity, but this seemed unusually harsh.

As Leaana finished the washing and began to dry the small wooden bowls and large flat stones used as plates, her father joined her.

"Leaana, I'm sorry for the severity of your punishment tonight. You're not a little girl anymore and must periodically be reminded of your responsibilities to the family. You must always remember to honor your family, both present and long-dead. Our ways and beliefs are old but have served us well for many years. Until you are grown and have added a family to your line, you must respect our ways and rules. Do you understand, my dear?"

"Yes, Pada, I understand, and I respect our ways. But…"

"Why did I use the strap on you?"

Leaana nodded.

"That was basically your mother's idea. You had her very worried. I had not thought the strap was necessary. After all, the meal was not over when you arrived. But, since even the hunters had returned to the encampment before you, your mother had thought something had happened to you. You know how she is when she gets an idea in her head. Had you not gotten back in the next few minutes, she would have called out all the hunters and even gotten me, Sagan, and Togan to go and search for you. You had her extremely worried. I would try to avoid her as much as possible tonight. Now, let me help you finish those dishes. Just don't tell your mother."

The explanation did nothing to ease her aching backside, but it did at least set her mind at ease. She would definitely make it a point to avoid her mother as much as possible for the rest of the night.

As Leaana was going to bed, her mother found her. Found her doesn't really describe the encounter; it was more like a hunter cornering her prey. Most of the family had already turned in. Leaana had been talking with Sagan in his room while petting Togan. She and Sagan were the only two people Togan allowed to touch him. When she left Sagan's room to go to hers, Leaana had to cross the family room. Her mother was standing in front of the fold of deer hide that served as the door to Leaana's room.

"Leaana, if you are ever that late again and worry me like that, then not only will you be washing our dishes but the dishes of the entire encampment! Now go to sleep, and I'll see you in the morning."

That was it. The matter was closed. Leaana's mother had ended the discussion before it ever began. She didn't fully believe she would have to wash the dishes of the entire encampment, but her mother had never been one for making empty threats. So, with this in mind, she decided it was best to get home quickly and not have to find out. Leaana dug her heels into Kada's side, urging her to go faster.

The days of being beaten for punishment were behind her now. Still, her mother was creative with punishments, so perhaps she would be made to wash the dishes of the entire encampment.

It would prove interesting if her mother tried to make good on her threat. Over the next several nights, Leaana would be forced to go from house to house doing the dinner dishes. Some dwellings would welcome her. That is the sort of thing that a girl of Leaana's age should be doing. Never mind the mark. It meant nothing. She was a girl and should do the work that all girls must do. As word spread of her duties, some families would probably save up a few nights worth just as an "I told you so."

Then there were the houses where she would not be welcomed. In these houses were those who believed she had indeed been marked. Washing the dishes was beneath her as a familiar, which would offend her animal guide. In fact, many of them believed she did this sort of work too much, and that is why her animal was so long in joining her. They would most likely save one or two dishes for her, but that would be it.

Leaana wasn't sure which she dreaded more, the houses where the workload would be greater. Or the ones where everyone would be on edge to keep from offending her or her non-existent animal guide.

Leaana was thrown from her reflections as she almost fell from Kada's back. Kada had made a quick turn to avoid running into a dogwood tree. The tree was showing the first of its white flowers, a sign that spring was truly here. Time to think about that later. For now, best to concentrate on riding. Pulling back on the reins again, she slowed their pace. Leaana didn't want to get home late and be sore from falling off Kada.

A short time later, Kada broke through the last of the trees and into the clearing made by Romin. She was at the top of a hill. Leaana looked down at the home of the people she had known all her life. The encampment of Romin was laid out in a circle. At the center was the great council ring with its nine totems. One to each of the animal spirits that control life and the fire that must always be kept burning to honor the spirits and keep them warm. Just outside the council circle were the homes of the council members and the fire keepers. The council members were the ones responsible for honoring each of the animal spirits. Each council member was selected by their love of that spirit and the way they kept its teachings. If there was a familiar in the encampment, he would serve as leader and guide to these nine. As for the fire keepers, they made sure the sacred fire did not go out. Usually, this position was kept by one family and would change with each turning of the four seasons.

The next ring of huts was occupied by the hunters and their families. This was where she lived. As her father was a farmer, normally, they would be located somewhere in the outer rings. However, her family had been allowed to move into this ring when she and Sagan were born. It was the council's way, and the people's, of honoring the family of the next familiar. Leaana could pick out her house even from this distance. It looked like her mother was outside looking for her. Better ride faster. At least there would be no more trees to have to dodge.

After the first two rings of homes, the circular nature of Romin was not as well defined. Families tried to get as close to the council circle and sacred fire as possible without entering the first two rings. Here, the encampment sprawled out much the way Leaana believed the cities of the elves did. She had never been to a city. She heard about them from the elves that traveled through Romin every year on their way to the cultural festival. She enjoyed the elves' visits. She loved the performances they provided and the stories they told of faraway places. Maybe one day she could travel and see them. Ah, well, time to dream later. Best get home now.

Chapter 6

Sagan awoke after sleeping deeper than he ever had before. He stretched. Every muscle in his body hurt. The recent exertion had taken more out of him than he had realized. Sagan winced in pain as he sat up, his shirt heavy and sticky from the blood of the deer. He wanted to lie back down instead of forcing himself to sit.

"I must get my bearings," he said. "How long have I slept?"

Looking at the sky through a break in the trees, Sagan noticed the sun was halfway down in the sinking sky. Night would soon be approaching.

"I must get up and figure out some way of getting the deer back to Romin," he said. "If only Togan had let me bring Karr with us."

Sagan stood, his legs screaming in protest. He would sleep well tonight, even after such a long nap. Looking around, Sagan inspected his surroundings. He was in a relatively dense part of the forest, the trees forming almost a solid canopy overhead. Only a few gaps here and there allowed light to enter. The limited light at least kept the undergrowth down. Large piles of leaves from the trees covered the ground. The deer was lying just as it fell, the large gash in the neck allowing the blood to spill onto the ground, staining the leaves.

Then it occurred to him something wasn't right. Where was Togan? When he had laid down, Togan was next to him. Now the wolf was nowhere to be seen. Perhaps he had wandered off. That would not be unheard of, but it would be unusual. Togan had wandered away a lot when he had first claimed Sagan as his pupil. Back then, it had been from frustration trying to get Sagan to understand what he wanted before their link was fully established.

After that, Togan left him a few times more. This was the first time they had been apart in almost two years.

The last time Togan left was when Sagan had ignored his wolf senses and was almost killed in a stampede of wild horses. Sagan had wanted to follow the hunters as they searched for new horses. The hunters had a head start, so Sagan was riding hard to catch up with them. He was using his wolf sense of smell to track the hunters so he could follow them without being seen. Togan was running alongside the horse, keeping pace, lending his senses to his two-legged pup. Suddenly Togan stopped. Sagan pulled his horse up and looked back at the wolf. Togan whined, sniffed the air, and headed off in a different direction as fast as he could run.

"Togan!" Sagan yelled. The hunters and horses are this way! I can smell them! We're getting closer. Where are you going? Come back here!" The wolf stopped, sniffed the air again, and let out another quick whine before darting away along his new path.

"The hunters are still too far away to see us. Where are you go...." His protest had been broken off in mid-sentence as a tremendous thundering began to ring in his ears. Turning to look in the direction he had been riding, he saw an enormous cloud of dust rising into the air. The sound of hundreds of hooves beating on the ground struck his ears. No wonder the smell of the horses had been getting stronger; they were heading right for him. Frantically turning his horse and galloping to follow his animal guide. Sagan looked back as hundreds of wild-crazed horses topped the hill and began to descend upon him.

His horse reared, startled by the stampede, and threw Sagan to the ground. Sagan landed hard on his right arm and heard something crack. A tremendous pain shot through his arm as he tried to get up to run after Togan. It was no use. The stampeding horses surrounded him now. Jumping this way and that, Sagan managed to keep from getting trampled. But the herd was growing denser, and soon he would not be able to move fast enough to avoid the thundering hooves. His life would soon be over, and he had not even become an adult.

Suddenly, there was a loud growl in front of him, and a horse bearing down on him dodged to one side. It was Togan. Togan was in the middle of the herd, nipping and barking at the animals enough to make them miss Sagan. Sagan could see the wolf jumping this way and that. A bark here, a quick bite on a shoulder there, the horses were trying to dodge the mad wolf. Togan's white coat became a blur of motion behind the dust the horses were kicking up.

Just as quickly as it had begun, it was over. The last of the horses ran past Sagan, and he had escaped relatively unscathed. His arm was broken from being thrown, but that was all. Sagan considered himself lucky and thanked the wolf for saving his life by throwing his arms around the wolf's neck and giving Togan a huge hug.

When he released the wolf, Togan took the opportunity to bite Sagan on the rear end. It wasn't a deep bite, but it still hurt. This was Togan's way of saying, "You fool. Listen to what your nose is telling you, and get out of the way." Togan then ran off and was gone for a long while. Long enough for Sagan's broken arm to heal.

What had he done wrong this time? He thought he had understood what Togan had wanted him to do. Was Togan mad because he lost control and had eaten the deer meat like a wolf? Oh well. No time to worry about that now; he had to figure out how he was going to get this deer home.

A twig snapped to his right. Sagan turned, drawing his knife. The smell of the dead deer could be attracting scavengers. He was going to have to defend his kill. Readying himself to do battle, Sagan crouched low to make himself a smaller target and moved closer to the stag.

Trees rustled and parted, and then Karr stepped through with Togan close on his heels. The wolf had gone back to get Karr. Togan had a rope wrapped around his neck. Sagan didn't want to know where Togan had gotten it. He would most likely hear about it in the morning, though. The rest of the people in Romin weren't as comfortable having a wolf around as Sagan was. Most likely, the owner of the rope would come looking for it and give him and his father a lecture about keeping Togan under control.

Taking the rope from Togan, Sagan made a quick bridle for Karr. Karr seemed relieved to have someone around besides a wolf snapping at his heels.

After making the bridle, Sagan grabbed three long, straight branches and tied them together in a triangle. Dragging the angle below a large overhanging tree limb, Sagan laid it on the ground. Going over to Karr, he guided him under the same tree limb and tied him there. Picking up one corner of the wooden triangle, Sagan laid it over the horse's backside, securing it to the horse with a short rope tied around its middle. Sagan then cut three short lengths from the rope and tossed the remaining rope over the tree limb.

Now for the difficult part. Sagan began by tossing one end of the rope over a large branch and tied the other end of the rope to the hind legs of the stag. Walking back to where the rope hung loose, Sagan pulled out the slack. Sagan took his big hunting knife from its sheath and stabbed it into a large root at the base of the tree as hard as he could. He reached as high as he could on the rope and pulled with all his weight. The rope went tight, and the back end of the stag swung into the air. Now sitting on the ground and holding onto the rope with all his strength, Sagan reached down with one hand and looped some of the rope around the hunting knife. Letting go of the rope, the back end of the deer began to fall until the rope was pulled tight on the knife. Working quickly, Sagan backed Karr and the wooden triangle to the raised back end of the deer. He then tied the hind feet of the deer to the top of the wooden frame with one of the short lengths of rope. Sagan then removed his hunting knife from the tree to relieve the tension on the rope. This done, he unlooped the rope from around his knife handle.

He repeated this exercise with the front legs and then secured the deer's head to its front legs to protect its horns. The antlers would make a wonderful trophy. Walking in front of Karr, he then began to lead the horse back to the encampment. Karr struggled under the weight of the deer. The stag, being half carried and half dragged because of its size, had not fully fit onto the frame. So burdened, Sagan began to make his way back to the encampment.

The journey was slow. Navigating the dense trees with this large cargo was more difficult than Sagan had thought. Several times he had to backtrack in order to find a way around one obstacle or another. After what seemed like an eternity, they broke from the trees into the plains leading to Romin.

Sagan's muscles ached. The exertion of running down the deer, followed by the exertion of tying it up, was now combining in his muscles, making them hurt more than he thought they could. It felt like every fiber in his muscles had been ripped apart and were trying to go in their own direction. If Karr wasn't burdened so already, Sagan would climb up on his back and ride the rest of the way, but the horse could barely handle the weight of the deer as it was. If Sagan stopped to rest, the horse might get too tired and collapse under the added weight. Plus, it was getting late, and Sagan needed to get the deer home so it could be cleaned before it spoiled.

As the trio entered the farmlands surrounding Romin, the workers stopped and stared. Some nodded their heads as if this was a totally expected occurrence, but most stood in awe at the sight. A sixteen-year-old boy was bringing home by himself the largest deer any of the farmers had ever seen. A few workers left their fields and began to follow Sagan, his wolf, and his horse. No one dared offer assistance. The completion of the hunt would be lessened if anyone helped Sagan with his prize until it arrived at its destination.

Sagan stumbled, the crowd that was gathering behind him gasped. Togan, realizing how tired his pupil was, caught up and walked beside him. Sagan reached down and touched his mentor, and it refreshed his energy reserves. He could complete this. He must complete this, if not for himself, to honor the great gift and lesson that Togan had taught him that day. Sagan entered the first row of huts, children ran out to see the sight that had attracted so many followers. Joined the procession, each trying to get a good look at Sagan and his wolf.

Someone in the back of the crowd began to chant his name. "SAGAN, SAGAN, SAGAN" soon, others joined in until the mass of people following him were all chanting his name, drawing even more spectators from their homes. Before long, the path Sagan was walking along was lined with people as the noise of chanting reached ahead of the parade.

Sagan was almost totally unaware of what was going on around him. He was so tired all he wanted to do was get home and climb into bed. Once he reached his tent, he could give the deer to his father, who would make sure it was cleaned and used properly. His father would most likely give the deer to one of the other hunters for preparation. Sagan would receive the horns as a trophy and most likely the pelt to use for a blanket or rug. His family would get the best of the meat, and the rest would be distributed as far as it could to the farmers of the encampment. The bones would be used to make jewelry, tools, knife handles, and the like, then the fat would be turned into oil to burn in lamps. No part of the deer would be wasted except the horns; those were truly just a trophy.

Sagan finally reached his house. The chanting of the crowd following him had brought others here to see. There were so many people that Sagan's family couldn't even see him approach. His mother finally managed to push through. She screamed when she saw him.

"OH, Sagan, are you alright? Are you hurt? Where did all this blood come from? You look hurt…."

Sagan had totally forgotten about his blood-soaked face and clothes. "I'm fine, mother. The blood is all the deer's. I am not hurt, just tired. Extremely tired. I will tell you about my hunt later, right now I must get some rest. Father, will you please see to the deer? Make sure it is cleaned and distributed properly."

That said, Sagan gave the rope he had been leading Karr with to his father and turned to the crowd. "I don't know why you chanted for me or followed me on my return. I have done nothing extraordinary. I have simply done my duty as a member of this encampment. I do what I am able to help everyone."

Sagan turned and went into his family's tent; he crossed the family area to his small private room. Opening the flap of hide that acted as a door, he allowed Togan to enter the room, he followed, collapsed on his bed, and almost instantly fell asleep.

Chapter 7

Leaana returned home to find a small crowd gathered outside their tent. Leaana climbed down from Kada and led the horse around back to the small tie-up behind the main tent. Leaana's family tent was laid out differently from most – it was the crowning achievement of Tarn, the chief builder. Her family home was actually four tents connected together. The large family tent in the center was where the fire pit was found. The family would gather around the fire pit for meals and discuss family business. Leaana's mother and father slept here close to the fire pit. It was impossible to go anywhere in the tent without passing through this room. The room itself was square. The ceiling rose in the center to an open point which allowed the smoke from the fire pit to escape. The fire pit was exactly that, a small hole in the center of the room lined with stones to help hold in heat.

One of the four walls of the tent was the main entrance. On the other three walls were openings covered in animal skins leading to connecting rooms. Leaana had the room to the right of the entrance, and Sagan's room was on the left. Leaana's two younger sisters shared the room at the back of the family tent. The other three rooms were also square with pointed ceilings. The ceilings' tops were perhaps the house's most unique part. The points of the ceilings were attached to tubes made from reeds and animal skins. These tubes ran to circular openings close to the center of the top of the main tent. The tubes were used to transfer heat from the family fire to each of the smaller tents in the winter. During the summer, the animal skins would be removed from the reeds so the wind could pass through the tubes and help cool the rooms in the summer.

The tent had been designed as a tribute to Sagan, Romin's first familiar in over a hundred years. The design worked well. Even better than Tarn had thought, and since then, he had been overwhelmed by requests from other families to redesign their tents in a similar fashion.

Leaana finished tying up Kada and walked around her room to the front of the tent so she could go inside. Leaana's mother spotted her across the crowd and very quickly moved to catch Leaana before she entered the tent.

"I'm sorry I'm so late, mother." Leaana began.

"Hush child, you have arrived before dinner, and this is no time to worry about the time of day. Have you heard?" Leaana's mother asked.

"Heard what?" Leaana asked.

"What your brother has done?" her mother replied.

"No. Is that why all these people are here?" Leaana asked, looking back at the crowd surrounding their tent.

"I am amazed that you haven't heard. Really sometimes I think you go around with mud in your ears. The entire encampment is talking about it. Your brother has killed Ralnar, the fabled phantom deer. Only three other hunters in the encampment have ever seen him, and none have seen him long enough to put an arrow to bow. Your brother brought him to the encampment by himself, and according to the hunters, the deer had no arrow wound. It had been stabbed to make the kill."

Leaana was stunned. How had Sagan done such a thing? She knew he was a skilled hunter, and his link with Togan made it possible for him to track animals that most could not. How had he gotten close enough to the phantom deer to put a knife in it for the kill? Surely the deer would have run away.

"Where is Sagan now?" Leaana asked.

"He is in his room asleep. He came home and presented the deer to the encampment like he had not done anything extraordinary. Then he went into his room and immediately went to sleep with Togan beside him. Now hurry. You have enough time to remove Kada's bridle and get her to the grazing grounds before dinner. We will discuss this more later."

Leaana quickly went back around the tent, grabbed the rope that served as Kada's bridle, and began to lead the horse toward the grazing grounds, lost in thought. Her brother had accomplished an amazing feat. Killing a deer that was only a legend and apparently doing it without a bow. Truly, he was destined to be a great familiar. No familiar in the history of all the encampments had accomplished something this remarkable so young. There were stories of the many great deeds of the familiars. She and Sagan had listened to them eagerly as children. They had even reenacted some of them in their dreams and fantasies.

Sagan was beginning to act like the familiars of legend. What stories would be told of his accomplishments? Leaana would only be remembered as the sister of a familiar who was once thought to be marked herself. She would not become a legend, but she would know a legend. In the past, she had wondered what it would be like to have witnessed the great deeds that the other familiars had performed. Only now did she realize she would witness great deeds by her brother. Would they seem as spectacular to her since she knew him intimately? Would he become a stranger to her as his power grew like so many other familiars did to their families?

She would not let that happen. She would stay close to Sagan and help him as much as she could, whether he liked it or not. She could not imagine life without Sagan; he had always been there for her and seemed to be the only one to truly understand how different she felt. But then, even he did not truly know. He was different from the other kids and was treated that way, just as she was, but at least he knew his place; and knew what he was supposed to do. She did not even know her own life. Half of her life had been spent preparing her to live as a familiar in case one had chosen her, and the other half had been preparing to live life as a normal member of Romin.

Soon she would know for sure, though. If she entered her rites of passage with the other children of Romin, then at least she could begin establishing herself in the community as a normal person.

She reached the grazing grounds. The grazing ground was a large grassy field just outside Romin where the horses could roam freely. No fence or barrier was used to keep the horses near the encampment; the horses seemed to stay by choice. Perhaps they enjoyed the security offered by people or simply did not want to leave their source of food. Whatever the reason, the horses stayed.

Leaana untied Kada's bridle and sent her to run with the other horses. She immediately ran over to where Karr was grazing and whinnied at Karr. Karr looked up and began snorting and neighing to Kada. Leaana stood there for a minute, wondering if they were talking about the events of the day. She turned around and started back towards her home.

Chapter 8

It took several hours for Mayan to gather the Elders for the meeting. It took even longer to get everyone to stop discussing the same old problems, how best to distribute food, where to build new tents, etc. Finally, Pargo got control of the meeting and got everyone to settle down.

"Now, Mayan," Pargo began, "What is this all about? Why the urgent meeting?"

"It is about Leaana and Sagan, and their rites of passage. I think we need to reconsider our position on this."

"Mayan, we have discussed this already. We decided a month ago during the last snow that Leaana should go with the rest of the children for her rite of passage. She has no animal guide to learn from and help her survive. She is not truly marked. It is time for her to begin a normal life in the encampment."

"That may be, but can we truly be sure. Do we know the will of the spirits? Perhaps her guide has been delayed in its arrival. If she begins a normal life her guide, if it exists, will never be able to find her."

"Mayan, you care for the girl nearly as much as her parents do. You have kept us from training her as the other girls so she would be set apart for her guide. Now as she approaches adulthood you would deny her a chance at beginning a normal life. If she went alone on her rites she would not survive. Sagan has his guide and must go alone, or we risk offending Togan. The ceremony to begin the rites is in two days. Why do you bring this up now?"

"I…."

"I apologize for the interruption," One of the hunters outside the door that kept casual passers from entering the council tent while the council was meeting stepped inside the tent.

"Yes, what is it?" Pargo said lifting a hand to set the guard at ease.

"There is a great commotion in the encampment Pargo. Sagan has returned from his hunt."

"What is so unusual about that?" Mayan snapped annoyed by the interruption. "Sagan always returns from his hunt. Usually with a kill."

"From the rumors the kill is the unusual part." The hunter explained. "Everyone is saying that Sagan has killed Ralnar the phantom deer. It is also rumored that there is no arrow wound."

"If there is no arrow wound how was the deer killed?"

"That remains to be seen. There is blood on Sagan's mouth and clothes."

"Is the child alright?"

"He is walking, his animal guide beside him but seems to be moving very slowly."

Tarn stood, "We must go and see this for ourselves. It must be verified if the deer is in fact Ralnar."

"But what of the matter we were discussing?"

"Mayan," Pargo began, "we will meet again tomorrow morning after the first meal and hear your reasons for raising this issue. But at this point I still feel the issue is closed. But out of respect to you we will hear you out trusted healer. Now let us go and see what our familiar has done."

Mayan stood still as everyone else left. He would hear soon enough if the rumors were true or not. Right now, he needed to think. He made his way back to his tent. It was a short distance from Pargo's since both were on the inner circle. The early evening air was crisp, still reminding one that winter that had just passed. The cold air helped to clear Mayan's head and relax him. Reaching his tent, Mayan threw aside the outer flap and entered allowing the flap to fall closed behind him.

Mayan's tent was simple, but constantly cluttered. Bags of herbs hung all around drying for use in medicines, their scents intermingled to give the air a heavy, fragrant scent. Most found the scent overwhelming and did not tarry long inside the healer's tent. Mayan loved it. He would at times throw a bag of the herbs into his fire to make one scent predominate. Grabbing a bag of chamomile leaves, he did just that. Soon the soothing smell of the herbs filled the tent, helping to further relax and calm him. The meeting had not gone well, but he still had time. He must figure out a way to convince the council to let Leaana and Sagan journey together.

He crossed his tent to where the history of the people was kept in a cabinet. Opening the cabinet, he carefully removed the ancient scrolls. Perhaps the answers he sought could be found here. There must be some precedent for what he wanted.

Sitting next to the fire, Mayan grabbed a piece of bread he had left on the warming stone. The bread was rich and full of honey and garlic, he began to read through the ancient scrolls. For hours he sat there reading and munching on the warm honey garlic bread. The scent of chamomile from the fire keeping him calm but alert. Scroll after scroll he read, trying to find something, anything, he could use to help his case.

After a while, he noticed he was having trouble seeing. He had been so intent on his research that he had let the fire die. The sun had set and there was not enough light in the tent to continue reading. Mayan stood, his old bones ached from sitting on the floor so long. A chill had crept into the room as the fire had died. Mayan had been so involved in his search that he had not noticed. Now, however, he could feel the cold inching its way into his bones and began to shiver. He walked over to his bedroll and grabbed his big bear skin blanket, where it lay folded at the foot of his bed. He wrapped himself in the blanket and turned, preparing to rebuild his fire. He stopped and stood motionless. In the doorway to his tent stood a large dog, no not a dog but a wolf.

"Togan, is that you?"

A soft whine was his answer.

"Well, my furry friend what brings you here? I wish you had come at a better time but right now I am deep in research trying to find an answer to a question that involves you, Sagan, and Leaana."

Togan entered the tent the rest of the way and sat down. He looked up at Mayan with a questioning look on his face.

"Oh, so you want me to explain do you. Ok, I am looking for a precedent that will enable me to send Leaana with you and Sagan when they pass into adult hood."

At that Togan let out a long mournful howl. The sound was incredible. Mayan had heard wolf cries before, but he had never been so close. It made him feel slightly uneasy. He knew he was in no danger from Togan, but wolves were powerful hunters and wolves had killed many brave men in his life time. The howl ended slowly fading to nothing. Almost immediately Mayan heard another howl in the distance. There was another wolf nearby and he was answering Togan's call. Then a second howl joined the first, then a third and a fourth. Not just one wolf but an entire pack was wandering close to the encampment tonight.

The pack, that was the answer he sought. Mayan looked down at Togan, but the wolf had already left. He wondered how much Togan understood of what had just happened. Had Togan known the answer to the question and come only to tell Mayan what he was missing. Mayan now knew what to tell the council tomorrow. It was so simple. He should have thought of it hours ago.

Suddenly Mayan realized that he was tired. The stress of the day had worn him to exhaustion, and he had been too worried to notice it. He crawled into his bed roll and prepared to sleep. He could sleep soundly now because he now knew what he would tell the council the next morning. He only hoped they would listen.

Chapter 9

Leaana was flying. She could see the ground far beneath her. The sun was just coming up and she could see it break over the horizon. The air was cool: she could feel it on her face as she moved. She flew down toward the ground a little and then began to fly up again. She turned away from the sun and then began to fly down again, this time lower than the first, and again climbed.

Leaana felt totally free. She could just keep flying forever, up, and down. She kept turning and flying down, then climbing back up. Why didn't she just keep flying in one direction at a constant height? Again, a turn and dive. Did she just see something off to the side as she reached the bottom of the dive? Another turn and another dive. She did see something. It was an elf, a relatively short fat elf. Why would she be seeing an elf? She climbed even higher this time and began a very quick dive. The ground shot up towards her; from the height she began the dive it would hurt when she hit.

Leaana sat up sweating in bed. The flight had been a dream. But what a dream, it had been more real than any dream she had ever experienced. She had loved the feeling of flying, of being absolutely free and separate from the world. If only people could fly.

Chapter 10

Pargo stood in the middle of the circle of elders. "We come this morning on the request of our trusted healer to hear his reasons for insisting we break with tradition and send Sagan Moongrower, our encampment's familiar, on his rites of passage with his twin sister Leaana. Leaana who was at one point believed to be marked herself but whose animal guide has not appeared. Mayan the floor is yours. May the spirits guide your words and may they guide our decision."

"Thank you, Pargo." Mayan said as he took his place in the center of the council circle. "I appreciate everyone's patience and understanding with me for bringing up an issue that everyone thought was settled. I hope you will understand the need for this when I am done.

"Two nights ago, as I slept, I had a dream. As you know, dreams are the animal spirits' way of speaking to us. In my dream I saw a wolf, a lone wolf running. As it ran it grew thinner and thinner until you could see the animal's ribs pressed against its skin.

"A second wolf joined the first. The two wolves ran together for a while. The second wolf staying healthy and the first wolf still thin but staying alive.

"A third wolf joined the first two. The three wolves ran together, and the first wolf regained its original form and all three began to grow. They continued to grow as they ran.

"What does this have to do with Sagan, Leaana, and their rites of passage?" Sigon the Chief blacksmith asked.

"Think about it for a moment." Mayan began, "Sagan is a wolf familiar as we all know. A wolf by itself is a powerful creature capable of surviving for many years. Two wolves can live even longer and grow stronger than one alone. But three wolves are the beginnings of a pack. A pack of wolves is almost unstoppable. In my dream a lone wolf starves, two wolves survive, and three wolves grow."

"I believe that if Sagan is to grow, and truly progress with his familiar he must learn to function as a member of a pack. I propose sending Leaana with Sagan as a pack member. Sagan will act as the pack leader caring for or working with Leaana as he sees fit."

Mayan scanned the room for some sort of reaction that might be on the faces of the elders. No luck. They sat there with their typical serious looks on their faces and were impossible to read. Mayan returned to his place and sat down, indicating that he had said what he had to say. Nothing happened. No one moved to continue the meeting. Perhaps he had made some progress after all. Finally, Pargo stood.

"Mayan, you have shed an interesting new light on this situation. A tradition that has always been cut and dried now takes on a new aspect. We know how you feel, and how passionate you are about this situation. While your passion is commendable, it may cloud our judgement. I ask that you retire while the rest of the council discusses your proposition."

"Thank you, Pargo, for your candor. I will leave now while the council is in discussion. I only ask that I be informed of your decision. You know my vote. Do not forget to count it."

With that, Mayan rose and left the council tent feeling relieved that he had at least made enough of an impression to make Pargo want further discussion. That, at least, was something. He walked briskly to his tent and threw a bag of herbs into his fire.

Chapter 11

Darmot sat on his throne, the only light in the chamber from a lone torch on the wall. Even this light was painful to his skin. The pain was worth it. A small price to pay for the power he now possessed. Soon Arctana and Subarta, the twin Elf Kingdoms, would know of his power as well. But not just yet. His forces were still not strong enough. He needed more people to convert.

Darmot was meditating. The deep breathing and mental exercise helped his body heal. Today, however, he was unable to still his thoughts. Twenty years ago, Darmot had left Arctana, the Northern Elf Kingdom, for the Dwarfgon mountains. He had left in disgrace, his once proud court reduced to himself and his two most loyal followers. He vowed to make enough money mining to hire an army to help him overthrow his cousin, King Aalan. Once Aalan was out of the way, he could then use the Northern army to unite the two kingdoms again under his rule.

For five years, he had toiled in the tunnels and caves of these mountains with little success. He had found enough to live on, but not enough to hire the army he needed. While exploring new tunnels looking for the riches he sought, he found his way into a strange chamber. A series of chambers cut out of pure stone. It was clear no one had been in these rooms for many years. The smell of mold was everywhere around him. Some of the rooms were furnished plainly, but some had elaborate decor. Excited by his find, he began to search. Perhaps this had been the palace of some ancient Dwarven king. Perhaps his treasure was still buried here, locked behind some ancient door. Perhaps his years of toil had finally come to an end.

His search of the ruins did reveal a treasure. Not one of gold and silver but of a treasure of knowledge. Behind a locked door Darmot stumbled onto a room full of scrolls. The scrolls were written in a strange tongue but somehow, he was able to understand them. The next year he did nothing but study the scrolls and explore his new home. The scrolls were the teachings of Duater, the spirit of the dead. The ruins he had found had at one point been a temple to Duater.

During his year studying the writings Darmot developed a powerful faith in Duater and realized that here he had found the object of his search. He had not found wealth but learned that Duater would give him the power he needed to achieve his goals. Duater would give him the power to exact vengeance on Aalan and conquer Arctana. After that it would be a simple thing to move through the human lands of Natarin as they had no formal army. That would give him thousands of new soldiers. Then he would conquer Subarta, the southern elf kingdom. With that conquest there would be no one left to oppose him. He would have extended his reign to the entire world and brought glory to Duater in the process. This was his destiny. This is the reason he had spent the previous six years in darkness.

Darmot spent the next year restoring the temple to its proper grandeur and preparing it for what was to come. When everything was ready Darmot left the temple at night and headed for a nearby Dwarf village. When he arrived, it was an hour before dawn. He had timed his trip perfectly so everyone would be asleep at this time of night. He crept into the village and went to the home of the food peddler he had been buying food from for all these years. He took the peddler's horse and harnessed it to a nearby cart. Creeping into the house he made his way silently to the bedroom of the merchant. Standing over the sleeping dwarf Darmot raised a club and struck the dwarf a quick blow on the head. With the peddler unconscious it was a simple thing to tie his hands and feet and carry him to the cart.

Darmot kidnapped each of the occupants of the next two houses in the same manner. Binding each person's hands and feet, placing a gag in their mouths and laying them in the cart. He stopped after the third house. He had six dwarves in the cart. That was enough for tonight, plus day light was fast approaching. He had what he needed. He must leave now so he could be deep into the mountains by the time the rest of the village awoke. He began the journey back to the temple leading the horse at first to make as little noise as possible. When he was a safe distance from the village he climbed into the cart and brought the horse to a brisk trot. He looked back to the unconscious bodies in the cart behind him. They were truly blessed. The next three days they would receive neither food nor drink. This would prepare them by purifying their bodies for what was to come. On the third day they would be born again. Duater would bless them through him, and they would begin a new life as servants of Duater.

By the time the sun was up Darmot knew he was safe. He had reached the solid rock ledges of the mountains. It would be impossible for a search party to track him over solid rock. An hour later he arrived back at his temple. He unloaded his unsuspecting cargo, all still unconscious from the blows he had dealt, and carried each one to a small chamber deep inside solid rock. He locked each one up individually so they could be purified for their new lives.

It wasn't long before it began. It started simply enough as each dwarf slowly awoke, to find themselves in pitch darkness. The screams started as questions trying to figure out what was going on. After a few hours they became more panicked. Darmot was stunned. Why were these people afraid? Didn't they know they were blessed and would soon be born again? He thought about talking to each of them and explaining what was happening so they would not fear. The screams, however, intrigued him. They were like nothing he had ever heard before. There was a musical quality to them which Darmot enjoyed. He decided to listen to It for a while. As the day grew on the song grew in intensity as the captive dwarves" terror increased. Darmot realized he relished this sound. He was saddened when the song ended for the day when the dwarves finally passed out from exhaustion.

The next day Darmot awoke with anticipation for the song to begin again — it didn't. A different sound was coming from the purification chambers today, moans and pleas for water and food predominated the sounds. These crying and moaning of the blessed disciples today were even more lovely than the sounds of terror that had predominated the day before. Yesterday he had thought the most beautiful sound in the world in the song of terror. But the song of agony was even more heart wrenching. If only they knew the wondrous new life that awaited them, they would not be suffering so much. But if they were not suffering then Darmot would be deprived of the joy of this strange music. He decided to let it continue. Soon they would suffer no more so perhaps this was needed for the purification process.

The third day the song was again different, less pronounced but still there. The dwarves no longer cared about food, all they wanted was water. They were promising anything they could think of to get it. Darmot listened closely again wanting to relish every moment of this song for as long as he could. The song of desperation was perhaps the best of the three he had heard. Would he get to hear these songs with each group of disciples? If so, he was getting an earthly reward from Duater for his worship. The songs of terror, agony, and desperation were something that only he would get to enjoy and truly appreciate.

At dusk Darmot went to the purification chambers and again bound the hands and feet of the dwarves. The blows to the head were unnecessary this time, the dwarves being too weak from hunger and thirst to fight back. He carried each of the chosen ones to the main worship chamber of the temple and knelt each before the main altar. Torches hung from the walls lighting the room in a soft glow. The dwarves flinched at the light having spent the last three days in complete and total darkness. The last of the blessed managed to find his voice and utter a curse at Darmot.

"Fear not," Darmot calmly replied, "soon you will be born anew and will begin a new life. All your suffering shall end, and you will thank me."

After the last of the chosen had been prepared Darmot placed a black stone on the altar in front of each of the chosen. He then went ahead with the Ritual of Raising and created his first goblins.

The goblins he created were magnificent. They were stronger than the dwarves had been and could see in the total darkness of the temple, which was good since even torch light was painful to Darmot's skin. For two days Darmot remained in total darkness allowing himself to recover from the ritual. By the third day his skin was still slightly tanned, but torch light no longer bothered him. He then performed the ritual on his two most faithful followers Carnell and Basara and created his first two raised elves that he named orcs.

Darmot sent his new orc and goblin servants into the surrounding caves rounding up other people to be raised for the glory of Duater. So, it had gone for the last thirteen years. Each time Darmot's skin healed enough for torches not to bother him he would send his servants out for more people to raise. Each time he would listen to the songs of terror, agony, and desperation and revel in each one. Each time he would conduct the ritual and raise the chosen to their new life it would take longer for his skin to heal. The larger the group to be raised the more sensitive his skin.

It has been two months since the last ritual and his skin had almost healed. His army was now quite impressive. He had nearly 3,000 goblins in his ranks with Fresmon the last of the mountain settlements still to be taken. This settlement promised to add another 1,500. In addition to the goblins, he had 1,000 orcs, and 400 raised humans, or ogres as they had been named. The orcs and ogres had come from the miners in the mountains, they had come to make their fortunes, and had no idea that they would be so blessed. Soon he would begin extending his reach, he would start by capturing the bridge at the Remis Plateau. This would interrupt trade but give him captives to continue increasing his numbers and then, then he would begin to exact his revenge on the elf kingdoms. They would fall and he would be able to erect more temples to Duater and raise everyone to Duater's glory. All would serve Duater and therefore serve him as Duater's priest.

"Your eminence." A coarse female voice interrupted Darmot's thoughts.

"Yes, what is it my child," Darmot replies opening his eyes and seeing Basara in front of him.

"The scouts you have sent into Natarin, the human lands, have returned. They report that they have found an encampment of humans less than a day's ride from the base of the mountains. This encampment is large and promises many to be raised to the glory of Duater. Perhaps even more than Fresmon. Shall I have Carnell send a raiding party?"

Darmot thought for a moment. A large settlement of humans would greatly increase his number of ogres. Ogres were the strongest of the raised races. While humans were naturally weaker than both dwarves and elves, they seemed to show a greater ability to change as was evident by their raised form. The average ogre was seven feet tall. Their strength was impressive: most could throw a horse with ease. In fact, some did this in battle to intimidate their opponents. Adding that many ogres to his ranks would make taking Fresmon that much easier and would help to accelerate his time table.

"Yes Basara, have Carnell prepare a raiding party. I want him to lead it. I need as many of the humans alive as possible. I should be ready to perform the ritual any day now so leave at once."

"Very good my lord he will depart tomorrow and should be back with in the week."

Basara left to relay Darmot's orders to Carnell. Darmot was left alone to consider how this increase in numbers could be put to the best use.

Chapter 12

Everyone in the encampment gathered around the council circle. The sacred fire had been built up until it was roaring. The sun had just set. It was dark, but the stars and moon were not out yet. At this time of night, the lighting seemed to be magical. Shadows were still well defined, but long enough to almost disappear as they ran into the darkness. Tonight, the Elders in the encampment would send her and the rest of the children her age on their rites of passage. She would soon be sent with the children and would begin to establish herself as a normal person, not a familiar. The dream of flight still stuck in her mind, though. If only it were true, if only she was a familiar. How her life would be different.

Pargo, the leader of the council and oldest man in the encampment, emerged from his tent. As he did so, the other nine members of the council stepped from their doorways as well. Each was dressed in the ceremonial clothing required by this night. Each member of the council was chosen because they were considered the master of their trade in the encampment. The council members also represented one of the nine animal totems that guarded and guided the encampment. The crowd grew silent as the ceremony was about to begin. Leaana had always enjoyed these ceremonies. Tonight, however, she felt a sense of dread, as what little hope she had left of being a familiar was about to be stamped out. The feeling of dread was matched almost equally with a sense of anticipation of being able to get on with a normal life as a member of the encampment.

Pargo and the rest of the council entered the ring of totems in unison. They immediately turned and began walking right to left around the circle.

Somewhere to the right of Leaana a drummer began beating a drum. Slowly at first, the lone drummer set the beat. Soon a second higher pitch drummer joined him, and the beat picked up a little. The council members are now walking in time to the beating of the drums. A third drum joins, even higher pitched than the second. It only sounds every 4th beat of the other two. On its sounding the Council members give a slight turn to the inside of the circle toward the fire.

The first trip around the council circle is complete. Suddenly, the rest of the drummers join in, and the slow methodical song erupts into a mad panic of overlapping rhythms. The council members were thrown into a rhythmic dance, still moving right to left around the circle. Leaana couldn't help but sway back and forth under the spell of the drums, and others were compelled to do the same. No one spoke. The only sound was the pulsating of the drums and the pounding of the council members' feet. Another complete circle around the sacred fire, the song continued, and the fire seemed to grow brighter and hotter even though no wood had been added. The flames seem to sway with the beat of the drummers, or maybe the drummers are playing to the dancing of the flames. The council members dance frantically in their circle, their shadows being thrown on the crowd by the fire seem to live and die with every beat of the drums.

Silence. Everything stops. No sound can be heard but the pop and crackle of the logs on the sacred fire now burning incredibly bright. The heat from the fire was almost enough to make Leaana want to move farther back and get behind someone as a shield from that heat. But she couldn't move. She was frozen in place, ears still ringing from sounds of the drums. The council members were frozen in front of their totems. The dancing and drumming stopping after the third trip around the sacred circle. The silence was deafening, no sound not even breathing could be heard over the crackle of the sacred fire.

Pargo took two steps forward, raised his arms over his head he shouted, "Arina, mighty eagle, Master of the skies, Giver of the bow, we ask that you watch over this ceremony and bless us with your presence."

Tarn, standing immediately to the right of Pargo, shouted with raised arms, "Larr mighty turtle, Master of the home, Giver of the knowledge of building, we ask that you watch over this ceremony and bless us with your presence."

Third in the circle was Mayan, "Sheta, mighty bear, Master of the healing herbs, Giver of writing, we ask that you watch over this ceremony and bless us with your presence."

The fourth elder was Sigon, chief blacksmith, "Duater, mighty Vulture, Master of the dead, Giver of weapons, we ask that you watch over this ceremony and bless us with your presence."

Next, was Manel, the elder hunter, "Roma, mighty wolf, Master of the hunt, Giver of the horse we ask that you watch over this ceremony and bless us with your presence."

"Matsaya," this was Novak the elder fisherman, "mighty fish, Master of the waters, Giver of food, we ask that you watch over this ceremony and bless us with your presence."

"Ozzul, mighty crow, Master of Song, Giver of language, we ask that you watch over this ceremony and bless us with your presence." This tribute was given by Arron the singer.

"Kran, mighty frog, Master of life, Giver of the knowledge of pottery, we ask that you watch over this ceremony and bless us with your presence." Gran the potter saluted his totem.

"Shamash, mighty snake, Master of the land, Giver of corn, we ask that you watch over this ceremony and bless us with your presence." Samon, the encampments best farmer made the last tribute.

Again, silence settled over the crowd. The wind blew slightly, and the fire seemed to grow even more. Pargo continued the ceremony. "We have paid tribute to the spirits which guide us through life. We know the spirits are with us as we proceed. We come here on this night, the night of the first full moon of spring, to send our children on the path to adulthood. Their rites of passage begin tomorrow morning. Tonight, we tell all what they must do. Tonight, the future will be decided."

A cheer erupts from the crowd, when it dies down Pargo continues. "Our encampment is blessed this night. We have in our midst a familiar. The first familiar that has been born in four hundred turnings of the four seasons. Tonight, he will begin his journey into adulthood and will begin to learn what is needed to take his place at the head of this council." Again, Pargo is forced to pause, as another cheer erupts from the crowd, this one louder than the first. "Sagan Moongrower step forward and bring with you your familiar if he will join us."

Sagan left Leaana's side and stepped into the council circle. He moved to an area between the totems and the council members, Togan at his side.

"Sagan Moongrower, as a familiar tradition dictates that you are to go through your rites of passage alone, only you and your familiar. Are you prepared to do this?"

"I am Master Pargo servant of Arina. I am prepared to go alone and survive with the knowledge and skills of my familiar. Thereby learning his ways and the ways of the animal spirits so I may guide the encampment."

"Well-spoken young Sagan. The council has decided, and this is by no small amount of discussion that you will NOT go alone."

Shouts of protest from the crowd. Sagan stood stunned, he was sure he would go alone did they doubt his abilities, had he failed in some way. What did Pargo and the council mean?

"Enough grumbling," Sigon bellowed, "do not disturb these joyous proceedings with your discontented words. The council has reached a decision. Do not upset the animal spirits by your protests and ill tempers. Allow Pargo to continue."

The crowd quieted. It was unusual for anyone but the head of the council to speak during this ceremony. It was especially unusual for Sigon, servant of the Vulture to speak, at any point save a funeral.

Pargo continued, "it is the belief of this council, that the animal spirits feel Sagan should be accompanied. Sagan's familiar is a wolf. A wolf is a powerful creature alone, this is true. But a grouping of wolves, a pack is almost unstoppable. Sagan will go on his rites and will rely on his familiar to learn to survive on his own. But one other will go with him. Sagan will be responsible for caring for or leading this other as he sees fit. Just as a lead wolf would do for a pack. The other to go with him is…Leaana Moongrower his twin."

Chapter 13

Leaana stood dumbfounded. She was in her room getting ready to go to the elves' carnival. The ceremony to start her rite of passage had passed in a blur after Pargo's announcement that she was to go with Sagan. She must be cursed. She had been looking forward to going with the other children on their rites. They were to go to and live in a small separate encampment and establish themselves and their places within the community. Leaana had been looking forward to beginning to prove herself as a normal person. But now that was not going to happen. She had agreed to go with Sagan. She and her twin would leave tomorrow morning before sunrise. Each of them would be allowed to take a bow with 24 arrows, a hunting knife, an ax, a bedroll, and clothing. Everything else they might need to survive, they would have to make during the journey.

When Pargo had made his announcement, Leaana had stepped into the circle beside her brother. Pargo asked if she would go with Sagan and accept his leadership and care during the month ahead. She had been too surprised to think, had she been able to, she might have protested, insisting she be allowed to begin a normal life. The shock had made her do what was expected of her; she had agreed. Pargo then told them what their rite would be. They must travel north to the Dwarfgon mountains and find one of the black stones used to line the sacred fire. Only familiars could gain entry to the temple that held the black stones. As a familiar, it was Sagan's responsibility to bring back a stone. Every familiar had at some point made this journey, so it seemed right to the council that Sagan made it now. Leaana would make the journey, relying on Sagan and Togan to help with her survival. She would hold the horses while Sagan and Togan entered the temple and brought out the stone.

The journey did not begin until tomorrow. Tonight, the elves were camped outside the encampment on their journey to Arctana, the Northern Elf Kingdom. They were not allowed in during the ceremony, but soon would be welcomed for entertainment and trade. Jugglers, acrobats, artists, and many different performances would take place all over the encampment. Leaana wanted to see as much as she could and enjoy this last night of childhood.

She finished removing the dress she had worn for the ceremony and slipped into her most comfortable deer skin tunic, the well-worn soft leather embraced her. She checked her family braids in the mirror. Everything was ready. She slipped on a pair of well-worn sandals and headed out to the festivities.

Already the encampment was alive with the sounds of the celebration. It had not taken long once the ceremony was over for the elves to descend upon the town. The encampment was the first of several that would be visited by the elves on their trip north this year. Last year the encampment had been the last stop as the caravan had been moving south. Leaana preferred to be at the end of the trip. When the elves were traveling north the performances were not perfected and there were always several mistakes. When they traveled south Leaana got to see the perfected performances. Leaana's parents preferred to be the first stop since they were more interested in trade than the performances because there would be more goods this early in the trip.

Leaana exited the tent and almost ran into a juggler that had stopped here to perform. She always thought the elves were funny looking no matter how many times she saw them. Their long legs and arms making them look incredibly tall and much like the scare crows that were used in the fields. Their pointed ears and eyebrows made them look happy all the time and always brought a smile to her face no matter how melancholy her mood.

The juggler stepped aside to allow her to exit without being in danger of being hit by the objects he was tossing. The juggler was managing to keep three knives and two flaming torches in the air at the same time. Leaana was sure the knives were dull but was impressed by the fact that he could juggle items of such different lengths so easily.

Passing by the juggler Leaana wandered aimlessly through the encampment. Not really paying attention to where she was going, stopping occasionally to watch different performances. Her mind always racing wondering what the next month would hold, and what her life would be like afterwards. Before long she noticed a large crowd in the middle of the encampment close to the sacred fires. The crowd seemed to be fascinated by something they were continually oohing and aahing. Stepping so she can see what the crowd is watching she notices a fat short elf, the first fat short elf she has ever seen, standing, turning in small circles and looking upwards. Her gaze was drawn upwards she saw a beautiful eagle flying, climbing…

"And now," said the short fat elf, "Aramin will begin to demonstrate the Eagles dive she is climbing now to gain height and soon she will seem to shoot towards the earth as if in free fall, but it is totally controlled. Eagles use this for hunting."

Leaana's gaze locked on the eagle. It was the most beautiful creature she had ever seen. Her breath seemed to catch in her throat and her pulse quickened. The short fat elf let out a sharp whistle and the eagle began its dive. Leaana watched fascinated. Suddenly the eagle's head pops up and it seemed to look straight into Leaana's eyes. The eagle then crashes into the ground with a bone rattling impact, and for Leaana, everything went black.

Chapter 14

Leaana woke feeling trapped. Every night for the last three nights she had been having the same dream. She was in a cage, riding in what looked like a wagon. There were other cages around her filled with birds. All the birds seemed to be hunting birds, falcons, and hawks. The wagon would bounce around shaking her in her sleep. She wanted to be free, she had something she needed to find. She had to get away. Tonight, however, the dream had been slightly different. She had seen the little fat elf that had been managing the birds during the festival. He was the key — he had her trapped. No, not her, but a part of her.

Leaana's mind cleared as the last of the dream faded. She must be tied to one of the animals in the falconer's cart. That is the only explanation for it.

After she passed out at the festival Sagan carried her home and put her in bed. She awoke the next morning and immediately left for her rite of passage with Sagan. There was no discussion, and no delay as was customary. Leaana had felt distracted since then. She had felt a pull from somewhere. Then each night she had the dreams.

She made up her mind. She was leaving. She had to. Sagan was still asleep and would probably be asleep for several hours. If she was quiet, she could gather some food and head off before he awoke. She would go and find the elven caravan and figure out why she was having these dreams.

Sagan and Togan had killed a small deer the day before. The meat was still drying over the fire. She didn't know how long she would be gone but she felt confident that she could forage if she had to. Taking some of the dried meat she prepared to leave. Sagan would be worried about her when he woke but he might try to stop her if she knew where she was going.

Leaana carried her bedroll and saddle bags with the food she had collected to where the horses were tied and untied Kada. Calming her mount, she tied her bedroll and laid her saddle bags on the horse's back. She began to lead her away from their small camp. Togan moved from the shadows and stood in her path. Kneeling Leanna spoke quietly to the wolf.

"Togan, I have to leave. I must go and find the elven caravan. I don't know if you understand me or not or understand why I have to go. I'm not even sure why I have to go but I must."

Togan leaned into Leaana and gave her a quick lick on the cheek. He then backed up and moved into the shadows again. Leaana was stunned. That was the first time Togan had licked her. With Sagan it was common but not with her, and she had more privileges with him than most. Leaana took it as a good sign. Leaana lead Kada a little farther from their camp, mounted, and then rode off into the dark prerising morning.

Chapter 15

Sagan awoke, his body still slightly sore and tired from his bonding with Togan the day before while hunting. Sagan wanted to use his bow, but again Togan had insisted that they run the deer down. Leanna had followed on Kada with her bow just in case a shot was necessary but, as before Sagan and Togan had been able to bond and run the deer down. Again, Sagan had killed the deer by using his knife. This deer was not as large as the fabled deer he had killed a few days before, but it was enough for his and Leaana's needs so it was large enough. As before Sagan had been so exhausted from the bonding that he had passed out. When he awoke, he found Leaana had already cleaned and skinned the deer, had a fire going and was starting to set the meat to smoke. He rose and helped finish cutting the deer and smoking the meat even though his body ached, and he was still tired.

This morning was better: only a few kinks and sore muscles to work out. Sagan got up and looked for Leaana. The sun was already a quarter of the way up in the rising sky. He had slept later than he thought. Leaana should have first meal prepared and may even have half of the camp packed by now. Again, Sagan looked around the camp. Leanna's bedroll was gone, as was Kada. The last of the meat that had been smoking over the fire last night was gone as well. Leaana was gone. She was supposed to be with him, part of his pack. How could she leave? Why would she leave? Sagan was going to have to go after her and find out. Quickly packing his belongings Sagan got ready to leave. He gathered his bedroll, packed the meat, and threw dirt on the few remaining embers of his fire. The rest of the deer carcass could be left for scavengers. He looked for Leaana's tracks. The smell of death from the nearby deer masked her scent so he would have to follow her tracks. There, he spotted her tracks in the dirt, determined her direction, and turned to go get Karr so he could go after his sister.

Togan leapt to his feet and charged Karr. Karr was normally not spooked by the Wolf's presence, he had grown used to Togan over the years, but a charging growling wolf was another thing entirely. Karr's years of instinct kicked in and he ran. In the opposite direction from Leaana had gone.

"TOGAN WHAT ARE YOU DOING? I have to go after Leaana, and she went the other way. Why are you chasing Karr?" Sagan cried as he set out in a run after Karr. Togan ran after him in a slow lope having scared Karr just enough to get him to run.

Sagan ran after Karr, chasing him over the gently rolling hills of the grasslands. After running over two small hills, Karr slowed and came to a stop. He began to graze, the initial panic from Togan's charge subsiding, and grass was always comforting to a horse. Sagan caught up to Karr and grabbed the rope he used as a bridle. Sagan threw himself on Karr's back, began to turn him back in the direction they had just come from when he caught a strange scent. The scent was a mixture of sweat, dirt, and had just a hint of death. He had never smelled anything like this before. Curious, he turned Karr in the smell's direction. Togan gave a low warning growl and took off like an arrow in the direction of this strange scent. Turning to follow, Sagan pushes Karr to a gallop. Togan was already topping the next rise as Sagan urged Karr to catch up.

Within a few minutes, Sagan could see shapes moving on the horizon. One slightly in front of a group of others. Togan still running full speed towards the shapes. With the strange smell getting stronger with every stride, Sagan could feel Togan feeding him strength. The feeling was exhilarating. Sagan almost wanted to jump from Karr's back and run with Togan, but knew that would cost valuable time. He dug his heels into Karr's side to encourage him to go faster. The shapes were becoming clearer now. The one in the front was shorter than the others and seemed to be running from the ones behind. One being chased by four, no make that five figures. Togan was getting closer to the strange figures, with Sagan still trying to catch up. He could smell them better now, sweat and fear from the first figure, then sweat, dirt, and the smell of death from the five figures giving chase. Sagan could feel the blood lust rising in Togan, he could tell Togan was preparing to attack. Reaching behind him, Sagan got his bow and an arrow from his quiver.

Togan ran past the front figure and lunged at the closest pursuer. Sagan took aim and let fly his arrow, hitting the second of the figures, giving chase. The impact of the arrow caused him to stagger and fall as the arrow stuck in the figure's arm. Togan had dragged his figure to the ground and was continuing to bite at its neck. Sagan began to taste the blood in his own mouth — it tasted strange, almost sour, not the normal salty metallic taste of deer blood. Sagan could now see the figures were not men, but some sort of creature with ugly misshapen faces and fangs in their mouths. Sagan was almost upon them now. The creatures had stopped with the attacks on their companions. One was approaching Togan, the other two looked at Sagan as he approached on Karr and drew swords from their belts.

Sagan rode Karr between the two, approaching him. Karr knocked one over as he ran by, then Sagan jumped from Karr's back onto the second, knocking him to the ground. Grabbing his hunting knife from his belt, Sagan thrust it at the creature's chest, only to hit something hard. A metallic ring sounded with the strike. The creature hit Sagan in his side, feeling the pain of the blow Sagan rolled off the creature and quickly rose to his feet. His opponent rose and stepped toward Sagan swinging with his blade. Only the increased speed granted to him by Togan saved Sagan's life as he quickly jumped back and avoided the strike. As the blade swung past him, the creature momentarily lost his balance, meeting no resistance to his swing. He stumbled. Sagan again used his enhanced reflexes to lunge in with his hunting knife again and strike at his attacker, this time hitting in the upper shoulder and penetrating the leather. The creature howled with pain, jerking away from Sagan. Grasping desperately to the handle of his hunting knife, Sagan managed to rip it free as the creature pulled away. The creature grabbed its injured shoulder and howled in pain. Sagan took a second to look towards Togan. The wolf had left his first opponent lying motionless on the ground and was attacking a second, again lunging for the creature's throat. Sagan noticed his arrow sticking out from the arm of the one Togan was now attacking.

Sagan could spare no more time looking at his wolf companion: his attacker was moving back in, now enraged with pain. The creature Karr had knocked over had also regained his feet and was approaching Sagan now, as well. Taking a lesson from Togan, as he so often did, Sagan jumped at his wounded attacker, catching him off guard, and plunged his hunting knife into his neck. There was no leather or metal here and the knife sunk deep. A quick gurgle was the only sound as the creature began to sink lifeless to the ground. No time to rejoice as he heard a footstep approaching. Again, his enhanced reflexes saved him as he quickly ducked below the strike from the other approaching creature. Pulling his knife from the lifeless form as it crumpled, he rolled forward to get some distance from this new attacker. Completing the roll, he sprang to his feet, jumped to his left to avoid a downward swing, and brought his knife up to his attacker's middle. Again, that metallic sound as his knife struck the attacker in the side of the chest. The vibration from his knife striking metal almost caused his arm to go numb. Jumping to the right, this time to avoid another strike, slashing again, hitting the creature's arm, slicing into the muscles there and causing it to drop its sword from the shock of the cut. Quickly, Sagan thrust his knife at the side of his attacker's neck again, the knife sinking into the soft flesh there. Another small gurgle, then nothing. Pulling his knife free, Sagan stood and looked around. A third creature approached, slightly more slowly after seeing his companions fall. Sagan's third opponent began a series of quick controlled swings, Left, Right, overhand, side, side. It was all Sagan could do even with his increased speed, to dodge each stroke. Sagan decided to try to knock the sword from his attacker's hand and brought his knife up. The sword crashed into the knife on a downward stroke. The knife deflected the sword and kept it from going into Sagan's head, and the force of the impact drove Sagan to his knees as the sword broke the blade of Sagan's knife. Stunned, Sagan waited for the next stroke and felt this was the end.

A menacing growl and a white furry form flew over Sagan's head as Togan jumped at Sagan's attacker and sank his teeth into the creature's throat. Togan's razor sharp teeth ripped the throat apart and blood sprayed into the air as Togan landed on top of creature. Sagan stood looking around. All five of the creatures lay dead, Karr was standing sides heaving as he pawed the ground unsettled. In the distance a horse and rider turned and rode north. Turning to look back he saw a short bearded man approaching — this must have been the person these creatures were pursuing.

The exhaustion from sharing energy with Togan was beginning to take hold: soon Sagan would pass out. Quickly he ran to Karr, grabbed his lead rope, and turned back to the approaching figure. The bearded man was there staring at him with a look of wonder on his face.

"Thanks for saving me Boss" the bearded man said as the sleep of exhaustion hit, and darkness took Sagan.

Chapter 16

The smell of wood smoke registered as Sagan started to come awake. His muscles ached, but not as much as he thought they would, not as much as the previous times he had used Togan's strength. Perhaps it was getting easier. Sitting up Sagan noticed a small campfire burning close to where he slept with a small bearded man sitting next to it. A tent was set up to his right. Togan stood next to him, eyes fixed on the man by the fire. Looking more closely, small might not be the best way to describe the man. He was short yes but fairly wide. Not overweight by any means but every inch of him looked well-muscled, this gave him a stocky appearance much like a tree trunk. Short, but solid.

"Ah so you are awake, Boss. Glad to see it. You slept very soundly, was almost afraid one of those nasty Orcs had killed you. I would have checked you over while you slept, but your furry companion wouldn't let me that close. You seem fine now Boss. Nice work taking care of three Orcs by yourself, not seen any one move quite that fast Boss."

"Um…thank you, I guess. What is an Orc?"

"Those nasty creatures that were chasing me. Orcs they call themselves. Not seen them around much before Boss. They seem to come out of the Northern part of the Dwarfgon Mountains. Not sure where from. I've lived there most of my life and not seen them around before. Two other creatures appeared around the same time — Goblins which are a little shorter and Ogres, which are tall and incredibly strong. Interesting dog you have there Boss."

"He's not a dog, he's a wolf, and I don't have him he has me…sort of…Who are you?"

"Sorry, Boss where are my manners, I am Masque, and I've been running from those Orcs for a while. I was getting tired, and they almost had me. I sure am glad you came along. Saved my life, that's for sure. I am in your debt."

"Are you a Dwarf? I've never met a dwarf before, we don't get any in our encampment of Romin."

"Yep Boss, I'm a dwarf. Why don't you come over here and warm yourself by the fire, tell me your name and we can talk a bit. With where you are lying, I'm almost having to yell for you to hear me Boss. But that wolf wouldn't let me get much closer."

Now that Masque mentioned it Sagan realized he had just been sitting staring dumbfounded at him while this conversation had been going on. Feeling slightly ashamed he stood, brushed himself off and approached Masque. Reaching the dwarf's side Sagan extended both arms crossed them at the wrists and held his hands open in greeting.

"I'm Sagan, and this is my animal guide Togan," Sagan explained hands still extended.

Masque stood, looked at Sagan's hand position, shrugged his shoulders and extended his hands crossed at the wrist as well. Sagan grasped Masque's hands and they shook once. "Interesting form of greeting you have Boss. Glad to meet you and the wolf. Did I hear you say that Togan is your animal guide, does that mean you are what your people would call a familiar?"

"Yes, I am a familiar, what do you know about familiars?"

"Not much Boss, only rumors and legend, though it will be interesting to find out how much of the legends are true. Based on how you handled those orcs at least some of the stories must be true." Masque resumed his seat by the fire, turned and removed a small pot. "May I offer you something warm to drink Boss?" Masque poured a liquid from the small pot in to a small metal cup. Sagan took the cup and smelled the liquid — it had a sweet citrus smell with a hint of cinnamon. He took a sip, the warmth of the liquid almost burning his mouth, but he swallowed quickly feeling the warmth seep into his tired body. It tasted like orange and cinnamon. "Orange tea

Boss, one of my favorite drinks on a cool night."

"Thank you," Sagan sat holding the tea in his hands. "How long did I sleep?"

"Not long Boss, a couple of hours, or shifts as your people call it. But like I said you slept deeply. I wasn't sure how long you would be out Boss, so I set up camp. Would like to have been a bit further away from those rotting Orcs but at least we are up wind of them for now."

Sagan rose, looked around and saw Karr tied to a small tree stump nearby. Sagan walked over to Karr, grabbed his saddle bag and pulled out some of the dried deer meat. "Are you hungry Masque? I have plenty."

"As a matter of fact, I am starving Boss. Thank you. It's been several days since I've been able to stop long enough for a decent meal. Had to eat on the run as it were."

Sagan walked back over to the fire carrying a small bundle of the dried deer meat and set it on the ground between himself and Masque. He also had a few slices of flat bread and some cheese. Masque took some of the meat and cheese, wrapped it in a piece of the flat bread and began to eat. After he had finished his first piece of flat bread and began reaching for another, Sagan asked, "so what is a dwarf doing this far from the Mountains? I thought dwarves never left the mountains."

"Well Boss, I leave the mountains a few times a year to trade with the human encampment closest to the mountains, Larin. I'm a blacksmith, you see, and I sell some of my knives and tools there. I also trade with the elves and other smaller human encampments. There are two or three smaller ones that Larin supports. I had finished trading in Larin and was heading east to trade with one of the smaller encampments when I ran into this band of Orcs marching through the countryside. I don't know much about Orcs, Boss, but I knew I wanted to avoid them. From what I've heard, people that meet Orcs rarely live to tell the tale or disappear altogether. So, I started heading south, trying to avoid them. Unfortunately, they saw me, and I guess they thought I needed to go with them Boss. So those five started chasing me. That was a week ago and I've been running ever since. So again, thanks for the help, Boss."

"Sure thing. It was really Togan's idea to help you out. We caught this strange smell and needed to find out what it was. Apparently, it was the orcs. We saw you running, Togan attacked one, and I joined in. Oh, no!" Sagan jumped up and ran over to where the bodies of the Orcs lay, bent over, and picked something up. "My knife, it's broken. All that's left is the handle. Going to be impossible to clean the next deer I kill if my food runs out."

"Sorry your knife is broken. May I see the hilt, um, handle?" Sagan handed the handle of his knife to Masque. Masque turned it this way and that examining it. "This hilt is made of antler. The artistry is very nice and adds a nice bit of showmanship to the piece. Not practical for fighting Boss but would be sufficient for cleaning game. I maybe need to talk to the craftsman that made this hilt Boss. I could use a supply for a few of my pickier customers. Don't find many antlers in the mountains big enough to make a knife hilt. But can't do much about that now, Boss, but I think I can help you out." Masque reached into a small pouch on his waist and pulled out a large knife. The blade shone in the sun and had a small curve to it. Masque looked at it briefly, shook his head, pulled the pouch open again, and looked down into it. He reached his hand in, even though the pouch did not appear to be big enough for his hand to fit in it. When he removed his hand from the pouch, he laid a small piece of metal on the ground beside his foot. Masque twisted the bottom of the knife handle and removed a small ball from the end of the hilt. He then grabbed the piece of metal on the ground and twisted it onto the end. Swinging the knife in the air, he thought for a second. He then grabbed a leather disc from the side of his belt and placed it on the handle, then screwed the metal piece back into place. Swung the knife again and then, reversing his grip so he grasped the blade, he handed it to Sagan.

Sagan looked at the knife. The metal piece at the bottom of the handle was a metal carving of a wolf head, done in amazing detail. You could see the teeth in the open mouth and almost see the fur. Above the wolf head was a series of leather discs increasing in size and thickness to the middle of the handle then getting slightly narrower just before a small metal cross piece then the slightly curved blade. Sagan took the knife from Masque. The blade glistened and was slightly blue in color. It seemed to be extremely sharp and light. Amazingly light for the size of the knife. Sagan worked it experimentally and it felt like an extension of his hand. Not like his old knife where you could feel the weight of the blade, this was almost like the blade wasn't there.

"That is a good knife Boss. One of the ones I was going to try to sell to your hunters, but I think you should have it to pay you back for the one you broke saving my life Boss."

"It's so light, and the blade looks like it is blue," Sagan marveled.

"Dwarven steel, hardest steel around. I told you I was a blacksmith. I made that knife, Boss. Any knives of this quality you find outside the Dwarfgon mountains I probably made it Boss. I thought the wolf's head was a nice way to personalize it for you. Oh, wait, almost forgot." Masque reached back into his pouch and pulled out a leather scabbard. "Wouldn't want you to cut yourself while carrying it around. It's probably longer than your old knife, Boss, so I don't think your old scabbard would hold it."

Sagan took the scabbard from him and placed the knife in it, untied his current scabbard from his belt, looked at it, and noticed that it seemed to be a bit short. Tying the new knife and scabbard to his belt, Sagan crossed over to Karr and placed the old scabbard in his saddle bag — the leather might be useful at some point, best not to waste it. "Thank you for the knife, Masque, and it has been nice meeting you, but I really must be on my way. I am traveling with my sister, and she ran off for some reason last night. I need to go after her."

"Well, Boss if you don't mind, I'd like to tag along. At least until we get to a town or village. After being chased by those beasties for a while, I really think there may be safety in numbers. Plus, I owe you my life. Least I can do is help you find your sister."

"I don't know, I'm on a quest for my village and am supposed to be learning to survive on my own. What do you think, Togan?" Togan let out a small whine and wagged his tail once.

"What does that mean, Boss?"

"Well, he isn't showing his teeth and growling, so I guess that means it's ok. Will you be able to keep up with my horse? I'll never be able to catch my sister walking."

"If you can take it slow for the rest of today and let me get a good night's sleep tonight, I shouldn't have a problem keeping up. I'm used to traveling on foot and can keep up a pretty good pace jogging. I may not be able to keep up with a gallop, but during the next few nights, I'll see what I can do to make it easier.

"Fine, but I'm not going to wait on you too much. I'll give you tonight to recover, but then I've got to set out after her. I think I know why she left, but I'm not sure, and I need to make sure she is alright before I continue on with my quest."

"What is this quest you're on, Boss?"

"I have to go to the Dwarfgon mountains and retrieve a sacred black stone for our council fire. Every familiar in history has done this as part of the rites of passage into adulthood." Sagan explained.

"Well, the mountains have gotten to be a very dangerous place the last few years with the arrival of orcs, ogres and goblins. You will need to be very careful, Boss. You might even consider not going once you find your sister."

"That is not an option, If I don't full fill this obligation, I will not be able to take my place in the Encampment. If I can't take my place in the Encampment, then my life as a familiar will not fully help my people."

"Well Boss just be careful is all I have to say."

"I will. Now let's get moving — our last campsite is just a short ways from here and I need to head back there to pick up Leaana's trail. We can camp there again tonight to let you rest but then we will start our search."

Masque stands, throws dirt on the small fire to extinguish it. Collecting his small pot and cups he seems to put them in the same small pouch on his belt from which he pulled the knife. Sagan unties Karr's bridle and begins to retrace his and Togan's steps from earlier in the day. Togan runs ahead smelling the air, Masque comes up beside Sagan and the two walked side by side into the sinking sky.

They arrived back at the camp Sagan had last shared with Leaana the previous day. Togan tied Karr to a log, untied his saddle bags and bed roll, from his saddle, and began to prepare the camp. Masque began to gather some of the small brush and dried grasses around to make fire.

"Hey Boss," Masque shouted over his shoulder as he scoured the ground for firewood, "I'm not finding much firewood around here. I think we may have to have a cold camp tonight."

Sagan sighed, during the walk back from the brief battle he had tried to get Masque to call him Sagan, but whenever Masque addressed him, it always came out Boss, "Yeah Masque, Leaana and I camped here about 3 days while we cleaned and smoked a deer I had killed to give us enough meat for our rite of passage. It took all the wood we could find around here to smoke the meat. Leaana was having to search pretty far and wide by the end of things to find enough to keep the fire going. These grasslands just don't have much in the way of wood. We have plenty of dried deer meat though and I'm happy to share if you are low on supplies."

"Thanks, Boss lost one of my bags while running and lost most of my food supplies. Kept the bag with my tools, a bit of metal and a few of the nicer weapons I was planning on selling. That knife I gave you would fetch a pretty penny at the Elven markets." Masque replied. "All this running has worked up an appetite. Hey Boss, what's your four legged friend doing there?"

Sagan looked up and saw Togan walk over the top of a rise, give a quick bark and then head down the other side, moving quickly. "Oh, Togan is just going to scout around a bit, making sure none of those Orcs are wandering around. If he lets out a howl, we will know we have company. Why don't you come over here and begin resting up? I will get you some food."

"Thanks Boss. While we are here, I'm going to start working on something that will help me keep up with that great lumbering horse you have there. I don't want to slow you down too much while you are trying to catch up with your sister." Masque opened the pouch on his belt and began pulling tools and metal out from inside.

Sagan opened the saddlebags and pulled out several pieces of smoked venison. The smoked meat was best if you could cook it in a pot with some water and make a stew of some sort out of it, but with no wood available tonight, they would have to chew on the bits of meat a bit longer. Sagan also pulled out some sharp cheese and a couple of small loaves of a bread

Leaana had made a couple of days before. The bread was made from oats Leaana had ground into a flour. Then she had stirred in some water, a bit of wild honey they had carried with them and had found a few eggs from the nest of wild pheasant. The bread was a bit heavy but very hearty and sweet from the honey. The sweetness of the bread would help offset the bitterness of the sharp cheese and smoke from the venison. Wrapping a piece of the bread around the cheese and venison made a satisfying meal. Sagan prepared three of the wrapped sandwiches for himself, and three for Masque while listening to the sounds of Masque building whatever it was, he was building.

"Masque?" Sagan asked as he handed the wraps to Masque, "how do you keep pulling all these things out of that small bag and where are these other weapons you were talking about?"

"Well Boss," Masque replied, "the bag I have is what we call a bag of holding. I am one of only a few dwarves that still know how to make them. Since we dwarves are so short, we had to have a way of carrying things that were larger than we were, so we developed these bags. I actually stitch a small part of the spirit world to the inside of the bag. By doing that it allows me to put anything into the bag that will fit into the top of the bag. It is like it changes the size of the item so it will fit into the bag. But unfortunately it doesn't change the weight of the items. So, I can only put as much in a bag as I can carry."

"Masque that is amazing how do you stitch the spirit world to a bag?" Sagan stared at Masque in wonder.

"Well Boss, 1t would take me 20 years just to begin to explain it to you. Just know it is an ancient dwarven art that like so many things that are old only two or three of us still know how to do it. The bags are very popular and are becoming very rare."

A sharp bark comes out of the darkness, "That bark means Togan hasn't found anything. He and I will keep watch tonight while you rest."

"Thanks Boss. I'm going to finish these wonderful wraps then work on my idea for about an hour then turn in."

"Have a good night, Masque. I'm going to sleep for a few hours, then take over the patrol from Togan. He will let us know if anything comes around." With that, Sagan rose, walked a small distance away from where Masque was working, laid out his bedroll, and laid down. Even with the events of the day running through his head, and his muscles still sore from bonding with Togan for the fight with the Orcs, Sagan soon fell asleep as the moon rose overhead.

Chapter 17

"Sire,"

"Yes Basara?" Darmot replied as Basara entered the throne room.

"Carnell has returned from the conquest of the Human settlement. He has brought you many new disciples for you to raise to our glorious new form." Basara said as she approached the throne and bowed.

Darmot sat a bit taller on his throne. "I am almost prepared. Once they have been through the 3 days of purification, I will be ready. How are things going with the preparations? Have you completed the move to the staging area?"

"Yes, my lord, all goblins, orcs, and ogres have been moved to the peninsula three days ride from here. That will keep our training and numbers a secret. It will help keep us hidden from the elves. Now that we are capturing the Remis bridge, someone is bound to start looking. A small guard unit of Goblins is here under my command to manage the violence that will pop up after the next ritual. Those guards are now busy placing the new disciples into isolation for purification. One more thing, Carnell seems agitated…"

The doors to the throne room slammed open as Carnell stormed in. He was still wearing his battle armor and dust from the road. Carnell, a large orc, and his armor made him seem all the more imposing. The anger on his face was apparent. The torchlight flickered through the room, casting strange shadows on the wall. His anger was so obvious that even the shadows seemed to move away from the oncoming storm and gather behind him. The darkness where he was walking seemed more absolute.

"They are dead," Carnell growled as he approached Darmot's throne.

"Who is dead, my love?" Basara purred, trying to calm the rage in Carnell. Rage was good. It made him a better warrior, but it also blinded him. It made Carnell plunge forward and forget strategy. It's better to calm him in order to get a more exact report.

"The orc patrol I sent after the Dwarf. They are dead — all of them." Carnell snapped, pacing the floor and growling. His fangs showed his obvious displeasure. "I have not lost an entire patrol of Orcs before. No one has been able to stand before them. Most have cowered or been overpowered. Now this."

"My love, losses are a part of this. It is not totally unexpected." Basara purred yet again. Approaching Carnell and beginning to touch him lightly to further calm him. "Calm yourself Carnell, silence the rage. Now, tell our Lord Darmot what has happened so we may understand."

Carnell violently shook off Basara's hand, her eyes flared, and a small snarl crossed her face. Carnell sighed and Basara again began to stroke Carnell forcing him to calm down. Carnell sighed again. The rage started to abate under Basara's ministrations. "We were a day from engaging the large human settlement known as Larin. I sent several patrols out in their sixes to find any smaller communities or settlements." Carnell began pacing as he reported. He was obviously still agitated and the telling of the story seemed to be building the rage again. "Our attack on Larin went as normal. The human hunters tried to fight back. Their unorganized tactics were defeated, and they cowered as they saw our strength. We rounded the humans up and were preparing for the march back here. The sixes returned. Most had five to ten humans with them, rounded up from smaller settlements. A scout for one of the sixes returned saying his five warriors had begun pursuit of a dwarf. They would return once he had been captured. We began our march back. As we were arriving back here the scout from the missing six caught up to us. He had been running for days to catch us even though our process was slowed by the captives. He had caught up to the warriors of his unit and they had been killed. The prints on the ground showed the dwarf they were pursuing. They also showed another person's prints, and what looked like the prints of a wolf. The throats of the warriors ripped out or slashed. Two people should not have been able to overpower a full fighting five."

"Carnell, I want the surviving scout brought to me now. He must answer for this loss." Darmot's eyes flashed with rage. This scout was a coward. His fighting five were dead. He reported the fate of the fighting five now he must complete his duty. The structure of the military units was fairly simple at this stage of the process. Groups of six orcs, ogres, or goblins worked together. One of them was lighter and faster than the other five. This one was trained as a scout and used as a runner for reporting movements and giving updates if needed.

Basara turned to one of the goblin guards in the room. "You heard my Lord Darmot, bring the surviving scout here at once." The guard clicked his boots and raised his two hands in front of him in salute. He turned and ran from the room knowing delay would not be rewarded. "Now come Carnell have a drink and refresh yourself from the road. Darmot will deal with this from here." Walking over to a small table in the corner of the room Basara poured a glass of wine from a crystal decanter. She handed it to Carnell.

"How do you expect me to drink at a time like this?" Growls Carnell as he slapped the glass from Basara's hand and shattered it on the floor.

Almost quicker than it was possible to see, Basara's hand flashed up and hit Carnell under the chin. The force of her blow lifted Carnell slightly from his feet and knocked him to the floor. Carnell growled and started to rise, a sharp pricking feeling at his throat stopping him. Looking up, he saw Basara standing over him, sword in hand, with its point resting against his neck. "I said have a drink and calm down," Basara growled through clinched teeth. "But if you insist on continuing to rage, I will be happy to indulge you."

"ENOUGH!!!" Darmot yelled as he rose from his throne. "Basara, put your sword away. Carnell, stay on the floor, so Basara doesn't have to put you there again. I love your passion for our soldiers Carnell. But if losing five does this to you, then I need to rethink my command structure. A war is coming and even with our superior numbers and quality of our raised troops, we will have losses. I can't have you raging and not thinking over every loss."

"My Lord, I'm…." whatever Carnell was about to say was cut off as the guard returned with an Orc in tow.

"Is this the scout that is the survivor from the unit that pursued the dwarf?" Darmot asked Carnell.

"Yes, My Lord," Carnell replied as he continued to sit on the floor following Darmot's orders to stay down. "This is the survivor of the six."

"Stand before me and Salute Orc." Darmot snapped.

The orc came forward and approached Darmot. Standing before him, he clicked his heels together and held both arms forward in salute.

"Your unit has been defeated. You have done your duty and reported their defeat. Now you must share in their disgrace, as all our units work as one." As Darmot finished this last statement, his arm moved. A sword seemed to leap from its scabbard into his hand. Then, as if part of the same movement, it slashed across the Orc's left hand slicing it off at the wrist. The orc screamed in pain and gripped the stump where his hand used to be. "Your first fighting five was defeated and you survived. You may still be useful, so you keep your life for now. Lose another fighting five and you will lose more than a hand. Carnell, get this one-handed scout out of my sight."

Carnell finally got up off the floor with what little dignity he could. He grabbed the orc by the back of the neck and led the whimpering injured soldier from the room.

"Basara, I worry about Carnell. He has always been rash, but lately it has been worse."

"Yes, my Lord, the raising to Orc has taken its toll. It seems to have enhanced his tendency to rush into things and not think. His anger is worse.

"As is your temper at times…one day you may try to humble him only to find him ready for you.

"I have Carnell totally under my control. He will never cross me, and I can use my influence to control him. He is a good military commander when he can be channeled in the right direction. Might I suggest sending someone else to investigate the deaths of the fighting five? I feel we should redirect Carnell and get him back under control."

"Who do you have in mind?"

"You don't need to worry about that. You have a ritual to prepare for. I will leave you now and let you begin your preparations. Would you like me to remove the hand?"

"No, leave it. It will be a nice focal point for my meditation as I prepare for the ritual of pain."

"As you wish, my lord. I will go now and prepare to avenge the death of our fighting five." Basara clicked her heels together and raised both arms in salute. She turned and strode out of the throne room. A chill of pleasure coursed down her spine from the violent display she had just seen. Darmot truly was vicious and strong enough to lead. His strength and violence excited her. She would have to find Carnell soon and pick another fight with him. Then she could fully enjoy him and relieve this pleasurable tension. But for now, she must seek out Spinel. From what she had seen, he should be able to answer any threat and exact the revenge that was needed.

Chapter 18

T*hat really is a beautiful hammer. The engravings on the handle make it really special. We truly are master craftsmen.*

Yes, and it's perfectly balanced as well. It will be very easy to swing. I'll be able to fight with this all day.

I still don't quite understand why you need something so beautiful and well made just to bang it into the side of someone's head.

Well, you are the poet and storyteller. How many of the great heroes in history have used a plain, unadorned piece of wood or stick of metal in their adventures? All the truly great heroes had truly magnificent weapons. This is no different. I am a truly great blacksmith and fighter, so I should have a truly magnificent weapon. Even if I have to make it myself. Which I do since there is no better Blacksmith around.

True, perhaps one day I will write the story of our adventures and I will try to give this hammer justice. Do we have a name for it?

Not yet. I am just completing it and have not gotten to know its personality. The name will come with time.

"Spinel, are you here?"

I believe that is Basara. She is a very dark but colorful character...not sure I fully trust her, though.

"Yes Basara, we are… um, I am here. What can I do for you?"

"I have a mission for you. I want to see if the combat skills I have seen you show on the training grounds are real. We had an entire fighting five get wiped out and according to the scout, it was by only one or maybe two people. If that is true, these people are better-than-average fighters, so I want to send someone who is a true master after them."

"Will I be going alone?"

"Yes. I want you to handle this personally. We have lots of patrols of sixes in the grasslands along the Animas rounding up small groups of humans. You can check with them for supplies, but otherwise, I want to know what you can do. You are unmatched in practice bouts, and you are definitely a great blacksmith. We have been impressed by the quantity and quality of swords you have produced for us."

"Well, Basara, if I am to make a weapon, I must understand how to use it. At least that is what I was taught. But if you know how to use it, then you should. I grew tired of making the weapons and wanted to use them. See this Hammer. I have just completed it for myself; it shall break the skulls of those who have wronged us. I look forward to proving myself to you."

"Yes, yes, your skills as a blacksmith have been too valuable to us to this point, as we have been building our forces, but now, we shall test your other skills. I expect you to leave within the hour."

"As you wish Basara," Spinel replied to Basara's back as she walked off, her request delivered.

If I ever do write our adventures, I'm going to have to embellish your conversational style. It leaves much to be desired.

Everyone's a critic. Let's prepare to leave. We finally get to prove to everyone that we are more than a great blacksmith and all this training won't go to waste. My father never truly understood that these skills should be used for more than just designing weapons.

Yes, I saw those memories. How long has it been since you have seen your father?

Well, as you know, Spinel has existed for three years. It had been 10 years before that since I had left my father.

That's right. I wonder what happened to him.

I don't. Now stop distracting me. We need to get ready to leave.

Chapter 19

Leaana drew rein at the top of the rise. She had been traveling hard for two days. Riding until it was too dark to see, sleeping a few hours, then continuing as soon as the light returned to the rising sky. Now she could see the Animas River below her winding through the plains. It seems wider and running faster than she expected. But this time of year, she knew it would be swollen from the melting snow in the Dwarfgon mountains. The Animas River almost divided the continent into two halves. It ran Southwest from the Dwarfgon Mountains, through the Remis plateau, the grasslands, and finally widened out and slowed to form the marshlands in the southwest. Leaana wished she could see the great falls where the Animas left the Remis plateau and enter the grasslands, but that was two days to the north. True, she could cross there but, if she went to see the falls, she would have to either double back here, or continue north and hope to catch Elven caravan at a later point. Better to cross here and catch them while they would still be relatively close.

Leaana figured by crossing here at the Silver Ford she would cut the corner and be able to catch the elven caravan within the next couple of days. The caravan would be following the main trade route from the south and would be using the Marshland bridge to cross the Animas. From there, they would turn north to head for the northern Elf Kingdom. If she was right, she should catch them after the Marshland bridge, but while still in the marshlands.

Leaana squeezed her legs together, and Kada began moving forward. She guided Kada down the winding path on the rise overlooking the Animas and toward the Silver Ford. She could see the ford now, it was named well.

There seemed to be a silver streak going across the water where the water streamed over the hidden rocks of the ford below. The Silver Ford was known to her people and used mainly by them. During the summer when the Animas was running normally, the Ford was used commonly. This time of year, it wasn't used very often. The river running as high and as fast as it is now made the ford more dangerous. Footing could be unsure and if you fell you could easily be swept downstream or worse tossed over and over in the swirling waters just on the other side of the ford.

As she drew closer, she could see two ropes tied to a pole. The base of the pole was partially underwater, and the lower rope disappeared into the water not too far into the river. The ropes were the only thing that helped secure travelers as they crossed the ford. During the summer, the bottom rope would still be under water but just barely. The top rope would be several hands above the water. Now the top rope almost appeared to dance in the spray it was so close to the surface. This crossing was not going to be easy, but it was her best chance. Drawing close to the pole she stopped Kada and dismounted. She rummaged through her saddle bag behind Kada and found a piece of the dried deer meat she had brought with her. Chewing on the smoked meat absently she went to inspect the ropes on the pole. Wading into the water she was surprised to find the water halfway up her calves while standing at the pole. She could already feel the pull of the current against her legs. Checking the ropes, she didn't see any signs of fraying on this end of the rope, and they seemed securely fastened. Looking at the river here she could see and feel the swirling current, could hear the roar of the water. Perhaps crossing here was too dangerous.

Kada whinnied nervously and started to pace toward Leaana. Leaana looked around, "what is it girl, nervous about the river? Yeah, I am too." Kada whinnied again this time Leaana heard something. Voices and what sounded like snarls. Looking in the direction of the sound she saw six figures topping the rise where she had just been. They were snarling and looked like they were carrying weapons. They pointed at her and began to run in her direction.

Leaana was afraid. What were these creatures and why were they running after her? No time to wonder about it. She leapt onto Kada's back and guided her over to the ropes. The lower rope was even with Kada's belly, and the upper rope was against her neck and Leaana would hold onto it as they crossed as well. Kicking her heels into Kada's side and talking encouragingly to Kada the two of them started across the Animas. After only a few steps the water was up to Kada's neck and washing over her back. The strength of the current was incredible. Leaana squeezed Kada's middle with all her might and held on to the rope that was brushing against Kada's neck with everything she had. Kada's eyes were wide with fright, feeling the current pushing against her but the ropes held. Her feet were finding purchase in the soft sand that had built up next to the rocks just past the Ford. The sand build up is what made the crossing possible. The rocks were never above water, so they were too slippery for footing but the sand that built up due to the rock barrier made the crossing possible. Moving slowly, they made their way across the ford. Leaana was concentrating on what was in front of her making sure she held on to the rope and that they were not washed down stream, she could hear nothing but the roar of the river now. She had no idea what was going on with the things chasing her, but she figured she could worry about that once they were across. They were starting to rise out of the water now as they approached the far bank. Taking a chance to glance over her shoulder she noticed the creatures were already at the pole on the far bank where she had just been and were starting their own crossing, using their hands going hand over hand on the rope and holding on so they didn't get washed away.

Leaana, now focused on the pursuit, felt the last of the current drop away as she and Kada found themselves safely across. Thinking quickly Leaana jumped down and pulling her hunting knife from her belt quickly cut through the ropes. As the tension on the ropes released the current began to sweep her pursuers downstream. They were swept away by the current. One creature remained on the far side. He was still close enough to the shore he had managed to climb out of the river before he was washed away. Leaana could see that he was screaming in fury, but any sound was drowned out by the sound of the rushing water. Then she saw what looked like a bow in his hand. Quickly she ran and jumped back on Kada's back. At that instant an arrow landed in the ground next to her. Urging Kada into a gallop Leaana rode off anxious to get out of range and put this entire incident behind her.

Chapter 20

Sagan awoke and quickly found Leaana's tracks going off to the southwest. For two days he followed Leaana's trail. Togan scouting ahead to warn if any orcs were around while Sagan alternated riding and walking Karr, keeping the pace down so that Masque could keep up. Masque jogged steadily along. Each night they would make camp, Masque would work on his invention, they would eat and all three would take turns keeping watch. Masque was amazed to see Togan curl up beside Sagan and sleep almost like a dog would with a child. It was so unusual to see a wolf behave this way. Masque continued to keep a pretty respectful distance from Togan. Whenever he got too close, the wolf's hackles would rise and a low rumble would escape from his chest. Sagan assured him that for Togan, that was a sign of affection. If he really didn't like you, his teeth would be showing when he growled, and you might lose a finger or two.

About two hours before sunset on the third day, they arrived at the Silver Ford. Sagan had been tracking Leaana, but after about the first day, he had decided this was where she was heading. She needed to cross the Animas River, which meant she was determined to find the elven caravan. She must still be trying to find out if the eagle she saw in the falconry show was her familiar.

The Animas River lay before them. The sun setting in the west, making the water glow with a red color instead of its normal silver. As the three companions approached the ford, Togan let out a warning growl. Sagan dropped to his knees and examined the ground.

"What do you see there, Boss?" Masque asked while staying back out of the way so he would not mess up the tracks that Sagan was examining.

"Leaana's tracks definitely lead to the river. She crossed here," Sagan said as he scented the air, "but I'm smelling Orcs. Their smell is faint, they have only been gone a day or so, and I see tracks here on the bank besides Leaana's. The tracks look to be the same age as Leaana's. So, they were either here when Leaana was or somewhere close to that time. I really hope she is ok."

"Well, Boss, we have another problem. The rope that is supposed to be going across the river to help with the ford crossing has been cut. There is no way we are going to get across this river here." Masque said as he reached down and began to drag the rope from the water. "It looks like it was cut from the other side, Boss. Maybe your sister made it across, saw some orcs on this side and decided to cut the rope so they couldn't follow."

"Maybe Masque. Unfortunately, I can't tell. What do I do now? I can't just let my sister wander on her own. I have to find a way to catch up with her."

"Well Boss do you have any idea where she may be going?" Masque asked while moving back from the bank to stand on a bit more solid ground.

"I think she is trying to catch the elven caravan that is heading to the Norther Elf kingdom for the festival. She saw an eagle in a falconry show that crashed into the ground during its performance and my sister fainted. Ever since then she has been convinced that the eagle is her familiar. She must be trying to find out and free the bird." Sagan dismounted from Karr's back and lead him back away from the edge of the river. Perhaps they should camp while they figure out what to do.

"Ok Boss. If you are going to catch up with your sister, I see you having two choices on what to do. One we go north from here cross the Animas at the bridge at the Remis plateau and then ride to cut the elven caravan off as they head north. The second choice, we head south and use the marshland bridge and hope we can chase them down. Personally, I think you would catch them quicker heading north Boss."

Sagan sighed as he looked at the sun, "You're probably right, Masque. It's just so frustrating not to be able to continue to follow her path and just hope we can find her. Looks like we only have about an hour or so of daylight left. Why don't we find a place to camp for the night? How are you coming on, whatever it is you are working on so you can keep up with Karr better?"

"Almost done with it Boss. After tonight you should be able to gallop whenever you want to Boss" Masque replied with a wink. "I agree we should find a place to camp. I have something else to discuss with you Boss as we settle in for the night."

Togan sniffed the air and let out a short growl. "Togan doesn't like the smell of the Orcs here let's move a bit away from the river bank before we make camp and try to find some shelter. There was a small grove of trees a little bit back might make a good place camp and be a bit more sheltered."

"Fine with me Boss. Knowing those Orcs are this far south has made me a bit nervous. I think we need to be more careful about being so visible. I know you want to hurry to try and find your sister, but I think we need to use caution. Which is what I want to talk to you about Boss." Masque said turning to head back the direction they came.

Sagan mounted Karr and turned him to follow Masque who had already started jogging towards the grove of trees they had seen earlier. Togan ran ahead, nose searching the air for any further sign of Orcs in the area. After half an hour or so they reached the grove of trees they had seen earlier. Sagan dismounted and tied Karr to a tree. Togan ran off and began to search the area, while Masque and Sagan began to set up their camp. Sagan ran a rope between two of the trees and hung his saddle blanket across it to make a shelter for them. It would keep the wind off them and keep them dry if there was any rain during the night.

While Sagan did this Masque began gathering wood and started a small fire for cooking. After the few nights they had already spent together making camp Sagan and Masque had established this as their common routine. Masque took some of the smoked deer from Sagan's saddle bag, and a couple of potatoes and put them in a small pot that Sagan had with him for cooking. He added some water and put it over the fire to boil.

The two companions sat down beside the fire to rest from the day's travel now that the camp was set up and dinner was started.

"So Boss," Masque began "I've been thinking about our situation. If orcs have made it down this far at least once, then we may run into more of them while we are searching for your sister. It might be a good idea for you to learn to fight so you can better defend yourself. I've studied just about every fighting style there is and will be happy to teach you, Boss. I know how to fight and will if I have to, but I am really a pacifist and refuse to unless I am directly attacked. Your strength and speed are a huge advantage in a fight Boss but, if you actually have some training you will be much more effective."

"You really think we are going to run into more of those things Masque?" Sagan asked.

"I do Boss. If they are this far down the Animas, there is no telling how many of them are between us and the Remis plateau. I really feel you need some combat skills, Boss, and something better to fight with than that hunting knife."

"Well Masque you claim to be the expert what do you think I need."

Masque reached into his bag and rummaged around a bit. "Well, Boss, first thing you need is a way to protect yourself from other weapons. I don't want to put you in armor because that would slow you down and your speed is your greatest advantage. So, let's try this." With that, Masque pulled something out of his bag of holding. He was holding what looked like a long glove with part of a sleeve attached to it. Mounted to the glove and sleeve was a small piece of metal. The metal looked like a small oval with a point at one end over the fingers. Another round piece of metal was on the underside of the glove, across the palm.

Sagan slipped the sleeve and glove onto his left hand. The oval of metal was only an inch or two wider than his arm, but was slightly raised by padding over the sleeve. The sleeve and metal extended from the back of the fingers to just below the elbow. A leather strap at the wrist and just below the elbow helped to secure it in place. Sagan marveled at how light it was. He could hardly tell he was wearing anything. Sagan flexed his hand and made a fist. His fingers closed over the metal square across the palm.

"That is a device of my own design, Boss. It protects your arm and bones from enemy weapons without you really having to think about it. This will give you a way to block sword strokes by just using your arm. With a shield, you have to think more about position and placement. This will be more instinctive. With your speed, it will give you a definite advantage and keep you light and able to move. The spike at the end gives you a bit of a weapon when you have to punch with your left hand. The metal rod on the palm reinforces your fingers to give your punch more power, Boss. I call it a Brield. It is a combination of a shield and a set of bracers."

Sagan moved his arm back and forth and around, getting used to the feel of the brield on his arm. It was so light it was almost like it wasn't there. Masque reached back into his bag of holding. This time, he brought out a sword in a scabbard. "This is the sword, Carameth. In the ancient dwarven language, that means Harvester." Masque turned the handle of the sword toward Sagan.

Sagan reached for the handle of Carameth and withdrew the sword from the scabbard with the sound of steel scraping on leather. The sword was about three feet long. The steel blade had a slight blue tint to it and Sagan could see small lines worked into the metal. Dwarven runes were carved into the blade close to a simple brass T cross piece. The hilt was wrapped in soft leather with a small bit of padding so that it rested easily in the hand. The sword felt like an extension of his own arm. There seemed to be very little weight to it and he handled it easily.

"While we travel Boss, I will start teaching you how to use these. I expect you to do what I ask when I ask it. The moves I teach you we will repeat time and time again until they become instinctive. It will take that much practice so you don't have to think when you are fighting and can just react Boss. Oh, and one more thing. After I finish my device, we probably should not have any more fires. They could tell the orcs where we are."

Nodding at this last statement, Sagan began weaving through the grove swinging the sword and pretended to be blocking with the brield. Masque watched his movement. "You have some natural grace and instinct Boss. We will build on that." Togan came back into the grove. Seeing Sagan moving around with the sword and brield he barked and began to run around with Sagan barking and leaping. Masque chuckled as he watched the two companions play together. He knew the hard work that was coming.

Masque reached into his bag. Time to finish the other device he was building. He would need it to keep up with what was coming. Dinner and a couple hours of work on his invention, then a good night sleep. Tomorrow the training would begin.

Chapter 21

Leaana's stomach growled. Her hunger pains were getting worse, but the worst part was the head ache she had from not eating. The past three days since she had crossed the Animas river at the Silver Ford had been an education for her. When she had rushed her way across the ford her saddle bags had come untied and washed down stream taking her food supplies with them. She still had her bow and the arrows that went with it, but she had been traveling through the southern marshes and game had not been readily available. She could have taken time to hunt but every moment she delayed put the Elven caravan that much farther ahead. So, she had pushed on. She slept fitfully at night as her stomach ached and rumbled. Luckily, she had not lost her water skin, so she had clean water to drink but as she wandered through the marshes, she wanted nothing more than to bathe. The thick sticky mud of the marshes caked on her and Kada's legs as they traveled. After a few hours it felt like she was one giant piece of walking mud.

She pushed on. Unable to have a fire to warm herself at night because of the dampness all around her, no food and covered in mud, the days and nights started to blur together and Leaana began to doubt that she had made the right decision in going off on her own. If she had talked to Sagan about her dreams and ideas maybe, he would have agreed to go with her. Then perhaps at least one of them would have kept their food stores while crossing the ford and she could at least have something to eat. But as it was, she was hungry, dirty, tired, and just miserable.

Then just before sunset on the third day she found them. She smelled the smoke from their cook fires first. The smell of wood smoke came to her from the distance, and she imagined how wonderful the warmth of those fires would feel. She thought of riding in to the elven encampment, asking for food, a fire and the chance to get clean. But she might be given a guarded escort as she moved around the camp, and it would make what she came to do nearly impossible. Best if she was undiscovered. Once she had found the Eagle, and determined if they were truly joined, well then, she would have to get them away. But after that perhaps she could hunt and rest.

She could see the smoke now. Rising above the scrubby trees of the marshlands. This was close enough for now. The sun would be down soon and under the cover of darkness it would be much easier to sneak into the elven caravan camp and find the eagle.

REST

The thought was so strong it was almost like her mind was talking to her. She was even more tired than she thought. She rode into a small clearing. The clearing was almost like a small island in the middle of the swamp. The ground was slightly higher here and there was a break in the trees, so the water and mud receded and dried enough for a bit of grass to grow. The grass would create a bit of soft place for her to rest and would be dry enough she could lay out her bed roll and roll up in her blankets without them getting sodden. She would be able to rest in warmth for a few hours. If only she could silence her grumbling stomach, then she would knew she would be able to rest well.

REST

Again, that thought came to her almost unbidden. Leaana dismounted from Kada, led her over to one of the little scrubby trees beside the clearing and tied the reins around it. She removed her blanket from where it was tied to the saddle and walked to the center of the clearing knowing this would be driest part. She laid out her blanket on the soft grass. Wrapping herself in her blanket she lay back on the grass, closed her eyes and as her body heat filled her blanket, warming her, she fell almost instantly asleep.

WAKE

Leaana sat up. She looked around. Leaana was alone in the clearing. Kada had folded her knees under her and laid down to sleep. She was probably as tired as Leaana. Leaana had been pushing her hard as well. Leanna could see where Kada had made a quick meal of some of the grass in the clearing. At least one of us could satisfy their hunger. Looking around again Leaana wondered what had woken her. She could have sworn she had heard someone tell her to wake.

She looked up at the sky, the half-moon was already low in the west. Close to Moonset. She had been asleep for 5 or 6 hours. That meant that she had two to three hours of uncertain light or almost total darkness before the sun began to rise. But once the sun did begin to brighten the sky she would still have about an hour of shadowy low light before the world was truly bright enough to see. If she was going to sneak into the elven caravan she had better get moving.

COME

There it was again. This time she was awake and alert enough to realize that she actually did hear the word Come. Well not actually hear it. It was more like it just appeared in her mind. It almost had a sound to it but was almost like a touch. Kind of like a high pitch and a feather. She imagined it would be the sound a feather would make if you could stretch it over a lute and strum it.

COME

Again. Slightly more urgent this time. Leaana got up, rolled her blanket and tied it to Kada. Untying Kada's reins she leapt onto her back and began riding in the direction she had smelled the wood smoke before she had slept. Now she noticed the smell of smoke was weaker, now more of a smell of smoldering ash as the fires burned low during the night as the members of the caravan slept. Soon, in just a few hours, she knew the members of the caravan would awaken, rise and stoke those fires again to cook their breakfast. With that thought her stomach growled again. Soon she told herself, soon she would take time to hunt. But she had to finish this first. The pull was stronger than ever.

COME

The feather touch in her head again. She rode through the marsh with a rededicated sense of purpose.

CARE

A feeling of danger and warning ran through Leaana. She realized she was riding too fast and too recklessly for this. She slowed her pace, dismounted, and began to lead Kada. Now that she was moving more slowly, she began to hear the sounds of the caravan in the distance. Small bell chimes from wind chimes, a cough here, someone snoring there. Then a vision over took her eyes, a smoldering fire, the bars of a cage, the cage swinging slightly in the breeze. Next to the cage is a Red wagon. Not just red, red was the primary color, but there were diamonds of blue painted around the middle and on the wheels. Leaana could even see a sign beside the door. The sign read "Falconer's Guild: Head Falconer: Fataso. Second Falconer: Parmarso: Come see the eagle Aramin and her amazing feats of aerial acrobatics."

Leaana tripped over a root and fell. The image left her mind, and she realized she had not seen the root because the image in her head and taken over her vision. It was almost like she was seeing that instead of the marshland around her. Through the bushes ahead of her she could see the first of the wagons of the elves' caravan. She had found them. Suddenly, somehow, she knew that the red and blue caravan she was looking for was in the third row of wagons from where she was.

Tying Kada to one of the bushes close to her so that she would still be screened from the wagons, Leaana took a second to listen and feel the night air around her. She attuned herself to the movement of the shadows and prepared to use all her stalking skills to ghost her way to the caravan she needed to find. Moving slowly, almost painfully slowly, Leaana passed through the screen of bushes and began to move towards the row of wagons. She reached the first wagon and crawled under it to take a quick breath.

STOP

The voice in her head again. Leaana froze, still crouched beneath the wagon in the first row. Not moving, barely daring to breathe, she waited. An elf carrying a spear entered the space between this row of wagons and the next row she was headed to. He walked slowly, pausing every once in a while and looking around. Leaana remained crouched and frozen under the wagon. The guard was doing his normal patrol and had already come this way 3 times in the course of his rounds. He stopped in front of the wagon Leaana was hiding under, turned around, looked behind him, then continued on his way to the end of the row. Turned the corner and began walking beside the wagons. The sides of two wagons were between Leaana and the guard now.

SPEED

Leaana didn't have to be told twice: she quickly crawled from under the wagon she had been hiding under and moved across the alley to the next row of wagons. She then quickly crawled underneath a wagon in that next row then paused before crossing the next alley. Looking out from her hiding place she could see the wagon across the alley had cages hanging around it and could see a board leaning against the side next to the stairs that one used to enter the wagon. Looking at the cages Leaana's heart leapt. There hanging on the corner of the wagon closest to her was a cage with the eagle she had seen in her encampment. If the sign she had seen in her vision moments ago was right the eagle's name was Aramin.

NO

Aramin didn't feel right for the name. The voice in her head seemed to agree. Then what is it, she wondered.

SCRILL

A sound almost like the sound an eagle would make when taking prey formed in her head but was almost word like. Scrill, was the closest sound Leaana could think that was close to the sound she heard.

YES

"So, your name is Scrill. Well either I'm going crazy, or I truly am a familiar and we are communicating."

SPEED

"You're right — we have time to figure out all this later — need to get moving" Leaana thought. Staying low Leaana crossed the alley between the wagons. She heard deep breathing and light snoring coming from the wagon that Scrill's cage was attached to. Standing up Leaana reached up and opened the cage door. She was about to reach her hand in to help the eagle out of the cage, but she hesitated. Here was a magnificently beautiful bird in front of her but at the same time truly dangerous. Her long curved beak was sharp and on her feet were talons that were nearly as long as Leaana's fingers. Those claws could rip through her flesh with ease. What was she doing?

CARE

"Ok if you say so I hope this isn't all in my head and you aren't going to rip through my hand with those talons of yours," Leaana thought. She then reached her hand into the cage and allowed Scrill to place one foot then a second onto her hand. She could feel the sharp ends of the eagle's talons pricking her skin but they didn't penetrate. Slowly Leaana withdrew her hand and Scrill from the cage. As soon as she was clear Scrill leapt from Leaana's hand flapped her massive wings and lifted into the air.

Leaana's vision changed again, now she could see herself standing beside the caravan looking up, then she saw the guard at the end of the row of wagons, about to turn the corner onto the row Leaana was on, as he continued his patrol.

Leeana's vision was hers again and she quickly ducked under the wagon next to her and froze. The guard with the spear rounded the corner and walked down the alley way between the wagons. Leaana held her breath and remained motionless. She used all the skills she had developed helping Sagan stalk deer in those few times she had been allowed to go with him, to stay still, and silent while the guard walked by.

The guard rounded the corner at the end of the row of wagons again and headed further into the elven caravan. Quickly Leaana crawled across the alley where the guard had just been and began to head back to where she had left Kada.

Over her vision, she saw Kada slightly below her and swaying slightly, no that was the limb that Scrill was perched on that was swaying. This time the vision didn't totally take over Leaana's vision and she was still able to see where she was going. It was still confusing as it seemed one eye was looking at her horse, and the other eye was still seeing the wagons she was crawling under but at least she could tell where she was going.

The sun was starting to rise. Very soon the elves would be waking and starting to stir. Leaana wanted to hurry but knew she would be more likely to be seen if she did. Still moving slowly and using the shadows to help conceal her, she made her way back to the bushes. Crawling under the bushes she soon found Kada right where she had left her. Scrill perched on the limb of the bush above Kada and waiting on Leaana to arrive.

SPEED

Scrill took off and began flying to the east. Leaana quickly untied Kada and jumped onto her back. One eye again seeing the earth from above. Only a short distance away Leaana could see that the marshlands ended, and the grasslands began. Riding quickly, they made their way east. Leaana's stomach growled again. But the pain in her stomach did not bother her as much now. Her heart was racing. She was a familiar. She and her animal guide had found each other, and she could communicate with an eagle, and see what the eagle saw. She rode into the east keeping her eyes on Scrill and following where she led. After two hours the ground dried and the rolling grasslands began to roll out before them, another half day riding and she would enter the western woodlands. Then she could find somewhere to hide with Scrill so she could hunt and get some proper rest. With a sense of joy and peace Leaana urged Kada to a gallop as Scrill continued to fly in front of them now heading to the northeast.

SPEED

Yes, ride hard now, get some distance between herself and the elves then maybe she could take time to set some snares or hunt. But for now, she would just rejoice that she now knew her place and had found Scrill. Once she met back up with Sagan everything would be ok again and they would return to the encampment, and she would know where she belonged.

Chapter 22

Fataso opened his eyes. The first light of the rising sun was just beginning to peek through the cracks between the shutters on the windows. Fataso looked around. The cages of the falcons and hawks used in the falconry show were hanging all around the inside of the Caravan. Parmarso, Fataso's falconry assistant, slept on the other small sleeping bench across from him. The inside of the Caravan was a really simple space. Two narrow sleeping benches stretched down the length of each side of the wagon. The tops of the benches would fold up, revealing storage below. The storage spaces had his and Parmarso's clothes and various supplies needed for their falconry shows. At the end of each sleeping bench, was a small closet. The closets had their cloaks and a few longer pieces of clothing.

The roof of the caravan was high enough to stand in the middle to move around. Down the middle of the roof a line of cages was hung, each holding a falcon or hawk. There were currently five cages. The hook closest to the door was empty. Normally, the cage for Aramin would be hanging there. Last night Aramin seemed very restless. In fact, in the last few days, ever since Aramin had crashed into the ground in the Natarin encampment, the eagle had seemed restless. The impact had not seemed to cause any physical damage to Aramin, but she had not been herself since it happened. Fataso had decided last night to hang her cage outside to give her some fresh air. He hoped this would help her with her recovery and would help her calm down. He had been resting her the last few evenings while they traveled and had been working with some of the other birds. This morning he planned on taking Aramin out of her cage and giving her some exercise, he needed to be sure she had no permanent injuries.

Parmarso was still sleeping. He would be asleep at least another hour. He was not an early riser. Fataso had always woken early. He contributed it to his early childhood living on a small chicken farm. On the farm, there had always been plenty to do. The family woke with the sun, got up, had a quick meal and gone to work. There had been eggs to gather, chickens to feed, crops to tend, chicks to check on, and all sorts of other things to do. He helped with it all. In all the years since his childhood, the habit of waking with the sun had never gotten out of his system. Getting up, he stood and got his clothes for the day out of the storage under his sleeping bench. Today would be another day of travel, so a simple tunic style. shirt and breaches of cotton would be the clothes of the day. Ducking below the cages, Fataso made his way to the rear of the caravan and opened the door. Stepping down, he looked at where he had hung Aramin's cage the night before and his heart nearly stopped. The cage door was open and Aramin was gone.

How could this have happened? None of the other elves in the caravan would have messed with the cage. They knew how unique Aramin was and how valued she was by Fataso and Parmarso. Fataso took a few deep breaths to calm down. Panicking would do nothing to help. Looking around he noticed some small soft foot prints near the base of the cage. Kneeling to examine the foot prints closer he noticed they were not the type of prints he would expect to see. These prints seemed to be made by a soft simple shoe or boot. The elves normally wore harder soled boots with a small heel especially while traveling. These prints did not have any sign of a heel print. So, someone from outside the caravan had been here some time recently and must have freed Aramin. The prints were very freshly made sometime in the last couple of hours. Looking around he found another few tracks leading across the lane separating his caravan from the next row. Moving across the lane he looked at the ground. There under the caravan he saw where the dew on the ground had been disturbed as someone crouched under this wagon. There more prints leading away back toward the edge of the encampment into the marshes.

Following the faint traces on the ground he made his way out of the elves camp to a small grassy area raised just out of the marshes. Looking around he found signs that someone had laid there, and he saw hoof prints. Someone with a horse had been there. Two lines of prints. One coming into the clearing from the South and one that seemed to be leaving the clearing to the Northwest. Did this mysterious rider have Aramin? That seemed to be the case or if the rider didn't have Aramin he or she at least was responsible for freeing Aramin. Either way Fataso needed to know what happened and why. He simply couldn't let the falconry guild down by allowing their most unique and interesting bird to simply disappear.

Hurrying back to his caravan Fataso ran up the couple steps leading to the door. Throwing the door open and calling out, "Parmarso, Parmarso, wake up!"

Parmarso sat bolt upright on his sleeping bench. "I'm up, I'm up, why are you screaming." The sound of sleep still heavy in his voice, his eyes not quite focusing.

"Aramin is gone, someone snuck into the encampment last night, opened her cage and let her loose." Fataso said as he grabbed a small bag from the closet on his side and, raising his sleeping bench to reach the storage beneath, began to stuff items of clothing into the bag. "I am going to try and track the person that freed her to see if I can find Aramin. I need you to continue on with the rest of the group. The falconry guild must be represented."

Parmarso more alert now, looked at Fataso almost in a panic "I am just your assistant you can't want me to continue without you. What if we have to perform? I am not ready"

Fataso stopped his packing. He crossed the small open space between himself and his assistant. Placing his hand on Parmarso's shoulder and looking him in the eye Fataso explained, "Parmarso, do you really think the wise leaders of our guild would send only two people on this journey to represent them if they didn't have full confidence in both of them? It is a long journey and one of us could be injured or become ill. The other would have to then carry on. I have seen you working with the birds. They listen to you, and you handle them well. You simply need the confidence to perform.

You may even be better with the falcons than I am. Aramin is mine. She is my responsibility, which is why I was chosen. You were chosen to go with me because you are the best the guild has to offer."

"You really think I'm good enough to represent the guild? I've watched you perform and the way you connect to the audience and the connection you have with Aramin is just amazing."

"Yes, Parmarso you can do this. Now I need to get moving before the trail gets old. I am taking one of the horses we use to pull the Caravan. Get with the camp quartermaster and get one of the spare horses so you can keep up with the group."

Looking at Fataso with a puzzled expression Parmarso asked, "How will you know how to follow the trail? I didn't know you knew how to track."

"Before I was in the falconry guild, I was a high ranking member of the trackers guild. I guided hunters in pursuit of game. An accident one day that resulted in a severe knee injury ended my days as a tracker. I still know how to track so I will be able to follow the trail. But the longer I stay here talking with you the farther away who ever I am looking for is getting."

Grabbing some food and stuffing it in his bag as well Fataso turned and hurried out of the caravan. Walking to the front where the horses were tethered, he selected a horse. The horse he chose seemed to be fairly calm while pulling the cart. Steady, a good worker, but not too spirited. Throwing his bag over his shoulder Fataso climbed onto the horses back. Parmarso came running around the caravan just as Fataso reached his seat on the horses back.

"Be careful Fataso. I will make you proud." Parmarso cried as Fataso turned the horse to ride back through the last few rows of the camp to where he had seen the other hoof prints.

"I know you will. Once I find out what happened to Aramin I will try and catch up with you. With any luck I will be back with the group before we reach Arctana." And with that statement Fataso kicked his heels into the horses sides. The horse accelerated. Fataso swayed on the horses back. He was not the best rider, but he would never catch someone riding if he was on foot. Regaining his balance Fataso guided the horse in to the marshes.

He found the hoof prints and began to ride to the northwest following the trail. Soon the elven camp was lost to sight.

Chapter 23

Leaana slowed Kada to a stop just outside the edge of a line of trees. The trees marked the edge of the Western woodlands. Her stomach growled again. Soon she was going to have to stop and find some time to hunt so she could get something to eat. Once she was inside the forest, she should be able to find a place that is sheltered enough to make a camp for a night to have a fire and cook. But first she would have to find something to cook.

"Schreeack" Leaana heard Scrill's cry from above. She looked up and saw the eagle flying low towards her. Just as she got above Leaana, something dropped on Kada's back. Leaana quickly grabbed at it to keep it from falling and felt soft fur. It was a hare. A rather nice size hare.

FOOD

The word formed in her mind. Again, Leaana was not sure if she thought it at that moment or if it was a message from Scrill. Looking up, she watched Scrill circle, then suddenly drop from the sky, vanishing from sight into the trees before her. A few seconds later she reappeared, climbing back to the sky and turning to come back towards Leaana. This time Leaana could see that Scrill was holding something in her talons. Once she was overhead, Scrill let go of what she was carrying. Leaana reached out to catch it and another plump hare landed in her hands.

FOOD

EAT

SLEEP

This time, Leaana was certain she understood. These were instructions from Scrill. Scrill has hunted for her. Leaana had never considered that Scrill would do that. She knew eagles hunted small game, but she was still getting used to the idea that she was not totally alone. Leaana kicked her heels into Kada's side and started to guide her into the cover of the trees. It did not take long, once Leaana was under the thick canopy of trees for it to start getting darker, even though the sun was still high in the pre-sinking sky. The thick canopy blocked the light and patches of sunlight streamed through in small breaks between the trees. The western woodlands stretched from the western side of the Animas River west and north all the way to the border with Arctana. She had been riding north and east, following Scrill. At some point, she would have to cross the Animas River again, most likely using the bridge above the falls at the Remis plateau. The woodlands would become more and more rocky as she got closer to the Animas and the Remis plateau. Leaana shook her head and laughed softly to herself. Her father had spent hours and hours teaching her the key points of geography for the land they lived in. Where the forest was, the plains, the mountains, and so on. She had hated the lessons. She didn't know why she should learn it or would ever need it. Now that she was on her own, traveling through the world, it was amazing how much she remembered. It helped her to know where she was and figure out the best path to meet up with Sagan.

Her vision shifted, Leaana now saw a small clearing, two trees that at one time had grown close together had fallen, when they fell, they separated slightly. The space in between them formed a small clearing. The clearing would be sheltered and fairly well hidden. Her vision was hers again. Looking around she saw a log lying on its side a little ways of to her left. On a branch close by she saw Scrill perched, waiting on her. As Leaana drew closer to the downed tree she saw that was fairly large. The roots of the two trees form the point of a V. There is a small opening between the bases just wide enough for her and Kada to enter. Once inside Leaana looked around. Leaves formed a soft covering over the forest floor. The clearing formed when the two massive trees fell was sheltered on two sides by the trunks of the trees. On top of the triangle is a massive tangle of branches from where the limbs of the trees intermixed as they fell. Here she would be protected from view, be able to have a fire and sleep to regain her strength.

Climbing down from Kada's back Leaana tied the reins to one of the branches. She then took her bedroll from where it was tied behind Kada's saddle and laid it out on the soft leaves covering the ground. Her bed roll looked so good. It would be nice to just lay down and sleep. Her stomach growled reminding her that she would not be able to sleep until she got something to eat. Leaana quickly gathered some tinder and fire wood. It was in ample supply from the two trees that formed her small camp site. She cleared some leaves from a small area so she would not catch the forest floor on fire. In the small space she laid out the tinder, some of the leaves from around, and some small twigs. She had some larger branches close by to feed the fire once she got it going. She took her flint from the specially designed pocket on the sheath of her hunting knife. Striking the side of the blade on the flint she threw some small sparks onto the dried leaves. Soon there was smoke, she blew on it and coaxed a small flame. Feeding some twigs, and then the small branches she soon has a fire going. Using her hunting knife, she quickly skinned the two hares. They were nice and plump having been feeding on the fresh spring grasses. Using the flat of her knife blade she drove two forked sticks into the ground on either side of the fire. She sharpened a stick and stuck it through the hares. She laid this in the fork of the two branches over the coals of the fire to heat. While the hares cooked, she walked over to Kada and got the water skin. Turning it up she realized that it was empty. The drink she just took was her last until she could find a water source.

FOLLOW

Looking up Leeana saw Scrill flying overhead and back out the entrance between the two trees. Leaana quickly rose and jogged to follow. Looking up she kept the eagle in view. After just a few minutes Scrill came to rest on a tree branch. The tree stood next to a small but quickly flowing stream. The water was clear and cool. Leaana quickly tasted it and then finding it clean and just a little sweet she quickly cupped her hands and drank great mouthfuls. She filled her water skin. Then she realized she was still covered in mud and grime from the marshes. She quickly removed her tunic and breeches and waded into the stream. It was not very deep, just midway up her calves but she splashed water on herself and rinsed off most of the mud. She quickly rinsed out her tunic and breeches removing most of the mud. It will feel good to be clean and have something clean to wear tomorrow. Gathering her water skin and damp clothes she made her way back to her campsite. She walked over to the small fire, threw another branch on, and turned the hares to allow them to cook evenly. The smell of the cooking hares started to fill the small clearing and she could hear fat occasionally dripping into the fire. Her stomach growls so loudly that it sounded like a small bear.

Soon the heat of the fire dried her skin, and she wrapped herself in her blanket. She hung her tunic and breeches from a branch to allow them to dry overnight. She looked up and saw Scrill perched on a limb nearby. It appeared that she caught a squirrel and was already making a meal of it. Leaana pulled one of the hares from the fire almost burning her fingers in the process. Quickly Leaana blew on the hot meat to cool it and began eating taking large mouthfuls. She ate so fast she hardly noticed what the hare tasted like. She finished one quickly. After the first hare was eaten, she realized she should probably save some of the second. She looked around for something to store the meat in. She realized that without her saddle bags she had no way to transport the meat. So best thing to do is eat it now. She would be able to hunt tomorrow or perhaps Scrill could catch something else as they travel.

Her belly full for the first time in nearly four days Leaana realized how tired she was. She built up the fire a bit so it would burn for a while to help keep her warm, looking up she saw Scrill still perched on the tree branch. "I don't know if you can understand me Scrill. But thank you, you have saved my life. I now know who I am and where I belong. I understand you can help me survive and we can help each other. Thank you."

SLEEP

"Yes, I will sleep now. Again, thank you." And with that Leeana stretched out next to the fire rolled in her blanket and was fast asleep almost before her head was on the ground.

Chapter 24

"Ok Boss let's start your training come over here," Masque pointed at a spot on the outer edge of the camp. It is just past rising, and the sun is still low in the rising sky, long shadows stretch across the ground. Sagan and Masque had awoken just before rising, had eaten a quick breakfast and were now getting ready to start the day. They discussed the night before that Masque would train Sagan for about an hour, giving him the beginning basic moves and then he would drill him as they traveled. The point was to maximize travel time in their search for Leaana while giving Sagan the combat training he needed. The moves must become instinctive, the only way to do that is through constant practice. Each day Masque will train Sagan on new moves and techniques and then drill him as they ride.

"Ok Boss, stand with your feet apart the width of your shoulders with your right foot slightly in front. Keep your balance on your toes so you can move quickly. Now Boss when I say One, swing your sword diagonally from your left shoulder to your right side at the waist. Two, swing the opposite, right to left. Three, thrust the blade forward. On four throw your brield up in front of you to block an oncoming stroke. Ready, begin One, Two, Three, Four, One Two three four" Masque called out. After a few minutes of repeating those four pose Masque added more. If Sagan had a question Masque would demonstrate. Soon Masque had taught Sagan 12 positions. Some defensive, some offensive.

He would start calling out the numbers in order. After Sagan got familiar with them and was moving quickly between poses, he would change the order and call out the positions at random.

"Keep your balance, Boss. Balance is the key Boss, never swing so hard that you fall forward or backward. Three, eight, one, ten, good. Faster, six, eight, four," Masque called, hardly pausing between numbers. Sagan moved almost in a blur, hitting each pose, then immediately moving to the next. Sweat was pouring off him freely. He could feel energy flowing from Togan. But it was not as much as normal. Just enough, he could tell to give him more speed and strength. Faster, he moved through the poses. The sword almost seeming to blur as it moved this way and that. Finally, after what felt like forever, Masque called a halt. Sagan slumped to the ground, his arms aching, so the sword sank to the ground. Sagan breathed in great gasps of air. He could feel the strength from Togan slow to a trickle, but the extreme tiredness that normally followed their bonding was not there. He had been able to draw the energy without totally exhausting himself.

"Well done, Boss, catch your breath while I finish breaking camp. We will ride for a while, then I will drill you on those same moves, but expect you to do them from horseback. All the practice will build your strength and timing."

With that, Masque went to work breaking camp while Sagan recovered. Sagan was already fit, his normal life of hunting and running with Togan kept him in good shape. The weight of the sword made his arms ache. But the sword was perfectly balanced, so it really felt like an extension of his arm. Soon the camp was broken down and packed away. Masque was tying a length of rope to Karr's saddle and the other end around his waist.

"Time to see if my invention helps me keep up, Boss" and with that, Masque pulls out what he had been working on the last three nights. Sagan came over to take a close look at what he had built.

A flat piece of metal, about two feet wide and three and a half feet long. Two leather straps went across it in the middle about a foot and a half apart. On each end of the flat piece of metal were two metal wheels. Carefully crafted with four spokes and curved pieces of metal.

"What is it, Masque?" Sagan asked in wonder.

"Well, Boss, I call it a chariot board. My feet go in the straps, and I stand balanced on the wheels. The rope is tied around me and as you ride, I am pulled behind the horse. This way, I don't have to run to keep up." Masque said as he placed his feet into the leather straps and balanced on the board.

"Shall we give it a try Boss." Masque asked while balancing on the metal plate.

Sagan put Carameth into its sheath and went to mount Karr. Climbing into Karr's saddle he touched his heels to the horse's sides and Karr starts walking forward. Looking over his shoulder he sees the rope begin to pull tight. Just as the last of the slack was pulled out of the rope, he saw Masque lean back just a little bit. Then the rope pulled tight, and Masque lurched forward. Sagan brought Karr to a stop. Masque fell forward and caught himself with his arms. Quickly he got back in place, smiled at Sagan and yelled.

"Let's try it again Boss. I'll lean back a bit more this time should help keep my balance."

Again, Sagan began walking Karr forward and again, Masque leaned back, this time he leaned back farther shifting his weight, so he rotated the plate so that the back of it was touching the ground. This time as the rope pulled him up right, he was able to compensate for the forward movement and he started to roll along behind Karr and Sagan.

After a few minutes Masque asked to pick up the pace and Sagan increased Karr to a trot. Masque kept his balance his knees flexing to absorb the shock from the ground and rocks. Soon Masque yelled for an increase in speed again and Sagan took Karr to a canter. Masque kept his balance. He gave a thumbs up and on they traveled. As the sun continued to climb in the rising sky Togan appeared. He had been away from camp in the morning when they awoke but now, he joined them. He loped beside Masque watching him bounce behind Karr on his unusual device. Masque was well balanced now and was moving with the rhythm of the ground.

"Ok Boss, time to practice again." Masque called out. Sagan pulled Carameth from its sheath as Masque began to call out numbers. "One, Two, Seven, Four…" and so on for an hour. Masque would let Sagan rest a while then the drilling would begin again. Every so often they would stop for water and quick meal and to let Karr recover. Masque would sit and rest his legs from having to keep them moving on his chariot board and Sagan would rest his arms. Togan would scout ahead during these times of rest. Several times Sagan would smell the scent of dirt and death that he now associated with orcs, he would be getting the smell from his shared connection with Togan, Sagan and Masque would then change their path and move farther from the Animas River. All the while still trying to move north trying to find Leaana assuming she is heading to the bridge at the Remis Plateau.

Every time they would adjust their course to avoid orc party Sagan would get increasingly worried. The orcs seem to be everywhere, Sagan began to wonder if Leaana had run into any of them. This fear kept him pushing for more distance. Each day Masque would teach him twelve new poses and those would be mixed in with the other poses Sagan had learned. Each day they traveled usually at a canter, until well after moon rise. Camp would be set up and Sagan and Masque ate a quick meal before sleeping a few hours. As soon as the sun rose, they would break camp and again begin their quick paced training and travel. Sagan now constantly keeping a steady flow of energy with Togan, this helped him keep up with the physical demands of travel and training. An added benefit of the constant flow of energy is Sagan's senses were becoming more and more acute he could now smell the orcs from a distance on his own allowing Togan to scout further and further afield.

After the first day of constant sword practice Sagans arms were aching. The second day Sagans arms were so sore he could barely lift the sword. Masque drove him hard though making him work through the pain. The third day Sagan was still sore, but the weight of the sword is becoming familiar making the work easier.

Masque was getting more exhausted every day. He was taxing himself both mentally and physically. Mentally coming up with new trials and challenges to use to train Sagan. The rigorous training is almost as hard on Masque's nerves as it is on Sagan's arms. But trying to keep up the training while riding the chariot board made it even more taxing on his energy reserves.

The chariot board enabled him to keep up with Karr at a canter, but it was very physically draining. Riding all day with legs bent to absorb shocks and to keep his balance, was using every bit of reserve energy. Eventually he was going to have to ask Sagan for a day to recover his strength. Masque knew that Sagan was worried about his sister, but he was not going to be able to keep up this pace for much longer. That thought running through his head Masque prepared to take Sagan through another training session. He would find a way to discuss his need for rest tonight at camp.

Chapter 25

Fataso easily followed the trail through the marshlands, hoofprints on the soft muddy earth and the crushed marsh grasses made the trail obvious. Trying to make up time on the thieves while he had a clear trial, Fataso pushed his horse, galloping as much as possible. He made good time through the morning hours while the trail was easy to follow. Now he was entering the woodlands. Here, the trail was not as clear. He entered the woodlands following a game trail. The shadows of the trees, the hard packed earth, made signs of the trail harder to find. Reining in his horse, Fataso dismounted and got down on one knee examining the ground. The horse was panting. His mount was used to pulling a heavy wagon at a slow, predictable pace all day long. The galloping they had been doing for the last few hours was something the horse was not accustomed to. Fataso would need to walk for a while to allow the horse to recover or it would be useless to him. "Just as well," Fataso thought, "I need to be closer to the ground here to stay on the trail."

There just a few feet in front of him a hoofprint in the earth. They did go this way. Continuing now slowly down the game trail, Fataso used his old tracking skills to find the path he needed to try and recover Aramin. A hoof print here, a broken twig there all showed that someone had passed this way before him. Reaching a decision, Fataso jogged down the game trail leading the horse. Trying to make up time on his quarry. At least he would move faster until he had to decide where they went. If the trail forked or intersected another, he would slow until he could figure out the direction.

The game trail wound around deeper into the woodlands. The trees grew tightly overhead, their branches almost covering the trail entirely. The shadows made it difficult to see. Luckily, the game trail seemed to be fairly heavily used, as it was fairly obvious. After an hour or so, Fataso was beginning to lose all sense of direction in the dark shadows. Unable to see the sun from the heavy overgrowth, made it difficult to tell which way he was going. The small game trail he was following soon ran into a larger trail. Here Fataso paused. Which way did they go? Again, he knelt and looked for tracks. Hmm, there were multiple sets of tracks here. Some hoofprints were much deeper. Larger, heavier horses and riders. Perhaps the person who kidnapped Aramin had joined up with a larger party. Fataso will just have to follow this new set of tracks and hope they lead him to Aramin. Turning to follow the new tracks down a wider trail, Fataso noticed some tracks were boot prints mixed in with the hoofprints. Some people were on foot, and some were riding.

Fataso continued following the new sets of tracks for another hour. He could see more light up ahead. Perhaps there was a clearing. At least in the clearing he could get his bearings. He could now smell smoke also. Perhaps he had found their camp. Hopefully his quest was coming to an end. Suddenly his horse stopped and pulled back eyes wide with fear. "What is it boy?" Fataso asked while stroking the horse's neck, "It just smoke from a campfire." Fataso's soothing voice and gentle stroke soothed the horse. He was still nervous but was at least willing to go forward now. Fataso continued down the trail. Now he could hear something. It sounded like grunting growling. His horse shied again. "Now you're starting to make me nervous," Fataso crooned to his horse. "I know I haven't really thought about what I'm going to do when I find these bandits. Perhaps we should wait here a moment while I figure that out. What do you say boy?"

Just then there was a crashing sound from the bushes beside them. Fataso's horse already on edge reared and jumped back causing Fataso to have to drop the reins or get pulled off his feet. The horse bolted running back up the trail they had been following. Fataso watched the horse go for a moment then turned in the direction of the crashing sound. There, coming out of the bushes in the direction they had been heading was a creature like nothing

Fataso had ever seen. Four feet tall, green skin, fangs in its mouth and claws on its hands. The creature was wearing armor and carrying a large club with spikes on one side. CRASH from the bushes on the other side of the trail came another one. Then one came out from the trees behind him. Fataso had just enough time to realize that he was surrounded by these strange creatures before the first one gripped his arm in a grip like iron. Then Fataso saw the arm with the spiked club go up, a sharp pain to side of his head then the world went black.

Chapter 26

Leaana awoke as the sun began to lighten the rising sky. The dense tree cover meant she could not see the sun, but the grey light of early morning was beginning to brighten the small clearing. Climbing out of her bed roll Leaana noticed a slight chill in the air. Shivering, she quickly grabbed her breeches and tunic from where they were hanging near the smoldering embers of her fire. Grabbing her water skin Leaana noticed that it was close to being empty. She walked down to the stream she had bathed in the night before and filled the water skin. Splashing water on her face, she cleared the last of the sleep from her mind. She cupped her hand in the stream and took several large drinks. Refreshed she turned to head back to the campsite. Perhaps she could find something to eat before getting on the road.

QUICK

Scrill's thought shot through her mind like an order.

QUICK

The urgency Scrill was feeling came through with the command and Leaana began to run. She got back to the small clearing and looked around. Scrill was perched on the edge of her saddle hopping from one foot to the other. Leaana could still feel the sense of urgency from Scrill, her adrenaline was beginning to flow. Quickly Leaana grabbed the saddle, Scrill took to the air as Leaana put the saddle on Kada's back. Grabbing her hunting knife, she quickly tied it around her waist.

QUICK

Leaana began to hurriedly mount on to Kada's back as she heard a crash behind her as something came though the bushes close to one of the downed trees that provided her shelter in this clearing. Looking back, she saw a creature. It looked like one of the things that had chased her at the silver ford, but here she could see more details. Its face had yellow eyes, a long pointed nose, and the mouth extended slightly with sharp fangs coming down from the top over the bottom lip. The skin had a greenish color to it. It was wearing thick leather clothing and had what looked like a leather helmet on its head. As she watched frozen in fear the creature sniffed the air. It let out a growl and looked around. It saw Leaana sitting on Kada and began to look for a way to get to her.

Leaana looked at the opening between the two trees that was her only means of escape from the clearing. She would pass very close to the creature as she rode out. She hoped it would not be able to reach her. Turning Kada she kicked her heels into the horses side. Kada already anxious from smelling the strange creature and hearing its growl, needed no further urging and immediately began to gallop. Leaana had to check Kada with her reins to keep her in control long enough to navigate the small opening at the base of the trees. Exiting the clearing Leaana heard a roar behind her. Looking back, she saw the creature chasing her only a few steps behind.

RUN

Leaana heard and felt Scrill's command and urged Kada to run faster. Only Leaana's skill as a rider kept them from crashing into trees. She seemed to be moving slightly faster than normal which meant she was able to help guide Kada as she turned this way and that through the undergrowth.

Suddenly another creature was in front of them. Leaana turned Kada to the right as the creature reached out a clawed hand and tried to grab her. The claws scraped along Leaana's leg. She cried out in pain. Then a brown shape flew past her head. Leaana looked back and could see Scrill attacking the creatures eyes. Her claws scratching and beak pecking until it had destroyed the creatures left eye. It cried out in pain and grasped its head where the eye used to be. Scrill flew up again and was away.

Leaana could feel moisture on her leg, she knew she was bleeding from the scratches that the creature had made on her leg. Surprisingly she didn't feel any pain from it but knew that was from the adrenaline she was feeling as she ran. When she slowed down, she was sure she would feel the pain. A third creature loomed this one she saw sooner and was able to dodge to the left without it scratching her leg. Then suddenly another one was in front of her. This one managed to swipe at Kada's legs. Kada stumbled and Leaana was thrown from her back. The creature that had swiped at Kada's legs reached to grab Leaana. A blur of brown feathers swooped past Leaana and a gash opened on the creatures arm where Scrill's talons ripped the flesh open. The creature howled in pain. Leaana jumped up and turned to run as the creature howled. As she turned, she ran right into creature she had dodged just a few moments before. An iron grip closed around Leaana's shoulder. A green clawed fist slammed into the side of Leaana's head. Leaana's vision clouded as pain erupted in her head. A second blow, more pain, then everything went black.

Chapter 27

Masque awoke, some sound had awakened him. Opening his eyes as he sat up and saw Togan standing by his feet. This was the closest the wolf had ever come to him. Masque's heart beat a little faster as a small rivulet of fear ran down his spine. Togan was standing with his head down sniffling Masque's legs. The sniffing sound was what had woken him. Togan raised his head and Masque could see the black eyes of the wolf staring at him. He could see the wind ruffling the fur on the wolf's back even though the sun was not up, and it was still in the dark of night. Traveling with a wolf in day light with him coming and going is one thing, Masque could almost convince himself it was just a large dog. But this, with the wolf standing over him his eyes staring into Masque's was a very different thing. Togan sniffed again, turned his head slightly to the side and moved it up and down almost like a nod once. Then Togan bounded away and out of the camp.

Masque sat still for a few moments. Trying to get his heart rate back under control. Since the day he had first met Sagan and his wolf familiar this was the closest that Togan had gotten to him. Even on that first day when they had saved his life and Sagan had passed out after fighting the Orcs Togan had only allowed Sagan within about 20 feet of him before he began growling and showing his teeth. Why had he come this close now? Who could understand the reasoning of a wolf? Better not to linger on the problem. Sunrise was still an hour away. Masque thought of going back to sleep but knew that after that encounter sleep was impossible. He got up, leg muscles aching from the days riding the chariot board. He walked over to their small stack of supplies and began to pull out some food. Best to get busy easiest way to calm down after a fright was to get back to normal routines.

Masque pulled out some of the dried venison they had been eating. He wished they could risk a fire. The cold food and the exhaustive pace were starting to wear on him. The venison was not bad. It had a good smokey flavor that overlayed the gamey taste of the meat. The deer that this was from had been fairly young as the meat was lean and not very tough even after the smoking process which sometimes turned meat into something similar to boot leather. Grabbing a piece of the flat bread, he wrapped the smoked venison in the bread and began to eat. He longed for a bit of mustard, or pickles. He always enjoyed mustard at home when he ate deer. The thought of home brought a brief bit of melancholy over him. He missed wife and children. He sat there thinking of home, while eating and watched the sun begin to rise over the eastern horizon. Streaks of pink and purple erupted in the few scattered clouds. The sky seemed to come alive with color and life. Strange how even when thinking about missing someone how something as simple as a sunrise can help you remember to enjoy living.

Sagan stirred as the sky brightened. His arms and legs felt heavy. His entire body was heavy. What was wrong with him? As he sat up, he felt tired, almost exhausted. He had not felt this way since he completed his first couple of bonding's with Togan. Then the sudden loss of the wolf's power and energy had left him drained and would cause him to pass out. Since then, he had learned to tap the strength with more control gaining the wolf's strength speed and senses as a steady stream. That was what was wrong with him. Togan's strength was gone, his senses were gone, the improved smell, the improved hearing, the energy was all gone. Sagan felt small and weak. After days of constantly having extra energy reserves to call on he now felt small and insignificant.

"Masque, have you seen Togan?" Sagan breathed weakly. Even his voice felt lessened and breathing seemed like too much effort.

"Boss, have I seen Togan? I'll say I've seen Togan Boss. Woke up with him sniffing me like I was something he was thinking about snacking on. He stood over me, Boss smelled me and then took off. I don't know what it was all about, but it made the hairs on the back of my neck take notice. I'll tell you that, Boss," Masque replied, still sitting on the ground staring at the sunrise.

"He took his energy from me, Masque. The energy I have been using to keep going all this time is gone. I'm tired. I don't think I can travel today. I don't think I can do much of anything today. We were making such good progress. How will we ever catch up with Leaana now?" Sagan breathed, annoyed and frustrated.

"Well, Boss, I'll tell you what. I may not have all the answers, but I'm beginning to think that your wolf friend there does. I am exhausted from riding the chariot board. I needed a day to rest, or I wasn't going to be able to make it. But Boss, I didn't know how to tell you. Perhaps ole Togan sensed how tired I am and decided to force us to rest today. I have a feeling that ole wolf has a plan and will help us catch up to your sister."

"Masque, you should have talked to me about easing up on the pace. I got so used to Togan's energy I didn't even think about how hard I was pushing us. I can definitely feel it now. Alright, we rest today, hopefully Togan will be back by tonight or tomorrow and then we push on. Agreed?" Sagan stood and walked over to Masque, holding out his hand.

"Agreed Boss. And I'll be sure to tell you next time I need a break. Now. Since we are being forced into this day of rest, why don't you come sit over here by me and enjoy this beautiful sunrise, Boss?" And with that, Masque shook Sagan's hand. They stood and watched the sun climb through the pinks and red colors of the rising sky. Then, as an early fog rolled in, they decided to light a fire, have a warm breakfast, and boil water to make tea.

Chapter 28

Leaana's head throbbed. She slowly opened her eyes, and the world spun around her. Blinking quickly, things started to stabilize. In front of her, she saw the face of an elf. Dried blood was stuck to the side of the elf's head, but the face was rounder than normal for an elf. The eyes were green and were looking at her with compassion.

"Easy there, young one. You've had a nasty blow to the head." The elf crooned, looking Leaana in the eyes. "Your eyes seem normal, so hopefully you were not too badly hurt."

Leaana looked from the elf's eyes and looked around. She was in what appeared to be a carriage of some sort. Large logs formed the walls with spaces between them. There were other elves and several other people in the carriage with her. It looked like everyone was chained to either the walls or the floor. Looking down Leaana noticed metal bands around her wrists that were connected to the wall she was leaning against. "Where am I?" Leaana asked, "And who are you."

"I'll answer your second question first. I am Fataso master falconer and representative of the Subartan Falconer's guild to the festival in Arctana. Even though the way things are now I doubt I will be representing much of anyone anywhere. In answer to your second question, you are in a goblin prisoner carriage." Fataso said leaning back against the wall next to Leaana.

"Goblin" Leaana asked looking around "What is a goblin"

Fataso pointed out of the carriage at a short green creature walking beside them. The creature had short legs, long arms, and claws at the end of its fingers. The mouth had fangs, the eyes were deep set and looked either angry, crazed or both. "From what I've gathered from listening to the conversations around us the short one's of those creatures are goblins. The midsized ones are orcs and the really tall one walking behind us is called an ogre. I don't know where they came from or where we are going but we are heading for the bridge over the Animas River at the Remis plateau."

Leaana's vision shifted. She saw the carriage she was in surrounded by fifteen to twenty of the creatures Fataso pointed out. Most were walking but a few rode horses. Four horses pulled the carriage she was in. It looked like there were at least 3 other carriages like hers in line all surrounded by more creatures. Leaana's vision shifted back. She sighed in relief at least Scrill was around. She looked up and there gliding above her she saw her. The brown wings spread wide as the eagle gently glided on the breeze.

Fataso followed the line of Leaana's gaze as she looked up concerned as he expected her to continue looking around instead, she looked up and smiled. Why would she smile? Then he saw the eagle gliding above them.

"Aramin," Fataso sighed. "I find you too late."

"Aramin?" Leaana's head whipped around to look at Fataso. "I thought you looked familiar. Are you the falconer that had Scrill, or Aramin as you call her as part of your falconry show?"

"Yes, she was the center piece of my show. The main attraction. It is because of her uniqueness that I was chosen to go represent the Falconry guild at this year's festival. I left the caravan to search for her and the person that stole her from me. Why do you call her Scrill?" Fataso looked at her with increased interest.

"I call her Scrill because that is her name. She told it to me when I rescued her from your captivity. I am a familiar and Scrill is my animal guide. Because you had her in a cage she could not come and find me. When you were in our encampment a few weeks ago our bond started forming and I was called to come and free her." Leaana said with anger starting to enter her words. Anger at the man that had imprisoned her animal guide all these years keeping her from finding her destiny.

FRIEND

The word seemed to be formed in her head. "What?"

"I was saying I did not imprison Aramin or Scrill as you call her when I found her, she was injured, and I nursed her back to health." Fataso said in a calm tone

"Not you I think I heard something from Scrill."Leaana said almost absently.

FRIEND

"There it is again. I think Scrill wants us to be friends. At least that is the word that is in my head. It's not an exact communication, more of a feeling of a thought than an actual word."

Fataso again looks at Leaana, fascinated. "I have no problem trying to be friends. Can you explain to me what is going on? What exactly is a familiar?"

Leaana leaned back against the post she was chained to sighed and said, "where to begin?" She took a few moments to gather her thoughts and then tried to explain to Fataso how certain people were born with the mark in their hair and received an animal guide. She talked about the nine different totem animals that it was possible to receive as a guide. She then explained how the animal and the familiar shared a special bond and that their souls were intertwined, which enabled them to share abilities. She even told him about her twin brother Sagan and his guide Togan. How they shared strength and speed, and Sagan could smell and hear like a wolf. She then told Fataso of the abilities she had, hearing Scrill's thoughts and the ability to share her vision.

When she was finished Fataso sat fascinated. "So, all these years you've known you were a familiar but didn't have an animal guide." Fataso asked.

"No, that has been my problem. My mark was not pure and there has never been a girl familiar, so no one knew if I was a familiar or not." Leaana sighed, annoyed.

"Well, why not just choose an animal so everyone would know?" Fataso asked.

"It doesn't work that way. Our animal guides choose us. The animal spirits know more about this world and the way it works than we do. The animals choose us and since Scrill was in your cage, she could not find me. When you drew closer to our encampment, our souls found each other, and I began to see what Scrill saw. When you were in our encampment, we fully joined. I guess that is why she got distracted and crashed into the ground," Leaana explained. "When Scrill hit the ground, I passed out at the same time"

"So that is what all the commotion was in the crowd. I could tell something else happened when Aramin…I mean Scrill hit the ground, but I couldn't tell what was going on. Plus, my attention was on Scrill. After all, she is the reason I am even here." Fataso replied.

"Why is Scrill the reason you are here?" Leaana asked.

"Well, you see, having an eagle as a falconry bird is extremely rare. Most of the time you have the smaller birds of prey, hawk, falcons, the occasional shrike or kestrel. But to have an eagle, especially one of the size of Scrill. Well, that is special. I have been training and working with Scrill for 5 years. Building trust, training her, learning from her, and developing our act that shows off the eagle speed and agility in the final dive. The Falconry guild finally was impressed enough to send me as the representative for the festival in Arctana." Fataso explained.

"Five years you have been training her? I wonder when she would have come to me if she had not been captive with you? Guess I will never know."

"I only have been training her for 5 years she has actually been with me six. Remember I said she was hurt when I found her? It took a year for her wing to heal and her strength to rebuild so she could fly again." Fataso said. "Now sit back and rest it's going to be a long day and I will tell you the rest of my story while you get over that headache"

Chapter 29

Sagan awoke. Sitting up and throwing off his blankets he looked to the east. The sun was just starting to creep over the hills in the rising sky. The red light of rising was just starting to give a pink glow to the world. Standing Sagan felt refreshed, stronger, and energized. The strength he received from Togan had returned. That must mean Togan was nearby. Moving quickly Sagan stirred the remaining coals from their small fire last night, finding the hottest ones he added a few twigs and blew lightly. The coals flared and soon a small flame began licking at the twigs. Sagan added a few more twigs then as those caught, he added some larger branches. Soon a small fire perfect for heating their morning meal was burning.

Turning back to the campsite Sagan saw three shapes moving to the south. Karr let out a scared whiney as his sensitive nose caught the scent of the shapes approaching. Quickly he moved to where Carameth was lying beside his bed roll. Picking up the sword he quickly tossed the scabbard aside and turned to face the new threat.

Standing at the southern edge of the camp was Togan. His white fur almost pink in the glow from the rising sun. Beside him were two other wolves. They were much shorter than Togan their heads only coming up to his shoulder. The one closest to Togan was as black as Togan was white. It was almost Togan's opposite. *Skanar* the word almost came unbidden into Sagan's head. The ancient word for shadow. Sagan assumed this was the black wolf's name.

The third wolf was solid grey except for a blaze of white down his chest. He stood next to Togan and Skanar tail flat out from his back. *Valonic* again the word came unbidden as Sagan examined the third wolf. Valonic was close to the ancient word for brave. Again, this must be the third wolf's name.

"Well Boss, it looks like we have some more furry companions with us." Masque said coming to stand beside Togan looking at the three wolves. "Hopefully these two new beauties won't try to eat me. Have you ever seen these wolves before?"

"No never," Sagan said putting the tip of Carameth on the ground and leaning on the pommel. "Masque the black wolf is known as Skanar, and the grey one is known as Valonic. At least I assume that those are their names those words kind of just appeared in my head as I was looking at them."

"So Shadow, and Brave one," Masque said, "if I remember my ancient Natarin correctly. Are they coming with us Boss, or have we stumbled into some sort of furry family reunion?"

At that comment Togan began to walk through the camp heading to the northeast with Skanar and Valonic following close behind. Karr paced nervously as the two new wolves walked past where he was tethered. Togan and his companions reached the top of the rise to the northeast, stopped, looked back at Sagan and gave a quick bark. He then bounded down the far side out of sight followed almost at the same moment by Skanar and Valonic. A few seconds later Togan's head reappeared of the top of the rise as if to say, what are you standing around for, we need to get going. Then his head was gone again.

Sagan sprang into action and began packing up their small camp. He put Carameth back in its scabbard and strapped it to his back. Grabbing his bed roll he quicky tied it into a neat bundle. Grabbing the horse blanket from where Masque had been using during the night, he quickly threw the blanket and light saddle onto Karr's back. He attached his bedroll to the tie hooks on the back of the saddle for that purpose and grabbed his saddle bags from where they had been lying next to the saddle. Tying them in place he then tied the rope that Masque had been holding onto to the central most hook so that he would be able to keep up.

While Sagan was breaking camp Masque took some of their venison and wrapped it in some pieces of flat bread. Placing the wraps on hot stones beside the fire he seared the surface making it slightly brown and crispy. He quickly ate his wrap washing it down with water from his water skin. What he wouldn't give for a cup of tea but apparently the wolves won't wait. They had better get moving. He handed the other wrap he had prepared to Sagan then threw dirt on the fire to put it out. Once the fire was extinguished, he mounted his personal chariot and got ready to head out.

Sagan mounted Karr looked over his shoulder to ensure Masque was ready and kicked his heels into Karr's sides setting him to a quick trot. Topping the rise to the north of the campsite Sagan could see the three wolves walking in the distance not far ahead. Apparently, they had kept to a walk once they were out of sight so they would not out distance Sagan and Masque by too much. Sagan kicked Karr up to a canter and after about half an hour they had caught up to the wolves who spread out from them so they could help keep watch. Togan led about 100 paces ahead with Skanar to the left and Valonic to the right again about 100 paces away. The wolves were running at a constant lope and Karr with his longer legs was able to keep pace at a steady trot. Togan turned and began to head north east heading for the Remis Plateau and the miles began to go by as Masque began to call out random numbers and Sagan began his practice again.

They had been traveling steadily for about two hours the sun now climbing midway up the rising sky when Sagan caught the scent of death and dirt he now associated with Orcs. The smell seemed to be coming from ahead of them. Sagan was preparing to change direction to avoid the orcs he could smell when Togan took off heading for the smell with Skanar and Valonic running to catch up.

Sagan yelled back to Masque. "Hang on back there. I think I'm about to see how effective your training has been." He then kicked his heels into Karr's side and began galloping after the three wolves. As he rode, he put Carameth into its scabbard and grabbed his bow from where it hung on the outside of his quiver. Sagan grabbed an arrow from his quiver and knocked it to the string. Better to take out as many orcs from a distance as possible. With the constant practice over the last few days, he knew he would be able to draw Carameth in a matter of seconds once the fighting got close in.

Suddenly, there they were. Six goblins running on foot and one on horseback behind them. These seemed shorter than the orcs he had fought before, they must be goblins. Sagan drew back and fired an arrow, almost not even seeming to aim. The arrow shot away and seconds later, the goblin in the lead jerked back and fell, an arrow sticking out of his neck. Togan was in the lead of the wolves, he ran forward and leapt over the fallen goblin and landed with his front paws in the chest of the second goblin, knocking him to the ground. This caused Sagan's second arrow to fly high, as he had aimed for the same goblin. Then Sagan was almost in the middle of them. He pulled back on the reins and brought Karr to a sliding stop. He leapt down, letting Karr run clear. Drawing Carameth, Sagan moved into the fight.

Chapter 30

Spinel watched the fight begin from horse back. Each of the three wolves was engaged with a goblin, snarling, biting, and jumping to avoid the sword strokes. The rider had shot one of his goblins while still charging in and Spinel knew that goblin would not be getting up again. But two of his band were approaching the human who was on foot now. The odds were firmly in their favor. But the dwarf, that was riding on a small cart behind the horse, seemed to be waiting. He looked familiar somehow, but Spinel couldn't see him clearly.

Spinel watched as the human in the group began to take on the two goblins that were facing him. The human moved smoothly but mechanically. The moves he used to fight were well rehearsed but not quite instinctive. The style of fighting seemed familiar. Just as the dwarf watching seemed familiar.

The human dodged a sword stroke, blocked another with what looked like a small shield on his left arm, then parried another stroke with the sword, then a side kick to the chest of one goblin, knocking him down to give him room to maneuver. Spinel watched the fight. The human was very fast, or the goblin soldiers were slow. The soldiers had very little training, relying on their increased strength, speed, and intimidation to win most battles. Like fighting with a poorly balanced club than the finesse of a rapier.

Suddenly, one goblin thrust at the human's side as the other goblin was swinging a side cut. The human quickly blocked the side cut with his shield arm while stepping aside to avoid the thrust. The thrusting goblin was off balance as he hit nothing but air and in what seemed like one fluid motion the human brought his sword down as he stepped out of the way and hit the goblin on the back of the neck, almost cutting his head from his shoulders. That goblin went down and now it was just one on one.

Spinel threw his leg over the saddle and slid down. Continuing to watch the battle as he approached, he could tell the other Goblin would not last long. Already he was behind in the fight just fighting defensively trying to stay alive. It would not be long until it was over. And then just like that with a quick flick of the wrist to change the swords direction from a downward diagonal strike to a side strike the battle was done. The human's sword tore into the goblins side and the goblin fell. Spinel did not mourn his fallen comrade. He did not even know the goblin's name. He had been a tool to use to help him find this upstart human and now it was time to finish it.

Moving into attack Spinel could see the human was just a boy, young fresh faced without even the beginnings of what human's called a beard.

He's very young

Yes, I see that

Are you sure we want to do this he is only a boy

Considering I would like to keep both of my hands then yes we want to do this now shut up so I can end this quickly

Then Spinel was into the fight with a crushing overhead blow he felt would break through the young man's defenses and leave him rattled by the force. Only to have his hammer stopped by the small shield worn as a bracer on his left arm. The block seemed to be done with ease with no sign of struggle to absorb the force or fear from the strength of the attack. Already a counter strike was on the way, a quick side stroke coming in from the right. Spinel stepped back slightly just enough to allow the point to pass in front of him and then was immediately on the attack again. The human dodged the next stroke and then it was almost as if they were dancing, stroke, dodge, attack, parry, dodge. Neither of them seemed to be able to get the upper hand. Spinel used all his increased strength and speed from the raising, but the human seemed to be able match him in speed, and he might even be slightly stronger.

Spinel heard a growl and from the corner of his eye he noticed that the largest of the three wolves had just finished off its opponent and was starting to head towards them. It was taking everything Spinel had to stay ahead of the human he was fighting there was no way he could fend off a wolf as well. This battle was not supposed to be this difficult, it was already supposed to be over. Reaching a decision Spinel quickly performed a feint attack with his hammer causing the human to back up one step. That was all he needed, Spinel did one quick back flip to gain a bit more distance then turned and sprinted back to where his horse was waiting. Grabbing on to the reins and the side of the saddle he quickly got the horse galloping not even bothering to get into the saddle. After they had run a few feet Spinel sprang into the saddle using the momentum of the galloping horse to help vault him up.

Well, that went well didn't it

We are still alive aren't we. We will have to be more careful next time and be better prepared.

The dwarf standing over to the side wasn't that...

Yes. I am well aware of who that was. He is unimportant. He will not fight so all we have to worry about is the human and the wolves.

But his presence does explain why the human was able to match you. The fighting style seemed very familiar.

Again, shut up I'm the fighter here you are just along for the ride.

Yes, because thus far this epic tale is not very epic and would not make a very heroic poem. At least from our point of view.

With that Spinel sighed and kept the horse galloping in case the wolves decided to give chase.

Chapter 31

Sagan slumped to the ground, breathing heavily, the sweat dripping from his forehead. Togan gave chase to the goblin, galloping away for a few feet just to be sure he really was leaving. Breaking off the chase, Togan trotted over to Sagan and licked a small cut on Sagan's left shoulder. Sagan wondered when that had happened. He didn't remember feeling it happen.

Masque walked over to Sagan looked at the cut on his shoulder and took a small clean square of cloth from inside one of the pouches on his belt and tied a quick bandage around the cut to stop the small trickle of blood that was welling from the cut.

"You did well, Boss. You took out the first two goblins quickly, even though one got a small cut on your shoulder there. But you handled them easily enough. That third one, the one that got away, Boss. He was something different. He seemed to have been trained by a weapons master."

"Yes Masque, he seemed to be able to predict how I was going to fight, where I was going to be. I never even really got close to hurting him. Why do you think he ran?"

"Well Boss, you may not feel you got close to hurting him, but he never really got close to you either. He could tell that you were evenly matched, and he wanted a chance to make sure he had the upper hand and at that moment he didn't. So, I figure we will see him again at some point. Well, Boss, it looks like our days of avoiding the Goblin patrols may be behind us. Your furry friends there seem to be more willing to take the fight to the Goblins that sit back and wait.

Sagan's breath was evening out as he recovered from the brief fight. "Yes, Togan seems to be more willing to fight, but I think if we had met many more at a time, we would have been in trouble. I really think two at a time is all I can handle. "

"Well, Boss, I don't like to fight but will lend a hand if directly attacked. So don't worry about defending me if it comes down to that. I can take care of myself, Boss. Let's move away from these dead bodies and have a drink and a quick meal. You need to rest just a bit before we move on. After the adrenaline wears off, you might start to stiffen up better to be on the move when that happens so you can stretch your muscles out."

With that, Masque led Sagan by the hand back the way they had come until a small rise separated them from the killing ground. Togan, Skanar and Valonic paced back and forth in a circle, keeping watch as Masque started a small fire and prepared to fix tea.

Chapter 32

Leaana woke. She had been dozing. Sitting up, chained to the post as she was dozing was all she could manage. At least the little she was able to sleep made her forget briefly about how hungry she was. The goblins would give her a small hunk of bread and a small cup of water each day. Enough to keep her alive, but not enough to satisfy her hunger or quench her thirst.

Shaking off the last of the sleep she realized that something had changed. The creak of the wagon, and tramp of goblin feet could still be heard but now a new sound was there in the background. A constant low pitched roar.

"Fataso, do you hear that, what is it? Can you see in front of us I hate being tied so I'm facing the back of this wagon."

"The sound you hear is the roar of the Remis falls. The falls formed by the Animas River running off the Remis plateau. We are approaching the bridge at the Remis plateau. It is quite a sight. You should look at it through Scrill's eyes so you can see it as we approach." Fataso replied.

Leaana just realized that she had no idea how to look through Scrill's eyes. She knew she could see through her eyes when Scrill had something to show her but had never considered if she could do it when she needed or wanted to. Leaana turned her thoughts inward looking for that tiny voice she hears in her mind and the pull she feels from Scrill. Feeling that touch of the eagle's consciousness, there just the slightest pressure in her head, almost like a vibration. She concentrates on where she feels the pressure and thinks SIGHT. Her vision blurs and Fataso and the back of the cart disappear from her vision replaced by a view of the cart from a tree branch near the road.

Then the world was moving as Scrill leapt from the branch and took flight. Over the cart surrounded by goblins and Orcs flying toward a cliff.

Here the Animas River met the Arctana river. Both rivers joined as they flowed down off the top of the cliff, falling nearly five hundred feet into the river bed below. On the other side of the falls, a road wound from the top of the cliff but was then lost from sight as it entered a cave mouth. The road they were on began to wind back and forth carved into the side of the cliff face. At the top of the cliff, where the two rivers ran through the rocky banks of the Remis plateau, stone towers could be seen supporting large cables. The cables extended from the towers on one side of the plateau to a similar set of towers on the other side. These cables were attached to boards to which the planking of the bridge was attached. The cables were as thick as tree trunks and, as Scrill flew over the top of the bridge, Leaana could see that it was wide enough for two carts to travel across it side by side.

The other thing she noticed were the other roads branching off from the Remis plateau in all directions. It seemed all roads lead to this bridge. As Scrill circled over the bridge to fly back towards Leaana she could see that goblins, orcs, and ogres were everywhere. The entire bridge was crawling with them and other carts carrying captives were already on the road heading to the northeast and the Dwarfgon Mountains.

"It's beautiful." Leaana said as the sun crept over the top of the Remis plateau and created a rainbow in the spray at the base of the cliff. "But it is also scary. There are goblins and orcs everywhere."

"That makes sense. The bridge here is the only way to safely cross the Animas River in the northern part of the continent. All travelers come through here at some point if you are taking any of the northern trade routes. They must be stopping any travelers that come along and capturing them. But why?"

"Well unfortunately I think we are going to find out whenever we get to where they are taking us." Leaana said. "I wonder where we are go…" stopping her speech in mid-sentence because she was distracted by what she was seeing now. On mountain top not too far from them to the southeast Scrill was circling a small party. Leaana could see three wolves and two people. Scrill went closer and then Leaana knew for sure. The white wolf was larger than the other two and was definitely Togan, and there lying on his belly looking in her direction was her brother Sagan. What was he doing here? Well probably looking for her. But he must leave, he must flee the goblin numbers were too great and he would end up in the wagon beside her. This thought in her head Scrill swooped down and let out a long screech then flew back up. Her brother looked up at Scrill then turned and spoke with the person lying next to him on the ground. Then they got up and started moving back down the mountain side, out of sight of the plateau.

Good they were leaving. At least that way her brother would not suffer the same fate she was in for. At least he would be able to lead their people. Leaana let go of the vibration from Scrill and lost the sight from the eagle. Looking in Fataso's face again tears began running down her cheeks. "I saw my brother he was on a mountain top to the southeast looking in our direction. Scrill swooped at him, and he turned and went the other way. Hopefully he can avoid the Goblins so he can go back and lead our people. I hoped I would see him again, but I am glad he is free and not going to face the same fate we are. Whatever that is."

"I'm glad he is safe. Don't give up hope. There may still be a way we all come out of this in one piece and see each other again. We don't know what they have planned for us or even where we are going. Until we have a reason to think something bad is going to happen it is better to have hope. Now, tell me about your brother and your life at home." Fataso grinned leaned back against the post he was tied too and settled in to listen to Leaana describe her brother and encampment. Hoping this would distract her at least for a little while from the fear they both felt.

Chapter 33

Masque was breathing hard, the exertion from the climb making breathing difficult even though he was in excellent shape. Years swinging his hammer as a blacksmith and travelling the countryside had kept him in shape. Before that the years of martial training to understand the weapons he would build had developed his muscles and endurance. Now this climb was making him breathe hard. Perhaps he was getting older than he realized. He looked up and could see the young human in front of him. This very young human, a boy really, not even full grown and he was learning to fight and kill just in order to survive. His innocence was being ripped away little by little. His determination to find his sister and his loyalty impressed him. His physical gifts and the speed at which he learned to fight were equally impressive.

During the last two days since they had first begun to engage the Goblin patrols instead of avoiding them this young man had essentially single handedly fought 3 more patrols with just the help of the wolves that traveled with them. The patrols seemed to be getting more numerous as they approached the Remis plateau so Masque had suggested they should look at what awaited them at the plateau before they got there. This climb was the result of that suggestion. Climbing to a mountain peak close to the plateau where they could look at the condition of the bridge and trade routes.

This mountain was normally considered unclimbable, but their furry companions had found a narrow game trail that led up the steep sides. Here they were, just reaching the summit, breathing hard, bruised, but not really any worse for wear. They had left Sagan's horse, and the small pony they had captured from one of the goblin patrols in a small cave at the base before they began the steep climb. The pony would be useful as they continued traveling because Masque would no longer have to ride his personal chariot behind Sagan, and they could run from Goblins patrols if needed.

Masque finished the last of the climb and now stood on the small flat area at the peak of the mountain. Here they could look at the Remis plateau, falls, and the bridge. There were no trees to obstruct their view because they were above even where trees would grow. The wind was cold here and there were even still patches of snow in some of the rocky areas that received little sunlight. Topping the crest, Masque stayed on his hand and knees to keep him from being as visible if anyone was looking their way.

The plateau and falls were a magnificent sight. The falls formed by the Animas and Arctana Rivers as they spilled over the plateau fell five hundred feet to a pool below. In the rock walls of the plateau, you could see layers of different colored rocks stacked up on each other. It was like someone had taken a knife and sliced through the side of the world and you could see all of it laid bare in that one rock wall.

Something else could be seen too, movement and activity. People were everywhere on roads and bridge of the plateau. This was expected at a major crossroads, but something about this traffic movement seemed wrong. Reaching into the pouch on his side, Masque pulled out a leather tube and two glass discs. Putting the larger disc in one end of the tube and the smaller one in the other. He then held the smaller glass disc to his eye and looked at the crossroads closer. He saw nothing but goblins, orcs and ogres. All the people moving around on the bridge and the crossroads were goblins, orcs, or ogres. He scanned around, saw a cart coming from the southeast, and looked at it. There were Elves in the cart that appeared to be prisoners. The goblins had captured and were controlling the bridge. No wonder no one had heard of the goblins. Anyone that came through here for trade would be captured or killed.

"Boss, it doesn't look good. The bridge is covered by our toothy friends. No way we can get across it. Here, take a look, Boss." Masque said as he handed the leather tube to Sagan.

Sagan put the tube to his eye and looked. Masque smiled to see the look of wonder cross Sagan's face as he marveled at how things are brought closer through the viewing device. Then watched as Sagan's smile turned into a look of concern, then worry, then outright despair.

"Oh no. Masque, they have her. They have my sister. There are too many of them for me to fight to get to her. What are we going to do?" Sagan sobbed as tears began to run down the side of his face.

Masque took the viewing tube back from Sagan and looked again. "Where do you see your sister, Boss?"

"There in the cart that is just starting up the road to the bridge," Sagan replied, his voice cracking with worry.

Masque looked again and found the cart Sagan had mentioned. Looking, he saw what appeared to be a human girl tied in the middle of the cart, surrounded by elves. The cart appeared to be escorted by 10 goblin soldiers. Five in front, and five in back. Even with the wolves and with himself finally committing to fight, there is no way they could defeat 10. The odds were too great. Plus, there were another 200 goblins, orcs or ogres all around the bridge that could lend a hand if any attack came. No, there was nothing they could do now. Sagan would have to accept that.

"Look Boss. I know you want to save your sister, but there isn't anything we can do now. It looks like a caravan heading out towards the mountains up at the top of the plateau. It has some more wagons that look like they have prisoners as well. I'll bet the wagon your sister is in will join that group." Masque's mind raced, trying to come up with a plan to help this young boy he was beginning to respect so much and was growing very fond of. Seeing the tears rolling down his cheeks was heart breaking after seeing the fierceness he had displayed while fighting the goblin patrols.

"Boss. Your Natarin encampment of Larin is only a day's ride away and the trade route to the mountains is a half day's ride from Larin. If we ride to Larin and talk to the elders there, perhaps we can get their hunters to help us rescue your sister. At least when they are on the trade route, there will be only the guards for the caravan and not all these other Goblins that are here at the bridge. It gives us a better chance, Boss."

Sagan looked over at Masque a glimmer of hope beginning to show through the despair on his face. "Do you think if we do that, we can free her?" Sagan asked.

"I think it is our best chance." Masque explained. Just then, they heard the screech of an eagle from above them. Looking up, they saw the eagle swooping down over them, coming within just a few feet, then speeding away, flying toward the Remis plateau.

"I think that eagle agrees with you, Masque. Alright, let's get off this mountain top and head for Larin." With that, Masque put away the viewing tube and they began the slow climb back down to where their horses were waiting.

Chapter 34

Sagan drew rein on Karr bringing him to a stop. His heart sank at what he saw. Before him is where the encampment of Larin should be. A large encampment found on the banks of a lake that is fed by the nearby mountain streams. Where there should be dwellings were piles of ashes. Nothing moved. Kicking Karr into a walk Sagan slowly rode into the edges of the ruined encampment. Masque following close behind. Both of them silent. Sagan made his way to the center where the sacred fire should be burning. There in the circle of sacred stones was nothing but cold grey ashes that matched the cold grey ashes that was all that was left of the dwellings.

"What happened here?" Sagan whispered.

Masque almost as quietly replied "It looks like the Goblins have been through here. They must have come through in force on their way to the Remis bridge. I am so sorry Sagan. I thought we would find help here not more sorrow."

Togan came trotting up beside them at this point sensing Sagan's distress he had come in from his outward patrol to help Sagan. Sensing the sadness, smelling the death and smoke in the air Togan let out a long howl of sorrow. Skanar and Valonic soon joined in, and the silence was filled with the mournful cry of the three wolves. Sagan and Masque dismounted and began to look around at the ruined area more closely. Some of the dwellings were still somewhat standing. Most, however, were simply piles of ash. Walking around Sagan found the charred remains of people. Men, women, and children that had either been killed in the attack or died in the fires.

One charred body was of what looked like a boy not much older than Sagan. In his hand he held the remains of a bow. His charred head was lying at his feet. At least he had died before he was burned.

"Masque. I can't stay here. I can't stay amongst these remains and dead bodies." Sagan said tears again running down his young face as he walked in despair. He walked to the center and knelt at the entrance to the sacred fire ring. There Sagan let out his own howl of despair as haunting as the wolves' cry had been. Seconds later Togan and the other two wolves join him as all four howl in a mournful tribute to the brave souls lost here.

After his howl Sagan remained kneeling, silence and stillness descended on the ruined encampment again. Larin was no more. It would have to be rebuilt eventually. To keep their connection to the spirit world the encampment would be rebuilt. The sacred fire would be relit from the original sacred fire in Arinin.

That fire had been burning continuously for thousands of years. For as long as humans could remember the sacred fire in Arinin had been burning. The part of that fire that had lived here in Larin was almost as old. Larin being either the second or third oldest of the human encampments. It was the first encampment to truly be permanent. The fish from the nearby lake had made following the herds of deer across the land unnecessary so its founders had stayed. Keeping a part of the sacred fire with them. It was heart breaking to Sagan, who as a familiar had been taught the history of his people so it could help him lead, to know this ancient part of fire had been extinguished.

After sitting in silence for a while Sagan rose without saying a word, walked to Karr, mounted and rode to the bank of the lake and began to ride along the bank to the Northwest, Togan running beside him and the other two wolves trotting slightly behind. Masque caught off guard by the sudden departure quickly mounted his pony and rode to catch up.

The two companions and three wolves traveled in silence for the next two hours keeping up a trot. Finally, Sagan reined in again. "Here. We will camp here on the edge of the lake. We are far enough away now that I can no longer smell the death there. Tonight, we camp. I will dance for the spirits of the dead in Larin, asking Duater to accept them in and guide them on the next part of their journey. Then tomorrow we need to try and come up with a new plan to rescue Leaana. But for tonight I must mourn and pay tribute. Masque, you have become a friend, but our dances are sacred and private things."

"Don't worry about it Boss. I'll go down to the lake and see if I can catch some fish. Kinda tired of venison anyway Boss. When you are done, send one of our furry friends down to get me and I'll come back. Hopefully with dinner. Then we can mourn together. I had some friends in Larin. I visited there several times as I was traveling around selling my goods. The blacksmith, there Rinnand, I believe that was his name, he always let me stay with him when I was traveling this way. He was a good man and an above average smithy. Be sure to honor him especially for me will you." With that Masque turned and started walking to the lake. His legs moving faster than he expected trying to be sure Sagan did not see the tears that lined his cheeks as well.

Sagan spent the next hour preparing. He gathered stones and placed them in a circle to make a fire pit. He then gathered wood from the driftwood that had washed up on the edge of the lake. The white sun-bleached dry wood almost looked like the bones of the dead as they were stacked to build a bonfire. Once the bonfire was ready, he found two more short but very sturdy sticks that he could easily hold in his hand. He would strike these together as he danced, since there were no drums. He laid the final two sticks across one another at the northern point of the fire circle. Now it was time for him to begin.

He removed his shirt, baring his chest to the night air. He poured some water into the dirt beside him, drug his fingers through the mud and coated his face. Normally, he would use the decorative paint of his people for this purpose, but he did not have any with him, so mud would have to do. He then walked over to Togan, placed his head against the wolf's head and took comfort in the soft fur and warmth there. He then stood, resolved for what he now had to do. Togan turned and, with the other two wolves behind him, ran off into the night, leaving Sagan alone with nothing but the fire pit.

Sagan walked to the pile of wood he had built into a bonfire. He took his flint and steel and struck them together, sending sparks flying onto a small batch of moss. The moss started to smoke. He blew on it, encouraging the sparks into a small flame. Then, placing the burning moss onto the small sticks at the base of the bonfire, he blew a bit more. The flames caught the small dry sticks almost instantly. Then, once a few of the larger branches began burning he rose, walked to where the two sticks lay crossed at the northern most part of the circle. He picked up the sticks and began to strike them together in a slow rhythm. He began to dance to the right. Stepping and turning in time to the beating of the sticks. He completed three circuits of the fire and then stopped, his breathing deepening as he focused on the rhythm and pattern of his dance. With a loud voice he called out, "Kran, mighty frog, you are the Master of life. I come before you now to honor those whose gift has been returned to you."

Striking the sticks again, he began to dance another turn around the fire. Once he reached the starting point again, he stopped and cried out, "Shamash mighty Snake, Master of the land, the bodies of these honored dead are returned to you as dust. Bless the lands they have lived in that it may be rich and fertile." He danced another turn around the fire. "Arina mighty eagle, Master of the skies, the skies have witnessed their lives. Watch over those of us that still remain." Dancing this time slightly faster. "Larr Mighty Turtle Master of homes, their homes are empty and sad, bring your comfort that happiness might return." Dancing faster still, "Sheta mighty bear, Master of healing herbs. Heal our spirits and help us record their lives that we may not forget." Another circuit of the fire even faster than the last. "Roma mighty Wolf Master of the hunt. The food and possessions of the dead will be divided to help those of us who remain." The dance is becoming almost frantic now. Sagan's breathing coming in rapid gasps. His voice cracking with strain as he yells, "Matsaya, Mighty Fish Master of water, we pour out our water skins, as those that have passed poured out their lives." Faster, must dance faster, "Ozzul Mighty Crow, master of song. Sing of the lives lost. Carry their names upon the wind that all may know and remember." The beat of the sticks is so close together now it is almost a constant sound as Sagan completes another circuit. "DUATER , MASTER OF THE DEAD, ACCEPT THESE SPIRITS INTO YOUR WORLD. JOIN THEIR SPIRITS AS THEY ARE MEANT TO BE." Sagan then dances three more circuits around the fire, screaming in agony, pain, and grief the entire time. At the end of the last circuit, he stops and throws the sticks he has been striking together into the fire. His breathing coming in rapid gasps. He falls to his knees the ritual done. Suddenly, he jumps up, pulls his hunting knife from his belt and cuts his hand. He holds the bleeding hand over the fire, allowing several drops of blood to fall sizzling into the flames. "I swear to all the Animal spirits. I will see the encampment of Larin restored. Larin's sacred fire will once again burn to honor you, Larr. This I vow with fire and my blood. May those two components combine to lock my vow." With that, Sagan turned his back to the fire and time of mourning and went to find Togan and to let Masque know it was ok to return.

Chapter 35

Masque went to the lake and tried to put the young man and his grief out of his mind. He tried to fish. What more calming past time could there be than watching the small waves of the lake splash against the shore as you threw a line baited with a bit of smoked venison into the water. After half an hour with no luck his curiosity got the better of him. For years he had visited the Natarins. And every time they had a ritual he was asked to leave. He had never seen the Natarin rituals. He had seen them dance some in celebration or for show. But a true ritual that they held sacred never. He wandered back towards where he had left Sagan. He found a small group of bushes where he could sit and observe while still being far enough away not to be easily seen by Sagan. He watched as Sagan finished building the bonfire and placed his head on Togan's head. Watched as the wolves ran off into the night. Then Sagan began to dance.

The dance had a trance like quality, it was almost as if Sagan was moving without thinking. Then he heard the first call out. The dance changed. Sagan's movements now resembled a frog. Not only did the movements match a frog but it almost looked like Sagan had put on a frog costume. That was impossible of course because he didn't have one with him. They had traveled together long enough that Masque knew all of Sagan's possessions. Then Sagan called out again, this time to a snake, again the dance changed movements resembling a snake, again it seemed as if he wore a snake costume. And so, it went with every new animal the dance changed to resemble that animal, and it looked as if Sagan wore a costume of that animal. The dancing got more and more frantic. Sagan called out to Duater the mighty Vulture master of death, then continued dancing three times around the fire. The last time he danced it seemed like others danced with him each dressed as one of the animals Sagan had evoked during the ritual. Perhaps the animal spirits really were with the Natarins. Perhaps they honored Sagan with their presence since he was a familiar. Then Sagan dropped to his knees, and all was quiet. Sagan was alone by the fire breathing heavily. Masque decided he had seen enough. He rose and quietly moved back to the lake side and threw out his line again. This time he got a bite and drew in the line with a nice sized orange tail on the end of the line. The orange tail was known for its sweet almost citrus flavored meat. They would eat well tomorrow.

Not long after his catch Sagan appeared and asked the age old question everyone who fishes is eventually asked, "Did you have any luck?" Masque showed Sagan the orange tail. They admired the size of the fish briefly and awkwardly the night air heavy with the sadness they both felt. Masque noticed what seemed to be a bandage on Sagan's hand.

"What happened to your hand Boss?"

"Nothing, I tripped on a rock in the dark and fell and cut it. It's nothing. Perhaps we should go and finish setting up camp. I have a fire going. We can sleep for a few hours and then cook that good looking fish for breakfast."

"Sounds good to me Boss. It's been a long hard day for both of us." Masque replied as he pulled in his fishing line one more time and stored it in the bag on his belt that never seemed to fill up.

Chapter 36

Leaana's throat was dry. The few sips of water she was given each day were enough to keep her alive but not enough to quench her thirst. It had been two days since they crossed the Animas River at the Remis plateau and they had been travelling steadily to the northeast since then. They were on a wide track that was apparently a major trade route. The ruts in the road were well worn but the extensive travel made them rough, and each bump could be felt in the cart. The ride was so rough it was nearly impossible to sleep. Hunger, thirst, and tiredness were her constant companions now. She was traveling though lands she had only heard about and never seen. When she had started out with Sagan on their journey to the Dwarfgon mountains she had been excited to see these new lands. Now it all passed in by in haze of discomfort. She and Fataso had talked to each other until their dry throats and tongues would not allow them to speak any more.

Trees lined the road here. The trees had what appeared to be a blue and black fruit on them. A memory stirred. She had seen that fruit before when traders from the north had come to visit Romin. They were called pumpells. They were about the size of an apple, had seeds on the outside like a strawberry but were mostly hollow on the inside and filled with water. They grew only near the Dwarfgon mountains where the cool waters of the mountain springs could feed them. Leaana reached into her mind and touched Scrill's presence. She pictured one of the pumpells. A few minutes later she heard Scrill's familiar screech she held opened her hands and Scrill swooped low and dropped a fat pumpell into her hands. She brought the fruit to her mouth, bit through the bitter skin, and began to drink. The water was sour, not sweet like she remembered, probably meant the Pumpell wasn't quite ripe, but the water was still like heaven on her parched throat. Way too soon the water was gone, and she was still thirsty. Another screech looking up another pumpell was falling from Scrill's talons. Again, Leaana drank. This went on till her thirst was slacked. Then she had Scrill bring pumpells for Fataso. Fataso gratefully drank as well.

Everyone Scrill bring them to all in the carts. Leaana thought the instructions. Previously they had communicated in just one word phrases. Even when she had told Scrill to bring the Pumpell to Fataso she had just thought Fataso and Scrill seemed to understand. Would she understand this? Scrill flew over the cart behind them that Leaana could see and dropped a pumpell into the cart. Good she had understood.

Before small band of trees were past them but Leaana knew that for the next day or so Scrill could fly back to this grove if needed and bring them water. Perhaps they would find more pumpell trees as they grew closer to the mountains. The water had even helped with her hunger. The water from the pumpell fruits was filled with nutrients and Leaana felt better than she had in days.

The guards noticed the eagle flying back and forth from the trees to the carts. They noticed the pumpells landing in the carts and the prisoners hungrily drinking their contents. A few of the guards threw rocks or shot arrows at the eagle in an attempt to stop it or frighten it away. After the eagle dodged all attempts to stop it and continued to bring the fruit most of the guards gave up. Th commander of the caravan wondered why an eagle would do that. It seemed too controlled for a wild bird. But other than giving the prisoners a little bit of comfort it wasn't going to hurt anything and now the guards wouldn't have to feed or water the prisoners. He decided to ignore the bird and its deliveries. Since he ignored them, the rest of the guards decided to ignore the eagle also.

The pace of the wagons slowed and Leaana saw the walls of the mountains starting to rise around them.

"We are entering the Moose Herd pass." Fataso said. "Years ago, this pass was discovered by following the herds of Moose that traveled through the mountains. It became the main trade route into and out of the Dwarfgon mountains."

Leaana stared at the rock walls around them. She was excited to see the mountains at last. She was also scared not knowing what waited for them at their destination. Now that they were in the mountains, she felt they must be getting closer to where ever they were going. The pass turned more north, and the sun disappeared behind the rock wall. Soon it would be night. Perhaps she would be able to sleep some this night since at least she was not thirsty and starving thanks to the pumpells. She reached into her mind and felt Scrill's presence and thanked her for bringing them the fruit. Then she settled back against the post behind her back and tried to get comfortable waiting for and praying for sleep.

The next day Scrill managed to fly back to the grove of pumpell trees and again Fataso and Leaana, and most of the rest of the prisoners were able to quench their thirst. Again, the guards decided to ignore the eagle and just decided not to feed them at the end of the day.

The caravan of guards and prison wagons continued up Moose Herd pass for two days then it turned and went due west for another day. They finally stopped outside what looked like the entrance to a building that had been carved into the mountain side. Leaana saw through Scrill's eyes that all nine of the animal spirits had statues on the outside of the building. This place must have been built by Natarins long ago. The caravan they were traveling in consisted of about 100 goblins as guards. They had been taking turns sleeping as they traveled so the caravan had not stopped since they left the bridge. In addition to the Goblins there were about 10 wagons similar to the wagon that Leaana and Fataso were in. Most of the wagons contained between five and six prisoners, all Natarins. But she and Fataso had ended up in a wagon with other elves. The prisoners were cut loose from the wagons now and made to stand just outside the temple. All total there were about fifty humans and about fifteen elves it seemed. An elf with dark colored skin walked out of an upper window of the building and stood on a raised balcony. Raising his hands to the crowd he spoke.

"I am Darmot. Fear not for you are blessed. Soon you will be Raised to a new form and will take your place in the world as you should. You will join my army and together we will conquer the twin elven kingdoms and you will build a new life upon the ashes of those kingdoms. Basara, see to their preparation for the ceremony." With that Darmot lowered his arms, turned and walked back into the building.

A female Orc began shouting orders to the goblins around them. Whips began to crack, and they were herded into the building through the main chamber then down stairs. Leaana was near the front only three people had moved before she did when the whips began cracking. Now each of those people was shoved into a small room with a door shut and locked. Leaana was pushed by the female orc, Basara, into a small chamber carved into the rock of the hall way. The room was so small she could reach out and touch all the walls just by stretching out her hands. Almost immediately after she was shoved in the room the Door was slammed shut. No light came in from around the door. It was dark. The total darkness that comes from being under ground. Leaana could still see some though. Her eyes had always been able to see in very low light even before she had met Scrill and her vision had become even sharper. Not that there was anything to look at. Four bare rock walls, a rock ceiling and a rock floor. At least the floor wasn't moving. She was terrified, thirsty and hungry. Scrill had not been able to get to the pumpell grove in the last two days, so she was thirsty again. She sat down, let out a scream of fright, heard others do the same then began to cry. Sobs wracked her body until finally from sheer exhaustion she fell asleep.

Chapter 37

Spinel rode up the road to the Remis bridge. Crossing the bridge once he went into the Goblin base camp. He had driven his horse hard, escaping from the young man with the wolves, and now it had come up lame. He needed a new mount, a tracker, and a double force of Goblins. That should be enough to capture or kill the young boy and his wolves and end this annoyance once and for all. Riding into the camp, he immediately turned to the grazing fields to find a new mount. Dismounting from his horse, he scoured the available remounts and saw a brown and white paint horse. It looked fairly young and in good condition. Much better condition than a lot of the old farm horses they had captured. This horse looks like it could run for days without issue. Just what he needed to catch up with his quarry.

"Horse master, I need a new mount. I want that brown and white paint over there." Spinel barked.

"And why should I just give you another horse? Look what you have done to your current one." the horse master spat, taking the reins of Spinel's current horse.

Spinel reached to a chain around his neck and pulled out a small Medallion. "This is Basara's sign of approval. I am on a special mission for Basara. Now, if you want to cause me problems, I am sure Basara will straighten this all out when we get back to the temple." Spinel growled at the horse master.

"Basara, you say" the horse master's fanged green face seemed to go white at the mention of Basara's name. "No there is no reason to mention this to Basara, here take the paint. Best horse in the field right now. Just came in a day or so ago, has been cleaned up, fed and watered and is in great condition." The horse master continued to rattle as he began to take the saddle and bridle from Spinel's old mount and place it on the paint horse. "She has been a bit scared of us but seems to be calming a bit. That fear will keep her in line, though, shouldn't give you any trouble." With that, he finished saddling and tacking the paint up and handed the reins to Spinel. The paint reared in fright, pulling back at the reins, Spinel kept a firm grip and turned to the horse, growling slightly. The paint reared again but seemed to realize escape was not possible and calmed down.

"Your right, horse master she does have spirit. Now point me to the commander. I need to recruit a couple of sixes to go with me."

The horse master pointed to a large orc overseeing the traffic crossing the bridge. Spinel leapt into the saddle and began to ride toward the commander.

That medallion around your neck is not Basara's sign of approval. Where did you come up with that?

"Will you shut up, it worked. I knew a lowly horse master would be afraid of Basara and I needed this horse. I hope using her name again will work with the commander so I can get the troops I need"

I hope you are right for both of our sakes. I've been dead once but I am enjoying being alive again. I don't really want to go back to being dead just yet. I have some great ideas for a new Saga once all this running around and fighting is done, I hope I can write again.

"Well don't get your hopes up,"

"What did you say?" the commander barked.

"Nothing," Spinel quickly replied. "I am Spinel, on a special mission for Basara,"

"Yes, yes, I was wondering when you were going to show up. I have been given instructions to give you whatever help you need. But I quite frankly don't have time to mess with you." the commander said. Looking around he raised his hand and shouted "Marnon come here." A small goblin came running up to the commander. "Marnon here is the acting quartermaster. He will get you any help you need just don't bother me with the details." With that the commander turned his back on Spinel and started barking orders as he walked away.

Two hours later with fresh supplies and two fighting fives under his command, and one other mounted Ogre that was supposed to be good at tracking, Spinel set out in search of the young boy, the dwarf and the three wolves. Their time was up.

Are you sure you can do this especially to him?

"Yes, I'm sure. He means nothing to me. Hasn't for years. I will be able to do whatever I must."

They rode back towards where Spinel had fought with the young man and the wolves. After half a day they saw wolf prints and not too far from that they found hoof prints. The prints were in soft ground so at this point even Spinel could see them. They were angled east and slightly north. Now that they had found the trail Spinel decided they should make camp. The sun was low in the setting sky and the lengthening shadows would make tracking difficult. The goblins traveled with very little equipment. They would sleep under the stars. There was a large tarp tied to the back of the tracker's saddle they could set up in case it rained but otherwise they would sleep in the open. The goblin foot soldiers did not seem to mind being wet or uncomfortable. They simply followed orders. The ritual that transformed them usually made them insane. This made them violent and obedient. Perfect for soldiers. Only a few like Spinel were able to come to terms with what happened to them, and this made them the officers of the army. Because they could actually think.

Once the halt was called and camp was set up the goblin soldiers removed their armor and set it around the fire to allow the heat of the fire to dry the sweat from the cotton lining. They wore simple cotton tunics and cotton pants beneath their armor. Most of these goblins had been in the field for weeks now and their under garments were sweat stained and they did not smell the best. Spinel and the tracker, that Spinel learned was named Coln, wrinkled their noses at the smell from the soldiers. They decided to be sure their sleeping space was upwind of the soldiers. Rations were given out. Rations were simple food of dried meat some crackers and a bit of cheese. A small fight broke out among the soldiers as one of the larger ones decided he wanted the dried meat of a smaller companion. The smaller soldier, however, was used to being bullied and quickly put an end to the bullying by breaking the larger soldiers nose for him. When the larger soldier tried again the smaller soldier simply gouged out the larger soldiers left eye. And that was the end of that.

Coln took a few minutes after eating to bandage the head of the goblin that was now missing an eye. Then everyone settled down for the night and began to sleep.

Needless violence and such great conversationalist we have for traveling companions.

"They aren't the most intelligent bunch, but they will help get the job done. I'm not here for the company. I'm here…"

Yes, we know why you are here but just keep in mind the stimulating conversation we had tonight for the future

"What choice do we have." and with that Spinel closed his eyes and tried to sleep. Knowing the next few days would be long as they tried to make up ground on the young man and the wolves. He and Coln had horses but the goblin soldiers were on foot and could only travel so fast so they would have to push them and travel early and late each day in order to try and catch up. Good thing the Goblins didn't complain or tire easily. The next morning, they would be on the trail as soon as the sun began to climb the rising sky.

Chapter 38

Sagan and Masque awoke the next morning. The sun was already a quarter of the way up the rising sky as they prepared their breakfast. Masque expertly cleaned and fileted the orange tail as Sagan relit the fire and prepared tea, as Masque had taught him to do. Masque set two flat rocks on the edge of the fire to heat. Once they were hot, he placed the filets of orange tail on the rocks skin side down at first to make the skin crispy, then after a few minutes flipped the filet over to cook the other side. He had found a few wild growing herbs, some thyme and rosemary and broke the leaves off the stems to lay them on the fish to add a bit of flavor. Once the fish was cooked, he removed them from the fire and placed them on some other flat rocks to use as plates. The rosemary and thyme set off the citrus flavor of the fish with just a hint of smoke from being on the side of the fire. It was nice to eat something besides the smoked venison they had been eating for the past few weeks.

There was not much conversation over breakfast, as both Masque and Sagan were still dealing with the loss of the encampment of Larin and the events of last night. The air was heavy with sadness and tension. After they had eaten and were enjoying their tea, Sagan finally spoke.

"Masque, we came to Larin to recruit hunters to help me free my sister. Well, that is not possible now. Larin has been wiped out. There is no help. We are on our own. I don't know what to do next. This was supposed to be a simple adventure to the mountains with my sister. Go retrieve a sacred stone from the mountains for the fire circle, learn to act as a member and leader of a pack from Togan while we went. Now we are fighting monsters.

My sister has been captured by them and I feel totally lost."

Sagan's voice was low, almost breaking as he admitted his thoughts to Masque. Masque had come to respect Sagan for his strength and straightforward personality. Now his respect for him only grew as he saw he was willing to be vulnerable to maintain his honest personality. Other people less sure of themselves in this situation would never admit they didn't know what to do. They would bluster and come up with some crazy plan that would most likely get them killed. Or they would take the coward's way out and just say that it was impossible and go home. But not Sagan. He was genuinely searching for answers to an almost impossible puzzle and willing to admit that he didn't know the next step.

"Well Boss, I wish I had a straightforward answer for you. But in this situation, there is no easy answer. We have a couple of choices, Boss. We can try to attack the prison convoy that is carrying you sister, but there are way too many goblins there for that to be really successful. We could try and draw some of the guards away and then hit it, but again, we don't really have the people for that. We can follow the convoy from a distance and try to wait for an opportunity to present itself. But Boss, none of those options have a very good chance of getting your sister back."

Sagan sighed. He had already figured there was not much chance of freeing his sister but he couldn't just give up. He had to figure something out. Togan came walking into camp. He picked up Sagan's saddle bag with his mouth and started walking towards the lake. He walked a few feet. Dropped the saddle bag then turned to walk along the lake shore. He stopped again after a few feet, looked back and waited.

"What is your furry friend doing Boss" Masque asked as he sat up and watched the wolves movements through the camp.

"I'm not really sure," Sagan replied but I think he wants us to follow him. "Perhaps he has an idea or knows something we don't know. My people have always believed our animal guides have a better understanding of this world than we do."

"Well Boss, he is heading to the mountains, and we are pretty sure that is where your sister is being taken. So, at this point I'm willing to proceed on a little faith if you are." With that Masque got up and started packing up camp. He rolled up his bedroll and tied it to his pony's saddle. Sagan did the same. The fire had been burning down and was almost out. As Sagan saddled Karr and Masque's pony Masque kicked dirt on the fire to extinguish it. Their camp had been simple, so it had only taken minutes to pack up. Togan barked impatiently then began to make his way along the shoreline again. Sagan and Masque mounted up and rode after the white wolf who once he saw them on horseback began a slow trot to eat up miles and took off around the lake to the mountains.

Chapter 39

Spinel called his small group to a halt. They had been on the trail of the young warrior and the wolves for two days. Traveling nonstop as long as they could make out the trail. They were now entering the ruins of the human encampment Larin. The boy had made his way here, probably looking for refuge after their encounter. He was so young he had to be frightened and wanting some protection, so he had made his way here. But he found no protection here. Larin had been raided by an advanced group of Goblins a week before they set up camp at the bridge. Larin was the closest encampment to the mountains and also the closest encampment to the Remis bridge. Their plans might have been discovered if the encampment had been left. Plus, the humans here would have greatly added to the number of ogres in Darmot's forces. The ogres' size and strength made them valuable prizes so Darmot would have had the encampment wiped out.

The small group of soldiers he was traveling with slumped to the ground. Goblins rarely got tired, but he had been driving them harder than normal trying to catch up with his quarry. According to Coln the tracks were only a day or so old here in the encampment which meant they were getting closer. He would let the goblin soldiers rest here for a few minutes while he and Coln rode ahead to see if there were any further signs.

Coln found the trail going out of the encampment and heading northwest around the bank of the lake a few minutes later. They rode following the tracks and found a campsite. The fire was still smoking, telling Spinel that he was just a few hours behind. The trail continued to follow the lake shore. Spinel told Coln to wait there and he rode back to collect the goblin soldiers.

He roused the tired soldiers got them on their feet and got them moving back to where Coln waited.

Soon they were back together and pushing the goblins hard trying to gain on the young warrior. The tracks were harder to see here even though they were on the sandy lake shore, but the tide had come in and washed some of the tracks away. But they would just follow the lake shore until there was some sign that they had gone in another direction.

Four hours of steady travel brought them to where a stream emptied into the lake from the mountains. Spinel knew this stream. It came down from the dwarven town he had grown up with and made a narrow pass from the mountains to the flatlands. It was not traveled heavily because of how narrow it was. Most of the time a horse had to be led though the pass due to the rough narrow uneven footing. Most travelers didn't even bring horses with them and would just travel the pass on foot.

Coln pointed at the ground and showed Spinel a wolf footprint leading into the pass. A second smaller wolf print was close by the first with two hoof prints nearby. So, they had entered the mountains through the Centipede pass. They would be traveling slowly down this pass so he would be able to catch up with them easily. Night was approaching. The sun was already dipping behind the mountains now that they were this close to them. Spinel decided they would camp on the edge of the lake and enter the pass tomorrow. It would be a cold camp tonight. Now that they were getting closer to his quarry, he did not want to risk the light of a fire being seen.

They moved back down the lake shore a few hundred yards to get out of the wind blowing down from the mountains through the pass. He ordered the goblins to eat and rest for the night. The goblins were so tired they didn't even bother taking off their armor after they ate before they collapsed to the ground and were almost instantly asleep. Coln walked to the water's edge and began fishing, casting a light line into the water repeatedly.

The Centipede pass, that seems to be stirring up some memories for you.

Yes, my father and I would use that pass sometimes when he would take me trading with him as I was learning my craft.

That should be pleasant memories why do you seem bitter.

My father never thought my work good enough. He taught me all the particulars of his trade, and I had started crafting my own items. But he always seemed to think I needed to learn more. After 75 years of learning from him I was ready to start my own trade, break out on my own. My father didn't think I was ready, so I left. And my father and I haven't spoken since then.

Well then, if this goes well perhaps you will get the chance to clear the air with him.

I told you before I don't want to discuss this now quiet down so we can get some rest. I don't know if you can feel how tired our body is or not since I have control of it, but we need to rest. Good night. With that Spinel rolled himself in his horse's blanket to help fight the chill of the night air and quickly went to sleep.

Chapter 40

Leaana could feel that Scrill was close. In her small dark chamber, she tried to take comfort in the fact that her eagle was close by. The hunger and thirst she was feeling were almost overwhelming. She didn't know how long she had been in the small rock room. The darkness was always present, so it was hard to mark the passing of time. She had slept in fits never knowing how long she slept. When she was awake, she could see only the darkness. Perhaps it had only been a few hours because she had not had anything to eat or drink since she had been here. With how thirsty and hungry she was, it felt like it had been longer than a few hours. From outside her door, she heard cries of fear, moans of pain and other desperately crying out for food, water or just any help they could get.

Her vision blurred and suddenly she wasn't in darkness anymore but looking down from a rocky outcrop on a large chamber. A row of black stones sitting on what looked like an altar. Black stones. The black sacred stones of her people that she and Sagan had been sent to retrieve. So, wherever Scrill was looking down on must be the source of the sacred stones. She had reached her and Sagan's final destination. Where she had been sent to go with him all those weeks ago. Funny how she had still reached it even though it would do her no good now. Hopefully Sagan had decided to return home, and not come here. If he came here, he would probably be locked in a cell just like her. Their people would never know what was going on and not have the benefit of a Familiar to lead them.

Her vision returned to her. She heard footsteps. The screams from around her grew louder. Suddenly her door was thrown open and torch light flooded the room. After the total darkness of her chamber the torch light seemed as bright as the sun, and she shielded her eyes. Clawed hands reached in to grab her as a goblin pulled her out of her cell. She was shoved in a slow moving line of other prisoners. As her eyes adjusted to the light she began to look around. She could see a long line of prisoners in front with Fataso closest to her. He was right in front of her. As they came to the next cell, the door was pulled open and the person there made to get in line behind her. Three people were behind her as they were led down the corridor.

The corridor opened into a large chamber. Leaana recognized it as the room that she had seen from Scrill's vision. She was turned and forced to kneel before the altar. Rows of prisoners behind her also kneeling and right in front of her was one of the black stones. She looked around trying to find Scrill but she could not see the eagle anywhere amongst the rocks. The light from the torches cast too many shadows on the rock ledges above them where Scrill would be watching.

The person who had named himself Darmot walked out onto the altar and began speaking.

"For three days, you have been purified. For three days, you have been given no food or water, so you could be cleansed. For three days, you have sung the songs of fright, hunger, and thirst and now your souls are prepared. You are ready to be raised. Transformed and brought to your true nature." After saying those words, Darmot began chanting.

Leaana watched in fright as light appeared behind Darmot and grew to replace the wall behind him. There was a white plane with dark shapes moving across. Darmot stepped back on to the edge of the plane and immediately one of the dark shapes seemed to enter him from behind. Then a beam of light shot from Darmot's fingers into the Black stone of the person on the end of Leaana's row only 3 people away. The dark shape moved down the beam of light and into the stone and then into the person. The person convulsed and screamed as their body began to transform. No sooner had it happened to the first person in the row than a dark form entered the second in the row. They screamed as well.

Leaana watched as the first body contorted and changed into an Ogre. The second began the same transformation. Then the third person and finally the one right next to Leaana had a form moving towards it. Leaana was terrified, knowing she was next. She heard Scrill screech and looked as a beam of light came from the stone and hit her. Her mind pushed the energy back. Suddenly, her mind was filled with another. But it was not painful, it was familiar. Then she noticed she was flying towards the back of the room, then turning to go back to the front. She heard Darmot scream and fall back. The white plane disappearing. The three ogres that had been formed beside where she had been kneeling were screaming in anger. Then she noticed her body wasn't there. She had thought she was just seeing through Scrill's eyes, but her body wasn't there. No sooner had she realized this than she felt her feet grabbing something heavy and Fataso screaming "No I couldn't possibly…" Then they were lifting, flapping and flying hard and fast. Up and out a crack in the ceiling, Fataso's screams trailed off, and he got quiet.

Leaana could not believe what was happening. She was flying. She looked to her left and saw a massive brown and gold wing. Looking to the right was the same. She looked down and could see the earth moving below them. She could look back and see Fataso grasped in two large taloned feet, apparently having fainted, whether from fear or exhaustion Leaana didn't know. The feeling was thrilling.

WELCOME

Scrill's voice in her head, except now it felt closer, like it was all around her.

JOINED

The voice was loud and comforting. Like a warm memory. Leaana heard the single words but was able to understand more meaning. They were joined now. The ritual had made them join. Could they separate again or were they permanently an eagle?

YES

Yes? But to which question.

SEPARATE

Yes, they would be able to separate again. Good but how, well she would worry about that when the time came right now, they needed to get away.

Find some place safe. Then go find Sagan and Togan. Just wait till he saw this. Suddenly their wings missed a beat, and they dropped a bit from the sky Scrill quickly recovered.

WEAK

REST

SOON

Three words the most she had ever gotten from Scrill at a time but she could tell from Scrill's thoughts that Leaana's weakened state from starvation and thirst was taking its toll on them. They would not be able to fly much longer, especially carrying the weight of Fataso with them. They flew higher, flying up to a mountain ledge high along a sheer cliff where goblin search parties would not be able to follow them. They placed Fataso on the ground and then landed. Scrill shoved Leaana's mind, and she felt herself shrinking and pulling away. She stood on her own. Her mind surprisingly quiet with out Scrill's thoughts. She looked down, noticed she was not wearing any clothes, quickly pulled Fataso's shirt off of him and threw it over herself. As soon as she had his shirt on, she collapsed from fatigue. Then everything went black.

Chapter 41

Togan led Masque and Sagan up the centipede pass. The further into the pass they go the more nervous Masque became. They stopped for the night earlier than normal because the high walls of the pass caused the sun to sink below the mountain walls and with the long shadows and uneven footing it became too dangerous to continue. One of their horses could miss a step and hurt their leg then they would be in trouble. Sagan and Togan of course could continue on Sagan's night vision improved by his wolf senses, but Masque would be left by himself, and Sagan couldn't do that. He had come to like the old dwarf and respected his wisdom. He could tell that something was bothering Masque. So, after they had set up their simple camp and were eating dinner Sagan decided to see if Masque wanted to discuss it.

"What's bothering you Masque ever since we entered what you call the centipede pass you have been quiet, what is it?"

"I'm afraid of what I'm going to find at the end of the pass Boss. I am from a dwarven town called Fresmon. It lies at the beginning of the centipede pass in the mountains. Another four or five hours tomorrow and we will be there. I used to use this pass when I was going out to trade with the people of Larin. There were times of course when I would use Moose Herd pass which is the main pass through the mountains but on occasion, I would use this pass. If I was traveling alone and not part of a larger trade caravan. Boss, I am worried about my family in Fresmon. After seeing what happened in Larin I am worried that Fresmon might be the same, or worse. It might be fine. Fresmon is not directly connected to the Moose Herd pass, so it is not as easy to get to as some of the other Dwarven towns. But I just have a bad feeling."

Sagan could understand Masque's worry. He was worried about what was happening with his sister. It had been several days now since he had seen her captured at the Remis plateau and he had no idea what had become of her. She had to still be alive and, okay, any other thought was impossible for him to believe. It was the not knowing that made it difficult and now Masque for the night and a few hours tomorrow would be in that state of not knowing. But then he would know and that could be so much worse.

"Well Masque, let me help distract you. What is the next step in my training? I could use a good workout."

Masque thought for a moment then said "Boss, best thing for you now is just constant drilling so take a ready stance, ok good and here we go, five, eighteen, three…" Masque began calling different positions at a rapid and seemingly random pattern. The randomness of the call kept Sagan having to constantly shift his weight as he moved from position to position to keep his balance. Occasionally Masque would call a halt, tell Sagan to assume a position and correct some minor breaks in form or balance. But otherwise, the practice went smoothly and quickly. Before long sweat was pouring freely down Sagan's back as he moved. Togan began jumping and snapping his jaws as he began to feel the effort that Sagan was putting forth. Then suddenly Masque pulled out two hammers from his belt and attacked Sagan. Still calling position for Sagan but now sparring with Sagan.

Sagan was amazed at how fast Masque was and how small his movements seemed to be. After the first few minutes of the practice Masque stopped calling positions and let Sagan move as he wanted. For an hour they sparred Sagan using every move and every ounce of speed he could to try and break Masque's guard. Masque on the other hand either simply blocked the sword with a hammer and a small movement of the wrist or simply wasn't there when the strike was over with. After an hour Masque called a halt and stepped on Sagan's sword after a quick downward strike from Sagan had found nothing but air. Masque looked in Sagan's eyes to make sure he knew the fight was over then lifted his foot from Sagan's blade. Sagan stood breathing heavily. Masque appeared to have not even broken a sweat while he avoided everything Sagan could throw at him.

"Masque that is amazing. I knew you could teach it, but I didn't know you could move so quickly. You made defending yourself look easy."

"Well Boss after 175 years of studying how to fight I would think I know what I'm doing."

"Yeah, too bad I don't have 175 years to practice. Here I thought I was getting better."

"Oh, don't think I didn't have to work to keep away from you. You are wickedly fast and strong. But since I taught you, it helped me predict your next move. A normal opponent doesn't have that advantage Boss. So, Boss you were behind from the start."

Sagan nodded. That made sense. Hot and sweat stained now, Sagan walked the short distance down to the mountain stream that flowed through here to make the pass. The bank was slightly wider here, which is another reason they had stopped when they did. Reaching the stream, Sagan removed his shirt and pants and stepped into the water. Cooling himself and washing off the sweat and dirt from the constant training and traveling. He rinsed the sweat from his shirt and pants, then put them back on and let them begin to dry as he sat by the fire.

Masque handed Sagan a cup of tea he had prepared as Sagan washed. They sat in silence, sipping their tea. Masque worrying about what he would find tomorrow, and Sagan worrying about Masque. Once they had finished their tea, they each laid in their bedrolls and tried to sleep.

The next morning, they awoke before the sun climbed over the edge of the mountain walls. They breakfasted in silence and packed up the camp. The sun finally climbed over the mountain walls, and they began their journey. It was later in the day than they normally would have stayed in camp, but they needed the light to safely traverse the winding trail through the pass. They rode in silence. Togan leading the way, followed by Sagan, Masque and then Skanar and Valonic, who had turned up in camp during the night. It was a pleasant enough day with blue skies overhead; the temperature rising slightly now that the shadow of the mountain was off the pass. The wind shifted. It had been steadily blowing down the pass back toward the lake; now it was blowing up the pass into the mountains.

Togan growled, and Sagan stopped smelling the air. "I smell goblins. They must be behind us coming up the pass."

"Let's pick up the pace. After we reach Fresmon, there is a wide area where we can set up a defensive position. The pass is very narrow just before the village so they will only be able to come through one at a time, which should make things a bit easier for us." Masque advised.

They kicked their horses into a trot, about as fast as they felt they could move on the narrow uneven footing of the track they were following. An hour later, they arrived at Fresmon. As they entered the town, the rock wall to their left fell away. The stream they had been following on their right went into the rock wall and the town lay before them, nestled in a circular valley with mountains around it. No one moved. The town was silent.

Masque pulled his pony to a stop, dismounted, and led it over to a small stable yard close to the mouth of the pass. Sagan did the same.

"I don't like how quiet it is, Boss. I am afraid my worst fears have been realized." Masque breathed.

"We don't know that the town is empty. Perhaps everyone is simply hiding." Sagan said, trying to put a note of encouragement into his voice.

"Well, Boss, I don't think I have time to investigate it right now. If you are smelling Goblins, they can't be too far behind. Get your bow and sword ready, and let's get ready to meet them. With the look of this town, Boss, I think I might want to lend a hand and give a little payback." Masque said as he drew his two hammers from his belt. "Boss, you take them out with your bow as they come through the pass there. If any get through, I'll be over here by the wall waiting." Masque took his position beside where the rock wall fell away and the pass began, Skanar and Valonic across the opening from him.

Sagan nodded, he took his quiver from his saddle and hung it over his shoulder grabbed his bow and took up a position where he could see down the first 50 or so feet of the pass before it curved back with the river. Togan took position beside him, his hackles up and teeth bared. Sagan put an arrow on the string, made sure Carameth was on his back ready if any got past his arrows or Masque. Then he stood waiting for them to come.

165

Chapter 42

Spinel stood from examining the coals of the fire. They were still warm. That meant his quarry was only a few hours ahead of him. He got back on his horse and yelled at the goblin soldiers to move. They stood slowly he had driven them hard today. They were moving at first light and had been running most of the day. But it had paid off. He knew this place. From years before when he had traveled trading. If he continued to push the soldiers at the pace, they had been traveling they would be in Fresmon within the next two hours. That would give them enough light still to take out the young boy and his wolves. Then everyone would get a nice long rest and they could return to Darmot in triumph.

He barked orders. He got the soldiers running, sent Coln after them and he brought up the rear. They had numbers and the element of surprise on their side. The soldiers ran on. Just as Spinel predicted, in about two hours the pass began to narrow for its final approach to Fresmon. The Goblins formed into a single file line as that is as wide as the passage would allow.

The first goblin rounded the final bend and suddenly dropped an arrow sticking from its neck. The next goblin jumped over his fallen companion and then dropped as a hammer crashed into the side of his helmet. The impact of the hammer made a ringing noise that echoed though the pass and off the rock walls. The third soldier fell just as the first one did an arrow sticking from its neck. The fourth goblin struggled over its fallen companions only to meet a dwarf wielding two hammers and began to fight for its life. The dwarf never seeming to be where the goblin was attacking. The fifth Goblin made it through the narrow entrance and immediately moved to his left as an arrow flashed by his head. Teeth bit into his knee and he collapsed as his legs gave way.

Spinel watched as he approached as goblin soldier after goblin soldier dropped as they exited the pass. His entire force wasn't even through the last gap yet and already they had been cut in half. The sixth and seventh made it through and were moving forward. Spinel's horse reared as it approached the dead goblins lying on the ground. Spinel not being prepared for the sudden movement, fell from the saddle. The horse bolted back up the pass a short distance to get some distance from itself and the dead bodies. Spinel shook himself then prepared for his time to go through the narrow opening. He ran forward into the middle of the remaining goblin soldiers. The ninth in line was about to enter. He got right behind him with the tenth on his heels. Coln turned his horse and rode off not prepared to fight now that he had seen five of the soldiers cut down in a matter of seconds.

The goblin in front of Spinel made it through the gap taking an arrow impact on his breast plate. The goblin staggered from the force but the stone arrow head was not able to penetrate the steel of his armor. Spinel quickly dove around him to get into the clear ground past the narrow gap. Standing he saw two goblins approaching the young man now standing some twenty yards away. He was dropping his bow and drawing a sword from his back as a white wolf leapt at the goblin nearest to him. A growl to Spinel's right had him turning and dodging a leap from a smaller grey wolf. Spinel's dodge was immediately followed by a swing from his hammer that made contact with the wolves ribs. The wolf yelped in pain and retreated to the edge of the clearing where the stream went under the mountain.

The dwarf was now fighting the goblin that had followed Spinel though the gap. The goblin was moving slow fatigue slowing it down, so the dwarf was easily dodging its attack and deftly delivered a hammer strike to the top of the helmet causing another metallic ring to echo across the rock as another goblin collapsed unconscious. Spinel sprinted toward the young man with the sword, he was already engaged with another Goblin. Spinel knew this would be his best chance while the wolves were all fighting, and he could take the boy two on one.

As Spinel ran to engage the boy, the goblin he was fighting lost its head from a deft forward hand swing from the boys sword. The superior numbers had been eliminated it would just be him and the boy. Spinel yelled a battle cry and moved to attack.

Stroke after stroke, parry after parry, he and the boy fought. Spinel was growing tired, he felt like he had been fighting for hours. His attacks were slowing becoming less precise. Then the boy made a mistake. He over extended on an attack and lost his balance. He tripped on a rock and fell. Spinel had him, he took a step forward, raised his hammer to bring a crushing blow onto the back of the boys head and then felt teeth bite into his left arm as his right went up. The teeth tore through his flesh ripping his arm open to the bone. He screamed, dropped his hammer and grasped his left arm. The boy had regained his feet and was raising his sword for the killing stroke. Spinel heard someone yell. "Boss don't kill him!" He then felt the impact of the side of the boys sword on the side of his head and everything went black.

Chapter 43

"Boss don't kill him!" Sagan heard Masque yell at the last moment with a tremendous effort he pulled back on his stroke and turned his wrist so that the side of his blade impacted on the goblins head. The goblin dropped like one of his sisters dolls from when they were children his eyes rolling back into his head. Sagan panted gasping for breath. He thought he was dead when he suddenly lost his balance, tripped, and fell. The Togan had saved him by biting the goblins arm. "Why didn't you want me to kill him. I've fought him before, this is the one that got away from the first patrol we fought. He must have been tracking us ever since." Sagan asked wondering what Masque had in mind.

"I'm sorry Boss but I couldn't let you kill him. I recognized his fighting style and movements. He fights like I do, and like you do. I've only taught my fighting style to one other person. I don't know how but I think that goblin is my son." Masque knelt beside the still form and began to wrap a bandage around his bleeding left arm.

Chapter 44

"Your son?" Sagan asked "He's a goblin how can he be your son?"

"I don't know Boss I only know that the fighting style and movements he used are the same as the ones my son Stingal used when I taught him." Masque replied. He went over to Sagan's horse and took the rope that was tied to his saddle, cut a couple of small lengths from the end and went back to the goblin's side. "Now that I have the bleeding from that bite under control, I'm going to tie him up, so we don't have to worry about him when he wakes up Boss." With that Masque placed the goblins hands behind his back and tied them together then put a piece of rope around his feet securing them together.

That done Masque looked around the clearing where they had fought. Goblin bodies littered the ground where they lay. Masque was disgusted. The senseless violence and loss of life were a waste. "Here Boss. Let's carry them back into the pass a little ways hopefully that will keep them from smelling too badly." With that he began to drag the bodies at the entrance to the pass back out of the opening, clearing the way.

Sagan followed also grabbing one of the goblin bodies and dragging it clear. He rounded the first bend in the pass and heard a horse nicker. Looking up he couldn't believe his eyes. There stood Kada, Leaana's horse wearing a goblin saddle and pacing nervously. "Easy girl," Sagan crooned "take it easy." He spoke softly as he approached her. As he reached for the reins, she shied at first. She sniffed the air then her head was rubbing into Sagan as she recognized his scent. Kada was in bad shape it looked like she had been ridden hard and not properly cared for. She was covered in lather and still breathing hard. Her belly looked empty, and her knees were scraped but other than that seemed to be ok. Sagan led her through the end of the pass past the dead goblin bodies and tied her next to Karr. The two horses nickered a greeting to each other. They stood side by side, their noses and faces close to one another. Sagan knew he would need to cool Kada down properly and give her something to eat but that could wait a few more minutes.

Sagan and Masque finished putting the goblin bodies in a pile just past the last bend in the pass where the trail was just a bit wider. Masque told Sagan to go care for Kada, he would finish what needed to be done. Masque wandered into the town of Fresmon, and came out a few minutes later carrying a couple of bottles of oil. He took the oil and poured it over the goblin bodies. Then using his flint and steel he lit the oil on fire. Black smoke rolled into the sky as Masque burned the bodies. The task completed he went back to Fresmon to see if he could find anyone there. Not believing for a moment he would find anyone because they most likely would have come out to investigate after the battle was over.

Masque walked the abandoned streets of his home town. Nothing moved. It was strange to be here, and for it to be so quiet. He was used to the sounds of people talking or laughter coming from the homes. He made his way to his house, walked in, and found nothing. His wife's body was not there. All their belongings seemed to be intact, but there was no sign of his wife. Everything was covered in a layer of dust, meaning that whatever happened here must have happened several weeks ago. After searching the house just to make sure he knew she wasn't there, he came back to the kitchen. He walked over to a large wooden cask in one corner and picked up a mug that was hanging on a peg beside it. He opened the tap on the cask and rich amber colored beer came out. He took a long drink, emptying his mug in one long draught. He opened the tap again and refilled his mug. He went over to the table and pulled a chair over by the cask. His young friend would be ok for a few hours. It was time for him to mourn his friends and family in his way. By drinking lots of beer and remembering their laughter and songs. He sat in the chair and drank. If he had his way, he would not be able to stand within an hour or so. He drained his mug again, reached for the tap, filled it again and began to sing and laugh by himself.

172

Chapter 45

Fataso huddled against the rock wall behind him. Trying to keep as far from the cliff edge as he could. He had never realized he was afraid of heights. The Southern elf kingdom where he was from was mostly flat. It had a few rolling hills, but nothing like the Dwarfgon Mountains. Even the Remis plateau had been higher than anything in the Southern Elf kingdom, and it was small compared to the mountains they were in now. Now here he was on a small ledge with hundreds of feet of sheer rock below him. The ledge he was on really was quite wide, probably thirty to forty feet, but with his fear of heights, it felt more like it was five feet wide. Beside him, Leaana slept in his shirt. When had she taken it off him? He didn't know. It seemed that was all she was wearing. He had awoken to find himself on this ledge with her in a deep sleep. The last thing he remembered was seeing an almost blinding light surround her as the black form approached her. The black form had fled from the white light that had surrounded Leaana and gone back into the white plane that had formed on the wall during the strange ritual. Then Leaana had not been there. A giant eagle had swooped down, grabbed his shoulders, and lifted him into the air. They had flown out of the chamber through a crack in the ceiling and then he had seen how high they were. He must have fainted because he had no memory of landing here, just waking up and finding Leaana asleep.

Leaana stirred. She shivered as she awoke. The wind up on this bare peak was cold and could seep into their bones. Fear of falling was keeping him warm right now, but soon even that would not be enough to keep him warm since all he had on was his trousers. Leaana sat up, shaking her head. Her long black hair tossing and blowing in the breeze.

"Fataso, you ok?" Leaana asked. as she sat up and looked around. She was close to the edge of the cliff and looked over and down. "Wow, what a view, Fataso. You should see this."

"That's ok. I am perfectly happy with this solid rock wall behind me. At least I can't fall through the rock wall." Fataso said as he pushed back harder into the wall.

Leaana stood and rubbed her hands up and down her arms. "That wind is cold. Thanks for the shirt, by the way."

"You're welcome. You may keep it if you can tell me what is going on, how we got here and what we are going to do now?" Fataso said, still keeping himself firmly against the wall and cringing slightly as Leaana walked back and forth on the edge.

"Well, Darmot is apparently somehow turning humans into ogres. I bet he made the goblins and orcs as well. I saw a black shape enter the people beside me and saw them transform. Well, whenever it was my turn, something else happened. I joined with Scrill, then we picked you up and flew you out of there. We found this rock ledge, figured it would be safe, landed, and then I think I passed out."

Scrill screeched from above. Leaana looked up and saw her eagle fly over and drop something. She reached out her hand and caught a small rabbit. Scrill then flew off and back down out of sight.

EAT

The command came through her head loud and clear. Louder than it had been in the past. No longer was it a vague impression, now it was a clear voice.

"Fataso, I hope you are as hungry as I am. This rabbit is for our breakfast but I don't see any way to cook it so I think we will be eating it raw." Leaana felt around and found where the talons had pierced the rabbit's fur and begin to try and pull the fur back.

"My dear, right now my stomach is doing flips. I'm starving, but there is no way I could eat."

Leaana had now gotten some of the rabbit fur back out of way and began to chew on the raw meat below. It was gamey and metallic tasting from the blood, but she managed to tear off a bite. A few moments later, she heard Scrill call from above. She looked up as her eagle friend swooped down and dropped something behind her on the rock ledge. Walking back to where it lay, Leaana noticed it was a short old knife. The blade had a sharp curve to it, ending in a sharp point. The metal of the blade was rusted and the leather wrapping the hilt was old and brittle.

BEAK

The word again sounding in Leaana's head. She picked up the old rusty knife and noticed that in spite of the rust, the blade was still fairly sharp. She used this knife to quickly skin the rabbit she was trying to eat. This made eating the meat of the rabbit much easier, not having to get the fur out of the way first. Again, she offered some of the raw meat to Fataso, again he refused. His nervous stomach could not hold anything down.

A few minutes later while Leaana was still finishing the meat of the small rabbit Scrill returned and dropped two pumpells on the ground again just a little behind Leaana. She took one bite through the outer skin and greedily drank the water held within. She took the other over to Fataso. This Fataso did not turn down his thirst over powering his fear of heights. He greedily drank the nourishing water of the pumpell.

Scrill circled one last time and then landed on the ledge. Leaana dropped the bones of the rabbit to the ground and Scrill began to pick the last few pieces of meat from them.

The rabbit had been fairly small and had not had much time to fatten up since coming out of its winter sleep so it had not gone very far towards ending Leaana's hunger pains however she could feel some energy returning to her as her body began to digest the small amount of meat from the rabbit and the moisture from the pumpell. She shivered. The cold wind whipping across their cliff hideaway chilling her. She knew they would have to leave soon, or the cold would set in and that could be just as dangerous as running into a goblin patrol but much slower. She began to wonder how they would get off the ledge because the sheer rock face did not look climbable, so their manner of escape was unclear.

JOIN

Scrill thought it very matter of fact like it was obvious. "Can we join again?" Leaana asked out loud.

"What was that?" Fataso asked.

"I was just thinking of how we were going to get off this ledge and Scrill told me join. I was just wondering if Scrill and I could join again to fly down."

"Well, that is all fine and dandy for you, but I think I'm just going to stay right here." Fataso said.

"You'll either freeze or starve. I guess in our joined form we can carry you down like we carried you up here."

"Freezing or starving is preferable to falling to my death while being carried in the talons of a giant eagle," Fataso said his face turning white from fright just thinking about the prospect.

"Well, I'm not going to leave you here to die so you're just going to have to go with us whether you like it or not. Plus, I need you to carry your shirt that I am wearing." Leaana said.

"Carry the shirt? Why do I need to do that can't you just continue to wear it?" Fataso asked looking puzzled. At least that was a different expression than the pure terror from a moment before.

"Well, I'm not really sure if I can wear it or not. I was wearing a shirt and pants before I joined with Scrill the first time. When we got here and separated, I wasn't wearing anything. So, I borrowed your shirt, then passed out." Leaana explained.

"I can see that being an awkward situation if we were surrounded by people. Fataso said. "I'm probably going to be unconscious if I'm flying, so I'll just wear the shirt again and you can take it off me again.

JOIN

GO

SPEED

"Scrill is getting impatient. I think we should go." Leaana reddened at the thought of having to remove the shirt in front of him. "Close your eyes, please." Leaana said as she reached up to undo the fasteners on the shirt that was holding it closed.

Fataso reddened and closed his eyes. A few moments later, he felt the shirt land on his lap.

REACH

Leaana reached mentally for that place in her mind where she felt and heard Scrill's consciousness. A moment later, a bright light shone in front of her eyes and then she was looking down on Fataso and the world in extremely high detail. She could see the goose bumps on his flesh and the beating of his heart in his neck. She could see tiny cracks in the rock face she had not seen before. "Ready" Leaana tried to say, but it came out as a low-pitched bird sound.

Fataso opened his eyes and marveled. Before him stood an eagle, but different than any eagle he had ever seen. The eagle stood more than six feet tall, her plumage a rich brown and gold. The beak was curved yellow and as long as Fataso's forearm and the Talons were black and sharp and the size of his lower legs. The eagle bent its head down and picked up the rusty knife in its beak and then leapt from the ledge, spreading its wings as it fell through space.

Leaana watched as the rock ledge fell away, and she accelerated towards the ground. She felt her wings unfurl and the wind catch in them. Suddenly they weren't falling, but were pulling out into a smooth glide. A single flap or two and they were climbing up on the wind. The feeling of the wind blowing across their body and supporting them was exhilarating. Soon they were banking back to the ledge, and she saw Fataso, standing shaking his head as they swooped down then She felt his weight as they grabbed him and lifted him from the ground. He screamed as he saw the earth fall away from his feet. Leaana heard him scream. Then the scream died as his body went limp in their grip.

The details she could see were amazing. Even though they were hundreds of feet above the ground, she could see the movement of the brush as the wind blew it. They flew, riding the winds of the mountains, swooping, turning, and reveling in the experience of flying.

Then, in the distance, they saw smoke. A large black plume of smoke rising into the clear blue sky.

THERE

Scrill's voice in their shared consciousness, and they headed for the smoke. They flew for another few minutes and they topped a mountain and saw a town below them. Houses carved out the mountainside, others built from rock free standing. The town spread out below them; streets crisscrossed. No one moved the in town, it was silent. Then, as they reached the edge of the town, they saw movement, a single person standing brushing a horse. Leaana recognized the horse, and her heart leapt. It was Kada, her horse, and the person bushing it was Sagan. She had found her brother. They could be reunited and figure out what to do next.

They let out a cry, Sagan looked up and his eyes widened in surprise. They flew down close to the ground and dropped the limp form of Fataso gently to the ground. They landed and walked over to one of the nearby houses and ducked as they walked inside.

Leaana felt a push as her mind was pushed out of Scrill, a flash of light filled her vision and then she was standing in the house. Her body feeling drained and exhausted. Seeing a table close by her she grabbed the table cloth and wrapped it around her. She heard a familiar voice then, call out.

"Sagan" Leaana shouted. She looked back to the entrance of the house and saw Sagan standing there with amazement showing on his face. Then she collapsed, as the exhaustion took hold.

Chapter 46

Darmot awoke in darkness. Every part of his body was in exquisite pain. He reveled in the pain but didn't know what had happened. He had been in the ritual chamber in the middle of the Raising ritual. when things went suddenly wrong. One of the black forms came back from trying raise a human and had gone back through him into the white plane. It had almost taken his soul with it. He had been outside his body for a moment but had fought his way free and gone back. The will power it had taken to resist that pull was enough to exhaust him. He slammed back into his body, and it felt like crashing into a stone wall. He had blacked out.

He got up his joints screaming at the effort. He took the pain in using it to drive him. Exiting his sleeping chamber, he entered his audience room. Basara, his constant personal guard, at her post as usual.

"Basara," Darmot began as he went to sit upon his throne to relieve the pressure on his aching joints. "Report. What did you see during the ritual."

"My lord Darmot. The power hit a young human girl at the altar. There was a flash then a giant eagle swept through the room. The eagle flew down and picked up an elven prisoner we had in that group then flew out of a crack in the ceiling. I saw you collapse when the flash happened as the power seemed to flow back on you. I had you moved to your sleeping chambers where you have been for the past day. It is good to see you up and moving."

"A human girl stopped the raising. But how we have raised thousands of humans with out incident? What made this girl different?" Darmot raged. "Send out patrols. Find the giant eagle or find the girl. I want to know what happened."

"I anticipated your desires my lord, patrols are preparing now and will be leaving within the hour." Basara crooned

Darmot stood covering the distance between him and Basara in a single stride. Standing above her "If you are so good at anticipating my needs, and I have been asleep for a day why have the patrols not already left" Darmot asked in quiet fury.

"My lord," Basara began, calmly not giving into Darmot's intimidating tactics. "When you collapsed the sanctuary was thrown into chaos. As you know, during the ritual we only have a few Goblin soldiers on hand to keep the new converts in line. It took several hours to get the prisoners back into their cells. We then had to send over to the main force and request more troops be sent over for the search effort. All of this takes time. Believe me when I say I have been working as quickly as possible to begin the search." Her voice still calm her manner easy.

Darmot took a step back, took a deep breath, and said "Yes, of course. However next time simply kill the rampaging converts to save time and send for the additional troops right away. That could have saved several hours."

"Yes of course you are right my lord" Basara said her voice never wavering in its calm even manner.

"Over see the search yourself Basara, I want nothing to go wrong." With that Darmot turned and walked back into his bed chamber.

Basara stood, walked out of the audience chamber, and shut the door behind her. Two guards stood outside the door. She rammed her fist into the face of the guard on her right with such force that he was lifted from the ground and collapsed. That pompous wind bag Darmot. Thinking she did not know what was required. If she had killed the prisoners, he would have been furious about the loss of so many possible new soldiers. But he had to correct her. One day, perhaps, she would grow tired of his interference and eliminate the problem, but for now, she would continue to do his bidding. He had led them for many years and had built an almost unstoppable army. So, for now, he still had her loyalty. But her patience grew thin.

She saw the commanders of the troops that had been sent to help with the search. Gave them the last of their instructions. Reminding them they want the giant eagle or the girl alive. She then sent them out to search, hoping they would return soon, as Darmot was not a patient man.

Chapter 47

Sagan stood in shock. His sister was here, asleep, nearly unconscious, but here. He had to find Masque and tell him, but he didn't want to leave his sister's side. An eagle stood on a table, in the house where Leaana lay. He had been brushing Kada down after the hard riding she had been through, and making sure she wasn't hurt. He had heard a strange noise, a low-pitched screech. He looked up and saw the largest eagle he had ever seen fly overhead and place a person on the ground, then land close to a house. The bird walked into the house. He had walked towards the house to investigate. There had been a flash of light from inside, then, he had heard his sister's voice call his name. He ran and looked in the window just in time to see her collapse.

Togan walked up and sat next to Leaana. He turned and looked out the door to the house, keeping watch. Sagan could feel Togan's protectiveness over his sister and knew he would stay there with her. Sagan, letting Togan watch over his sister, walked back to the person who the eagle had placed on the ground. It was a relatively short, fat elf. Why would it be carrying an elf? He seemed to be ok just unconscious, like Leaana. His lips were cracked and dry and his cheeks a little sunken, but otherwise he seemed ok.

Where was Masque? The last time Sagan had seen him, he had gone into town. He left the elf's side and started to search for Masque. After going through about half the town, he began to hear what sounded like singing. A song would stop, he would hear a garbled voice, then laughter. The laughter he thought he recognized as Masque. He had heard him laugh some around their camp sites as they had traveled the last few weeks.

He followed the sound winding through side streets till he finally came to a house carved into the side of the mountain on the opposite side of the town from where they had entered from the pass. From inside, he could hear Masque's voice. The speech seemed to be slurred with the words not so clear and he was speaking in Dwarfish. Sagan couldn't understand the words, but after just a few, there was more laughter. After a brief pause and a loud belch, he heard the slurred voice start to sing again. The tune was lively, but Sagan had no idea what the song was about.

He entered the house and saw Masque sitting on the floor by a large cask, a large cup in his hand. The song stopped and Masque drained the contents of the cup and quickly turned to the tap on the cask and drew more liquid from it. Sagan took this opportunity to speak. "Masque, my sister is here. I'm not sure how, but I think she flew here."

"Boss! You're here! I'm drinking to the town! Celebrating their lives, telling stories about them and drinking. You say your sister just flew in; boy, her arms must be tired, Boss." With that, Masque let out a laugh loud enough to hurt Sagan's ears. It echoed through the house and down the streets of the town. He turned up the cup and proceeded to drain the contents again. This time, as his head went back to drink the last drops from the cup, he fell backwards, hitting the ground. Sagan could hear snores coming from Masque, and he knew he would be out for the rest of the night. Sagan had seen men passed out from drinking before. One or two of the town elders had done so the night after their rite of passage ceremony. They had been too fond of something called elvish brandy. Sagan searched through the house, found a blanket on one of the beds and covered Masque with it. He decided the best thing to do now was go back and watch over his sister and the elf until they awoke. He made his way back to where his sister lay unconscious on the floor.

He arrived back at the house where Leaana lay. As he entered, he saw she was still asleep. Togan was still sitting beside her, and the eagle was still perched on the table. Since there was nothing, he could do for her right now, he decided to explore the house. The front room they were in seemed to be a combination living space, and kitchen. A fireplace sat on one wall with logs neatly stacked beside it and a large black pot hanging on a hook on an arm so that it could be swung over the fire. Going into the back of the house he found what appeared to be a cold cellar. In the cellar he found potatoes, carrots, onions and some other vegetables in jars, tomatoes, okra, and beans. Coming out of the cellar and further back from the kitchen area he found two bedrooms each with large feather mattresses on the beds. The blankets on the beds were disturbed like the people that lived here had left in a hurry in the middle of the night. Some clothes hung neatly in a curtained space in each room. Wherever they had gone they had left their clothes behind.

Night was falling, the sun dipped behind the mountains. There was the beginning of a chill in the air and the wind was picking up outside. Sagan went back out the front of the house to where the horses were waiting patiently. He had noticed a small stable to the side of the house and led Kada, Karr, and the small pony Masque had been riding into the stable for the night. They would be warmer there out of the wind than standing out in the open.

After dealing with the horses, Sagan went to where the goblin they had tied up. He still lay recovering from the blow to his head. Sagan loosened his bonds slightly to allow the blood to flow back to his hands and feet. Then he picked the goblin up and carried him into the house as well. He laid him on his side next to one of the walls. Then he built a fire in the fireplace to keep the chill of the night air from settling in.

Leaana stirred, she sat up and looked around. "Sagan?" she asked as her eyes opened.

"I'm here Leaana," Sagan replied as he stepped to her side, helping her up off the floor. He enfolded Leaana in an embrace. A long hug taking comfort in the knowing that his twin was alive. Leaana stood there, arms by her side enjoying the hug but unable to hug back. Sagan broke the contact and looked at his sister.

"Why aren't you hugging me back?" Sagan asked.

"Because I have to hold this table cloth in place. I am not wearing any other clothes." Leaana explained.

"Why aren't you wearing clothes?" Sagan asked. "Did that elf out there steal them or hurt you? What has happened, where have you been? I've been looking for you and saw you had been captured by goblins. How did you escape?"

"Sagan, calm down. I want to tell you everything Sagan, but first, I need water and where is Fataso? Oh, and can I borrow something to wear?" Leanna asked as she moved to sit in one of the chairs around the table. As she sat the eagle moved to stand in front of her. Leaana reached up to absently stroke the bird's feathers. Sagan watched surprised to see such a casual interaction between Leaana and this large predatory bird.

"Is Fataso the elf the giant eagle brought in? If so, he is out in the yard. Let me draw you some water from the well outside and then I will check on him." Not even giving Leaana a chance to reply Sagan dashed outside to the well and drew a bucket of water. He found another bucket lying near the well and transferred the water to it. Bringing that back to Leaana he sat it on the table next to her. She immediately dipped her hands into the water and began to drink. He then went outside to check on the elf lying on the ground. The elf was still asleep, so he picked him up and carried him into one of the bedrooms in the back of the house and laid him on one of the beds. Covering him so he would not get chilled. Then he came back into the kitchen.

"The elf is still asleep. I have laid him on one of the beds in the back of the house. Why don't you search back there and see if you can find something to wear. Then can you tell me what's been going on?" Sagan asked.

"Sounds good. Oh, and do you have any food? I haven't really eaten for the last few days and I'm starving." Leaana asked.

"Food? How can you think of food now?" Sagan replied, exasperation in his voice. He wanted answers and food was the last thing on his mind.

"I have been a prisoner and starved for the last week or so and I am hungry I'll tell you everything I just need to eat." Leaana pleaded. With that she went back into the house to search for some clothes.

Sagan went back out to the stable and grabbed his saddle bag. He set a small portion of the smoked venison aside for Leaana to snack on. Then he took some of of the water in the bucket and poured it into the black pot over the fire. He went into the cold cellar and brought out some potatoes, carrots, and onions. He took the last of the smoked venison and threw it in the pot. He then cut the carrots, potatoes, and onions and put them in as well. Soon the smell of venison stew began to waft through the house as the water began to boil over the fire.

Leaana reemerged with the elf following behind her. "Sagan this is Fataso. Fataso this is my brother Sagan." she said as she gave Sagan a proper hug. A low growl came from the corner of the room where Togan sat.

"Oh yes, sorry and this is his animal guide Togan. I'm sorry Togan, I didn't mean to leave you out." Leaana explained. She quickly crossed the room and scratched Togan behind the ears. A low growl escaped from the wolf's throat. Sagan could feel the pleasure that Togan was experiencing. As she walked back to her seat she stopped, bent over and picked up the small, curved knife.

"Glad I hadn't lost this," Leaana said, "Scrill gave it to me. Called it my beak."

"Scrill?" Sagan asked?

Leaana sat at the table and started to chew on a piece of the smoked venison that Sagan had set out. She gave a piece to the eagle still sitting by her on the table. Her stomach growled as she could smell the stew beginning to heat.

"While we wait on the stew to get ready, I guess I can start explaining. First a few introductions. Sagan, Togan," Leaana began turning in her chair so she could address the wolf as well, "this is Scrill," Leaana indicated the eagle on the table by stroking her head. "She is my animal guide, and I'm a familiar. She had been held by the elves after she had been injured years ago. That is why she had not come to find me. When the elven caravan came through Romin, we found each other. I kept seeing visions from her point of view, so I had to go find her."

Sagan nodded. He knew the draw that familiars often felt when they were apart to be back together. He now understood why Leaana felt she had to go.

"Well, when you left to go find her why didn't you explain that to me? I would have gone with you." Sagan said disappointed that she had not done exactly that.

"Well, I didn't know if you would go with me, or if you would have thought I was crazy and just wishing for something. Also, I felt like it was something I had to do on my own. Maybe I had to go alone to prove to myself I was worthy," Leaana explained.

Sagan understood that as well. All his life being a familiar there had been high expectations placed on him. A feeling of having to prove to the encampment that you were truly worthy to be a familiar and ultimately lead. Going on a quest to free your familiar yourself could feel like a necessary step along that path.

Sagan looked around the kitchen area and found a ladle and some bowls. He served some venison stew and gave it to Leaana. He spooned out some meat with a bit of the broth and placed it in a small bowl and cautiously placed it in front of the eagle, being careful to stay far enough away that the beak or talons couldn't get him.

"Scrill is it? I don't know if you need something to eat as well, but here you go." Sagan said.

Leaana smiled at the thoughtfulness of Sagan to feed Scrill, and at how careful he was to keep his distance. She watched as Sagan served Fataso a bowl of stew, then began eating with gusto.

While Leaana was talking and Sagan was cooking, Fataso had looked around the room at Sagan, the wolf, Togan and Scrill perched on the table. This was definitely an interesting crowd. But no matter what or who he was with, it beat flying. The stew in front of him smelled good. Seeing that Leaana was beginning to eat, he also tucked in and started to enjoy the savory stew.

Sagan took a small portion for himself and prepared to sit. Before he could sit and begin eating, Masque stumbled through the door.

"Hey Boss, that smells good, and I could use something to settle my stomach." Masque sat at the table across from Fataso and took the bowl from Sagan's hand.

Luckily, Sagan had prepared a large pot of the stew using the last of their smoked supplies. At this rate, there would not be much left. He again served himself a bowl and began eating. Sagan introduced Masque to Fataso,

Leaana, and Scrill while everyone ate.

After they had dined, Masque made everyone a cup of tea and they sat around the table enjoying the hot drink. Sagan was tired. He had not really had a chance to recover from their battle with the goblins at the pass entrance. Tending to Kada, Leaana's arrival, preparing the meal, moving the prisoner, and introductions had kept him moving and thinking all afternoon and well into the evening. Sagan was proud of his sister and wanted to hear more about what had happened to her, but right now, he needed to rest. Valonic and Skanar howled from the distance. Togan sniffed the air, howled, and gave a quick bark. He then bounded out of the house. Scrill also took off from the table and flew out into the night.

REST

"Scrill says we should rest." Leaana says.

"Scrill says?" Masque asked.

"Yes, I get impressions of words from her. Only one word at a time, but it has been clearer since our joining."

"Your joining?" This time, it was Sagan asking the question.

"That is a long story, perhaps best saved for when we are all rested." Fataso replied.

"Yes, Togan, and the other two wolves traveling with us will keep watch through the night." Sagan said.

"Scrill is out keeping watch as well," Leaana pointed out. Not wanting it to seem like her familiar wasn't pulling her weight. "Why do you have two other wolves traveling with you?"

"That is a long story. That can also wait until tomorrow. Leaana. Why don't you take one of the beds in the bedrooms, and Fataso you take the one you were already in. You two look like you could use the rest. Masque and I will sleep out here and keep an eye on the prisoner."

"His name is Stingal, Boss. I'll make sure to loosen and retighten his bonds throughout the night I don't want him to lose a hand or foot." Masque said.

"All right. Goodnight, everyone we can finish catching up in the morning." Sagan said as he ushered Leaana and Fataso to the back of the house. Sagan went to the stable behind the house and got his and Masque's bed rolls. He laid them out on the ground in the main room. Sagan laid down, mind racing about his sister's return, but knowing that she was safe. After a while he finally fell into a deep relaxing sleep, the best sleep he had since Leaana left.

Chapter 48

Leaana walked into the kitchen area to the smell of bacon frying. The stew had satisfied her last night, but she was still hungry from the week of starvation she had been through during her captivity. She noticed several pieces of bacon already cooked and cooling on a towel. Masque was working at the fireplace cooking another pan full of bacon and had a second pan on the side that held potatoes seasoned with black pepper and sage. He had also made a loaf of bread and had some sliced and lightly toasted from the fire. Leaana was delighted. This would be the best meal she had had in weeks. She found a plate and began to serve herself bacon, potatoes and a couple of slices of bread. Fataso came out of the sleeping area and joined her filling his plate.

Sagan came in the front door he had been out in the stable making sure the horses had water and plenty of straw for the morning. He smiled as he saw his sister tucking into a large breakfast. Masque had awoken early and checked the cellar here and a nearby smoke house for items to use for the morning meal. He had found the potatoes under some straw in the cellar to help keep them cool and found the bacon in the smoke house. He had found flour and yeast and prepared the bread. Sagan prepared a plate for Masque and then one for himself. The sounds of everyone eating and enjoying their meal filled the house. They heard a moan from the wall near the entrance. The goblin tied up there sat up and moaned slightly. His arms were stiff from where they were tied in front of him.

"Masque, what are we going to do with him. I spared him because you asked me to. We still need to discuss who he is? But for now, what do you want to do with him? He's tried to kill us twice." Sagan said looking at Masque trying to decide what was in his mentor's mind.

"Well Boss. I know I told you that I thought he was my son. But I don't know how a goblin could be my son. But he sure fights like my son would."

"I think I know what may have happened to him." Leaana said. "I don't know if I can fully explain, but I may can give you some part of it"

"Alright Bossa, let's hear the tale. For now, I'm going to adjust his bonds and give him some breakfast. I'll put a loop around his neck and tie him to the wall. That way I can free his hands to let him eat. Once that is done let's hear your story. Ok Bossa?" Masque then rose from the table and went over to where the goblin sat against the wall and began adjusting his bonds.

Leaana leaned over to Sagan and whispered "Bossa?"

Sagan grinned "Masque has never used my name. He always calls me Boss. I guess Bossa applies to you because you are a girl. The only actual name I have heard him use is Togan's. And he only used that after Togan scared the life out of him one morning by standing over him as he was waking up and taking a good long smell. Before that he referred to Togan as Furry Boss. Still does most of the time. Gets a bit confusing when the other two wolves are around. Still we normally know who he is addressing."

Leaana still looked confused but nodded her head. Masque returned to the table and took his plate, put some bacon and some of the potatoes on the plate and took them over to the goblin. Leaana could see that the goblins hands were now free. With those claws on the ends of its fingers she wasn't so sure it was safe to have them free, but Masque seemed to know what he was doing.

Masque returned to the table and poured everyone a cup of tea from the tea pot he had kept on the back of the fire to keep it warm. "Alright now Bossa let's hear your tale."

"Yes, sis, let's hear it. But how about you start from when you left to go find Scrill," Sagan chimed in.

Leaana gathered her thoughts and began to tell them about her first encounter with the goblins at the Silver Ford, first hearing Scrill's voice in her head and seeing with her eyes. The escape from the elven camp and their first night in the woods.

Fataso joined the story here, telling his part about tracking Leaana and thinking she had joined up with a larger party turned out to be a group of goblins that had captured him.

Leaana told about being captured, meeting Fataso and their journey in the wagon up the Remis Plateau, across the bridge, through the Moose Herd pass and finally ending up at the temple with the animal totems.

At this point, Masque interrupted, "I know that place. Dwarven legend says that it is haunted by spirits and that entering it can cause you to be cursed. I believe at one point your people," he indicated Sagan and Leaana, "had performed some sort of rituals there. Not sure when they left it or why. I do know most dwarves give it a wide berth and won't go near it."

"Well, it is full of activity now." Leaana continued. She then described the small room she was held in and the utter despair she felt while waiting for whatever was to come next.

"The waiting is to purify you for the ritual."

Everyone's head turned to look at the goblin.

Chapter 49

Spinel sat and listened to the group talking as he ate his breakfast. His hands were free and the loop of rope around his neck was not tight, but he knew that if he moved, the knot would tighten and begin to choke him. Masque had done a good job of securing him while still allowing him to feed himself.

They are an interesting group, are they not? You know the young man; I believe his name is Sagan, and the white wolf seem to get along. Now you hear about this girl being able to hear the thoughts of an eagle and see through the eagle's eyes. Very interesting indeed

"It may be interesting, but it doesn't concern us. We are their prisoner, and it is only a matter of time before they most likely kill us. We have tried to kill them twice and now they will most likely want to kill us instead of leaving us to hunt them down again."

Perhaps if we give them something they need, they might be more likely to spare us. Knowledge, as they say, is power. The girl Leaana, I believe, is talking about being imprisoned in the temple. We know why; I think I will tell them.

"Don't…"

"The waiting is to purify you for the ritual."

Well, that got their attention. Everyone is staring at us now. Let's see what else we can find out.

Masque stood. He crossed over to where Spinel was tied up. "So Stingal, what do you know of the ritual, is that what changed you?"

"I saw it change others," Leaana said. "The humans that were before me during the ritual were changed into ogres. Somehow it caused Scrill and

I to be able to join. What were those black shapes coming from the white plane?"

"Oh, we know much about the ritual. We have been through it. The name is Spinel now. Not Stingal."

"We?" Masque asked.

"We. The black forms that Leaana is describing are souls from the spirit world. The ritual is placing a second soul into a body which causes the body to change from its natural state. So Stingal is here, as this was his body, and I am here. I am Cowren. We renamed ourselves Spinel as we were getting to know one another."

Masque walked back over to the table and sat down. "Boss, a second soul in a body, how is that possible. No wonder the bodies change."

"I'm not sure Masque all I know is it is not the way things should be. As a familiar I have an animal guide and our souls are joined together. That enables us to learn from each other and share abilities but a second soul actually being in another body."

"Maybe, since I am a familiar and had found Scrill is why I wasn't transformed it just joined our souls further. You remember hearing stories about some of the ancient familiars back when the world was young. They would learn enough from their animal guides that they would eventually become them. Isn't that what we strive for as familiars." Leaana said.

"But those are just myths. Since we started actually writing our stories down that has never been recorded. It is only a legend." Sagan replied.

"Ah but legends often have some basis in truth," Fataso said, "many times legends are exaggerated but often there is a basis for the story."

The discussion continued among the four at the table.

Perhaps now they will want to keep us alive. You see knowledge can be a powerful tool.

"Giving them too much knowledge can also get us killed by Darmot or his followers. You have opened our mouth enough now we need to shut it again."

Chapter 50

"We need to stop Darmot." Masque said. "Before he completely wipes the dwarven race out of existence. Most of our race lives here in the mountains and if all the dwarven towns are like this one and they have all been converted, there won't be many dwarves left. Stingal over there, or Spinel, as apparently, he is now called, was my son. He left to make his own way ten years ago. He moved to another dwarven village up in the far north part of the mountains. We have never been close, so we did not keep in touch. I think the last time I saw him was five years ago.

"Yes, and three years ago, the village I lived in was attacked by a band of ogres and we were all captured and converted. The mountains are full of empty towns now. Just like here." Spinel said, interrupting Masque.

That means the goblins must have attacked here after I left to go trading a month and a half ago. Which means my wife and my daughter are also gone." Masque said, his voice dropping. Pain showing in his eyes.

"How can we stop him? There are just four of us. We have already seen that there are hundreds of goblins, we don't know how many ogres and orcs he has?" Fataso said. "The odds are not really in our favor. I'm no warrior. I'm a tracker and a performer. But Leaana did save my life by getting me out of there, so I will help however I can."

"Good Boss, and we may need all the help we can get. I think we need a bit more information on the temple, how many goblins are there and any other details we can get out of our green skinned friend over there." Masque said. "You there, Spinel. How many goblins guard the temple?"

Spinel sat mouth shut, spine straight, staring defiantly at Masque.

"I asked you a question." Masque yelled at the goblin.

Spinel continued to sit, not saying anything.

"Bossa, you've been there too. What do you two remember about numbers?"

Leaana thought for a moment and then spoke, "I don't really remember how many guards were there. I know there were a lot when we arrived with the caravan, but when we went for the ritual, I'm not sure. When I escaped, I wasn't really counting. I was in a bit of shock that I was flying."

"I also don't know how many guards were there. There were probably five or six that guided our group from our preparation cells into the altar room for the ritual. How many were in the room before that I don't know." Fataso said.

"Why don't you three go look through the rest of the town for supplies? We are going to need food for starters, Boss. You remember the house you found me in last night? Well, that was my home. Go there and look for some arrows. We may need that bow of yours before this is all over, and I think I have some arrows that will work better than what you are currently using. I'm going to have a talk with my son and see if I can get any more information out of him." Masque said

"Are you sure Masque?" Sagan asked.

"Yes Boss. Go I need some time alone with my son."

With that Sagan, Leaana and Fataso left. As soon as they were out of the house, they heard Scrill call as she swooped down out of the sky and flew past Leaana's head. Togan came bounding and walked next to Sagan. Fataso flinched as the large wolf walked right past him. He had seen the wolf from a distance briefly the night before but did not realize how large he was.

Soon they split up and began searching the nearby houses for anything they thought might be useful. Leaana found the smoke house where Masque had gotten the bacon. Hanging here were several large haunches of meat they would be able to slice and already have it preserved. She made a note of the location but decided to wait to gather it since her small curved knife was still rusty, and she wasn't sure how well it would cut.

Sagan wandered through the town. Wondering how Masque expected them to stop Darmot and what he was doing. He found his way back to where he had found Masque the night before. His home was one of the ones carved into the side of the mountain. It was large and spacious with rock porch outside. He went in and like the house they had been in the night before the main room by the entrance was a combination dining and living space. Immediately off this room seemed to be the blacksmith shop Masque used. A large anvil stood in the middle of the room. Two big black furnaces stood against the back wall where it was just beginning to be carved into the rock face. A large pipe came out of the top of the two ovens and ran through a hole in the rock up and into the mountain side. Hammers, tongs, and other blacksmith tools lined the walls but no arrows.

He continued back into the house. The light quickly fading as he walked back into the mountain side. Sagan felt uneasy. It was dark, in the shadows of the hill side, and no sound came from outside. The silence and the dark were making him nervous. Togan growled, and his hackles stood up picking up on Sagan's unease. A door close to the workshop area turned out to be a store room. A lamp hung by the door. Togan took a second to light the lamp. It had a built in flint and steel on the side of the lamp to make lighting easier. That was a novel thing to Sagan. The steel was a small round rough wheel against a flat piece of flint. He turned the wheel and a spark leapt up and onto the lantern's wick. The oil soaked wick caught immediately, and yellow light poured into the room dispelling the darkness and lifting Sagan's spirits slightly. Togan stopped showing his teeth but his hackles were still up.

Sagan searched quickly. In a few moments he found a leather arrow case that had 48 arrows. The arrows were wooden perfectly balanced with large metal points at the ends. The points were three sided with a barb on each side. Once they entered a target, they would be very difficult to remove without causing further damage. The metal points would surely be better against the metal armor of the goblins than his old stone points. His arrows had been effective enough when he had managed to hit the gaps in armor but would not penetrate the armor if he missed the gap. He grabbed the bow case and saw a good looking pack lying next to the door. He grabbed that as well. Leaana did not have her saddle bags, or a pack of any kind and would need one at some point. Finding the items, he had been looking for, he headed back to the house they were using as a camp. Togan loping beside him still growling slightly.

As they all gathered around and went through the items, they had gathered Masque began talking.

"Boss, it is worse than we knew. Apparently Darmot has been converting people for years. He has an army on the southern peninsula below the mountains waiting to invade the elven kingdoms. He was planning on a few more large conversions to finish building his numbers then, he was planning on invading. Boss the good news is when he plans a conversion most of the goblins are sent away. They only keep twenty or so guards around to help subdue any of the newly converted. If we are going to stop Darmot's conversions that would be the time. That was all I was able to get out of him. Leaana, Fataso we need every detail you can remember in order to make a plan."

"What are we going to do with Spinel over there." Leaana asked.

"For now, keep him here Bossa. Boss, can you get the other two furry ones to guard him once we have our plan ready?" Masque asked looking at Sagan.

Togan growled and let out a short bark. A few moments later Skanar entered the house and sat by Spinel. Valonic was pacing back and forth outside the door.

"Well, I guess that is a yes." Masque said wonder in his voice at how much Togan truly understood about what was being said. "Now, are we all in agreement that we need to stop Darmot?"

Leaana, and Sagan looked at one another and then looked at Masque. "Yes, we agree." Sagan spoke with Leaana nodding her head.

"And you Boss?" Masque said looking at Fataso.

Fataso hesitated. He knew that Darmot needed to be stopped. But he was unsure how the four of them would be able to stop him. "I'm not sure how we can do it and I am not much of a fighter, but I will help however I can."

"Great now Fataso tell me everything you remember about when you were held captive in the temple"

They talked and planned well into the night when they finally went to bed, they had a plan worked out that was fairly simple. It relied on timing, and a lot of luck but it was the best they could do. They each went to prepare and rest because they did not know what the next few days would bring.

Chapter 51

Leaana flew through the crack in the temple roof she had used to escape. The crack was actually a small naturally occurring tunnel that ran vertically from the ceiling of the temple for about twenty feet and then turned to a steady incline up and out for another 50 to 6o feet. Her eagle vision made it so she could navigate the tunnel even in the low light of nighttime. She exited the crack in the temple and stayed close to the ceiling. She flew around the outer walls until she found what she was looking for, a small natural ledge just above and to the right of the main altar. She flew low over the ledge and carefully dropped the pack she was carrying. She quickly turned and flew back to the ledge and landed. She pulled her mind from Scrill and now felt the familiar feeling of separation begin just as she felt herself pull apart from Scrill. As she saw the blinding light of their transformation, she reached for Scrill's mind again, pulling energy back. She stood on her own feet with Scrill on the ground beside her. She was tired but did not have the overwhelming exhaustion she had felt the other times they had separated. Sagan had been right. By holding on to a bit of the energy, she was able to separate without collapsing.

She froze, listening. Hoping no one had noticed the light from her transformation and come to investigate. Minutes passed. No sound, no alarm being raised. She relaxed and moved quickly to the pack she had dropped. She opened the pack and pulled on the warm clothes she had packed. A fur lined set of breeches and fur lined tunic. She then strapped her "beak" to her arm. The knife she now referred to as her beak now bore little resemblance to the knife she had been brought by Scrill after their initial escape. Masque had offered to give her a new knife, but she had refused, feeling a sense of attachment to the blade. After her refusal, he examined the weapon. He cleaned the dwarven steel of the blade and removed the rust. He then replaced the leather binding on the hilt and made sure it was properly balanced. The knife now was smooth and sharp. The dwarven steel had rusted but not pitted over the years, showing the quality of steel they produced. While this blade did not have the blue tint and lines of artistry that Carameth had, it was still a good blade. Masque had also made a sheath for her so she could wear the short curved blade on the upper part of her left arm.

Now that she was clothed, she took a moment to untie Sagan's bow from the outside of the pack and quickly took a moment to string the bow. This was also something new for her. While she had always been able to draw and shoot Sagan's bow the strength needed to string it had always been beyond her. Now that she had joined with Scrill her strength seemed to have increased and she was able to string the bow. The arrow case Sagan had found was also tied to the pack and she now placed a few arrows point first in the ground so they could be reached quickly and easily. That done she sat back against the rock wall at the back of the ledge and waited.

To Leaana this had been the worst part of the plan. She had been sent in to wait and watch for them to begin preparations for the ritual. When they started preparing the sanctuary, she was to send Scrill to signal the others that things were ready. They would approach the temple and attack while the guards were assembled in the temple but before they could bring in the subjects for conversion. She was to protect them from above to make sure no one attacked from behind while Sagan, Togan, and Masque fought their way through to Darmot. Fataso would wait, hiding down the prisoners corridor. They hoped the guards that brought the prisoners in, would come in answer to the sounds of fighting. He would then work to free the prisoners and try to convince them to help fight to help even out the numbers.

If the prisoners didn't help then Sagan, Masque and Togan, would be fighting odds of more than four to one and even with Leaana taking a hand from above that was not odds they could expect to overcome for long.

She realized she was hungry. The energy she spent while flying must have made her hungry. She had some of the smoked beef with her and began to eat. One to satisfy the hunger gnawing at her and two to help her stay awake. It was dark in the sanctuary now and quiet. She could easily see herself falling asleep while waiting and miss the opportunity to tell the others to move in.

Time passed. Leaana unable to see the sun or stars, had no idea how much time passed. Her nerves were on edge, so it felt like it had been hours or days that she had sat here and watched. Then she saw it. A flicker of light as steel sparked against flint and a torch was lit. That torch was used to light a second and she saw a female orc moving around the room lighting torches.

"Fly" she thought to Scrill and immediately the eagle took off and flew up back out the way they had come. Leaana began to move slowly and quietly stretching her muscles. She stayed against the back wall out of sight waiting for the next step.

Chapter 52

Sagan, Togan, Masque and Fataso waited on top of the front entrance of the temple. They had climbed to the top of the mountain three mountains away from the temple and had then traveled over the connecting peaks to make their way to the mountain that housed Darmot's temple. They had then descended to where the front of the temple had been carved out of the rock to make the entrance. Standing on the roof of the entrance staying well back from the edge making sure they couldn't be seen by guards patrolling out from the entrance. The guards did not patrol, they just stood at position on either side of the door and of course most people did not think to look up.

They had ropes ready and when Scrill flew over to signal that they were preparing the ritual they would wait a few minutes to let the guards assemble in the sanctuary. Then they would descend on the ropes and attack. Fataso would break off and go down the tunnel beside the temple back to the holding cells to free the prisoners. Hopefully the guards assigned to bring the prisoners up would move to help defend from the attackers leaving Fataso free to release the prisoners.

The night was ending, and the sun was just beginning to climb into the rising sky when Scrill flew low and in front of Sagan making sure she was seen. Sagan nodded to Scrill and the eagle turned and flew back to the crack. Masque crouched and crawled forward to the edge of the entrance. Looking down he watched the guards waiting to see if they moved. Togan began picking his way through the rocks making his way down. The wolf, if seen, could be passed off as a natural occurrence, but he moved behind statues to avoid detection and got ready to jump.

After a few minutes, which felt like a year, Masque stood and moved back to beside Sagan and Fataso. "Ok Boss the guards just went inside. That must mean they are starting to assemble for the ritual. We better move Boss."

Tying the ropes to the statues, they threw the ends over the edge they quickly and quietly descended down the front entrance of the temple. Once down they moved to enter the temple. Togan jumped down and landed beside Sagan. Fataso moved over to the door where he and Leaana had been taken when they were brought as prisoners. Sagan drew Carameth. Masque pulled out his hammers and they entered the temple.

The room was round, a natural cavern that had been carved larger to make the sanctuary room. Goblins formed a half circle around the edge of the room. they could just make out two orcs on the main altar in front. One of those Orcs had to be Darmot. Togan growled and leapt at the goblin nearest him, and the battle began.

Togan's teeth bit into the upper arm just below the sleeve of the chain mail shirt. The goblin screamed in pain. All the goblins turned to see what was happening. Sagan decided to take advantage of the moment of confusion and swung Carameth at the goblin in front of him. The sword caught the Goblin at the neck and cleaved through. The head separated from the goblins shoulders and landed on the stone floor with a sickening wet thud. The body slumped and fell to the ground.

Masque had slammed his hammers into the side of the helmet of the goblin in front of him knocking him cold and he too fell to the stone floor. Togan was leaping for the throat of the goblin he had just bitten.

Sagan stepped over the body of the downed goblin and turned to the right to help Togan. Masque turned to the left, his back to Sagan. Sagan finished off the goblin Togan had bitten. Togan moved on and began attacking another goblin. Sagan also started fighting his third goblin now. Sagan could feel speed and strength feeding into him from Togan. He was moving faster than ever before. The goblins around him seemed to be moving slower, the entire battle seemed to be slowing down.

Sagan heard a hiss smack sound and saw an arrow imbedded in the neck of a goblin to his left. Leaana shot well.

Orders were being shouted from the altar now. Calling for the soldiers to form a defensive perimeter around the Altar. The goblins drew back to form a battle line to protect Darmot and the other orc on the altar. The female orc was giving the orders.

This momentary withdrawal gave Masque, Togan and Sagan a chance to take stock of how they stood. Seven goblins were already dead or unconscious. Sagan had killed 3, Togan had ripped the throat out of one, Masque had knocked out two, and arrows stuck out of the neck of one beside Sagan, and from the shoulder of one beside Masque. Sagan heard a hiss and saw an arrow flying towards Darmot. The female elf beside him threw up her left arm with a shield on it in and caught the arrow just in time. Then almost faster than Sagan could register what happened a blade was flashing through air back in the direction of Leaana. Sagan saw her drop as the knife flew past where her head had been only a moment before.

The goblins had gotten organized now and began to advance on the three fighters on the ground. Sagan could hear footsteps coming from a hallway off to the side and five more goblins entered the room and took stations close to Darmot and the female orc beside him. Hopefully that meant that the guards that were supposed to be bringing the prisoners were here now and Fataso could begin his part of the plan.

Sagan growled, he could feel the wolf blood lust rising in him. Togan growled beside him his hackles raised. Sagan began fighting again, two goblins were on him, and he was fighting desperately to fend them off. He heard a screech and saw Scrill swoop in and claw at the eyes of one of his opponents. He used the second of distraction with that goblin to thrust his sword into the middle of the other goblin he was fighting. He then turned back to the goblin Scrill had attacked only to see him fall, an arrow sticking out of his chest from where it had penetrated the chain shirt he was wearing. No time to rejoice, he was again fighting two goblins at once.

Masque dodged and struck dodged and struck. Always trying to stay one step ahead. However, he was also fighting two opponents at a time and did not have Sagan enhanced speed. He had taken a few cuts on his arms, blood flowed from the wounds. An arrow flashed by killing the goblin that had just caught him across his left arm with its claws. Luckily the sword attack had missed but Masque had been unable to avoid the slashing claws that had followed. Another arrow flew by another goblin fell. Scrill attacked his last opponents eyes and scratched them out with her talons blinding it. Masque quickly brought his hammer down on the blinded goblins head and knocked it out. For a moment he was clear no immediate threat. He took a moment to step back, retreating to the entrance to give himself a bit more time. He then took a clean cloth from one of the bags he had on his belt and tied a bandage around the claw marks on his left arm. The blood had been flowing freely from them and he was scared it would affect the grip on his hammer. The cut on his right arm had been a graze from a sword blade but was not bleeding as freely. It could wait a moment. Arm bandaged he stepped back in the battle attacking a goblin that was trying to step in behind Sagan.

Chapter 53

Fataso hid in the shadows. He heard the running of feet down the hall where he remembered the prisoners were held. He saw five goblin soldiers run past his hiding place and enter the Sanctuary. He waited another few minutes, counting to one hundred, then starting over and counting again. Making sure no other guards came running up. He heard the sounds of fighting begin again, and he decided he couldn't wait any longer. He drew the dagger that Masque had given him and began moving down the hall toward the prisoner cells. He entered a small room with a table in the middle and realized how lucky he was. There, on the table carelessly tossed aside as the guards ran through to join the fight, was a ring of keys. Picking up the keys, he moved through the room. He also found two water skins that were full handing on pegs by the door. He took those, also remembering that the prisoners would be half crazed from thirst.

He moved down the hallway and came to the first door. He fumbled with the key ring, trying two keys before he finally found the one that worked. Opening the lock on the door, he opened it. Laying sprawled on the ground was a human male. Weak, lips cracked from thirst, he lay there moaning. Fataso saw for the first time where he had been kept. He had been in total darkness, so he had not been able to see the cell when he had been in it. If it was like this one, it would have been small, which it had been. The room was only six feet by six feet and roughly cut directly into the rock wall. The door was large, but not totally square. It was oversized to block out light and was an effective barrier.

He looked again at the person on the floor. He lay not moving and weak, asking for water. Fataso thought about giving him the water skin but then decided against it. He had a limited amount. He would hopefully find some prisoners in better condition than this one, and he would need water for them. Even with water, this person would be no help in the fight.

Fataso moved on to the next cell, unlocked its door to find another prisoner sprawled and weak on the floor. This was not encouraging. He kept moving, unlocking door after door. He found a few of the prisoners still conscious and able to move. They were all weak, and all needed water. He opened every door he could find. Moving as quickly as he could. He was worried. This was taking too long. As he moved farther from the sanctuary, the sounds of fighting faded. He did not even know if the fight was still going on. But he still kept going until he found two doors in a row empty. He decided the rest of the cells would be empty and he started going back up the hall. He had opened about forty cells. In those forty cells, there had been fifteen humans that were aware and able to stand.

He gathered those fifteen people together and gave each of them a few drinks from the water skins. Making sure everyone had a little. There was not enough water for them to quench their thirst, but it helped a little. While they drank, Fataso was thinking of what was to come next. He was no fighter; but he owed Leaana his life. If he had to fight, he would in order to help repay that debt. Once the water was gone; he began speaking to them.

"My name is Fataso. I am here with a girl who can turn into an eagle, a boy who can talk with a wolf, and a dwarf. We are here to help you escape and stop the person that captured you. But we need your help. I know you are weak, thirsty, and hungry. We will see that you all get plenty as soon as this is over but for now, we need you to fight. At the end of this hallway is a sanctuary. There an elf named Darmot would have changed you into ogres. There are twenty guards and the friends I told you about are fighting them to try and kill Darmot. They are badly outnumbered and need you to fight with them."

"Fight with them. Most of us can barely stand and you want us to fight those monsters. We will be slaughtered like sheep." One of the men said.

"True, you may die fighting, but if you don't and my friends are killed, you will be turned into one of those monsters and lose yourself in the process." Fataso replied.

"Do you at least have any weapons for us?" a second man said

"No, I have a dagger but that is all. But they will not be expecting us so being able to do a surprise attack will help." Fataso calmly pointed out. He needed them to fight, needed them to attack if for no other reason than to create a distraction. He didn't want them to die but hoped they would agree to fight instead of waiting to be converted.

"I don't have time to stand here and argue with you. They are already fighting for their lives and will need help. I'm not much of a fighter but I'm going to help. You can come if you want." And with that Fataso turned and began walking back up the hallway past all the open cell doors. He heard mumbling behind him but resolutely kept walking. He entered the guard room at the end of the hall and stopped to wait and see if anyone was going to join him. A few seconds later he heard the slapping of bare feet on the floor and turned to see ten of the men walk into the guard room as well.

"Five of us stayed back to help the ones in the cells that are too weak to stand. They are going to see if they can find water to help get them ready to move. The rest of us are here to help however we can." A tall dark-haired man said.

"Thank you, now let's go" as he turned, he saw something he had not noticed before, leaning against the wall close to the door towards the rest of the temple were five spears. In their haste to check on the battle sounds the guards must have just gone to investigate with their swords and left the spears here. Turning back to the ten released prisoners. "I think we have found some weapons."

The prisoners gratefully took the spears. They paired off. Two men per spear. They followed Fataso out of the guard room through the hall and then took a right to head into the sanctuary. All eyes were focused on the fight raging close to the center of the room, so no one saw them enter. The men lined up two men on a spear and charged at the backs of the goblins as they were starting to surround three figures.

Chapter 54

Leaana watched from her position above the sanctuary floor. She had shot about half of her arrows. Killing 5 of the goblins as they were closing on either Sagan, Masque or Togan. Sagan and Togan seemed to not need her protection as much so most of her focus had been on Masque. She had been so focused on her job that she had not noticed the female Orc on the stage produce a bow and take aim at her brother. She saw the movement out of the corner of her eye. Looked in the direction of the altar in time to see the arrow released toward the crowd fighting below her. Her heart froze as she was terrified the arrow would hit one of her companions. As she watched Scrill swooped down and caught the arrow midflight. She snatched from the air with her talons. Much as she would do with an annoying sparrow she was hunting.

That crisis averted Leaana saw a new opportunity, she turned and let fly an arrow at the Orcs on the Altar. Her first arrow aimed at the armed female orc the Second following about five seconds later at Darmot. The female orc had reflexes as quick as a cat and caught the first arrow on her shield protecting herself. The second arrow was on a different line, she lunged with her shield to block the second arrow. She misjudged the arrow's flight slightly and missed catching it on her shield but took the arrow in the upper arm just above the area protected by her shield.

Leaana turned back to the fight on the floor now and saw ten men carrying spears charge the back of the goblin line just as it was starting to close the circle around Sagan, Masque and Togan. The five spears slammed into the backs of the goblins and parted the goblin line. She saw Togan jump over a fallen goblin and close his teeth around the throat of a goblin that was about to attack Masque from behind. Leaana shot and killed a goblin that was now approaching Togan from the back. Then Sagan was running past the goblins that had taken the spears. Their companions turning and attacking the spear men. But Sagan was free and running toward the Altar.

Leaana followed his path making sure a goblin did not try and stop him but there was nothing but the female Orc between him and Darmot. The female Orc raised her sword and attacked Sagan as he charged in. He caught it on his brield and they began dueling. The female orc was fast, but Her movements slowed by the arrow wound in her shield arm. Leaana knew she had an opportunity, took aim and shot an arrow at Darmot.

As she released the arrow, she saw the female Orc fall. Sagan leapt over her body and rushed Darmot. Darmot, however, was ready. He moved forward to meet Sagan, causing Leaana's arrow to go behind his head. Darmot drew a sword from under his robes and thrust toward Sagan as he charged at him.

Sagan, unprepared for the speed and suddenness of Darmot's lunge, threw his sword up and deflected the Darmot's sword to the side just in time. Darmot was already moving again, this time coming in with a side cut at Sagan. Again, Sagan was able to use his sword to catch and deflect the stroke. Sagan's arm vibrated from the impact. Darmot's strength was surprising. Another stroke, this one over hand coming at Sagan's head. This time, Sagan was able to bring the brield up to stop the stroke, leaving his sword hand free to attack. He swung as quick side cut at Darmot who simply took a step back, causing Sagan's strike to pass through thin air. They circled now, each attacking and blocking or dodging the other's attack.

Leaana watched as Sagan and Darmot battled. She looked back at the rest of the battle and saw a goblin circling behind one of the freed prisoners slice through the side of the prisoner and watched him fall. Then Leaana's arrow struck it in the back of the head and the goblin moved no more. She turned her attention back to Sagan and Darmot. They were moving too fast and were too close together for Leaana to get a shot and not risk hitting Sagan.

Sagan could tell that Darmot was a very skilled warrior and was matching him stroke for stroke. He had to end this quickly so he could get back and help Masque. He decided it was time to try something a little unorthodox. Sagan dropped to his knees and brought his brield up to stop the downward stroke he knew Darmot would attack with. Sure enough, the nearly crushing impact of the stroke impacted his brield. At that moment, using all the speed and strength he could summon, he thrust his sword up perpendicular to his brield, and using its length, pushed Darmot's sword into the ground. Once there, he put his knee on the sword, trying to stop Darmot from being able to pull it back.

This action also caused Darmot to bend over and bring his head closer to Sagan. His knee still holding Darmot's sword, he threw a punch using his left hand. The fist was reinforced by the metal rod crossing his palm from the brield and he made contact with Darmot's chin. The force of the impact rocked Darmot back and caused him to lose his grip on his sword.

Leaana saw Sagan drop to his knees. At first, she thought he was injured, then she saw his lightning fast move to trap Darmot's sword and deliver the punch to his jaw. Darmot straitened dazed slightly, and Leaana saw another opportunity. She shot again at Darmot.

Leaana's arrow slammed into Darmot's chest and less than a second later, as surprise entered Darmot's eyes, Sagan rose from his knees and swung Carameth and sliced Darmot's head from his shoulders.

Blood sprayed from Darmot's body as it slumped to the floor spraying Sagan as it went down. Sagan let loose a wolf like howl, the sound echoing through the chamber, Togan joined him. Leaana looked and saw that all the goblins in the chamber were down, either dead or dying. Three of the humans that had attacked with the spears were still alive seven had died at the hands of the goblins before Masque or Togan could get to them. There was even a goblin dead at the feet of Fataso. Darmot was dead and the fight was over.

Chapter 55

Leaana and Sagan watched as the last of the rescued prisoners climbed onto the wagon and prepared to leave. The fight in the temple had been just a day ago but it felt much longer.

After the fight had ended Sagan had needed a few minutes to get over the wolf induced blood lust. Sagan had actually bent over and taken a bite out of the dead body of Darmot before Masque was able to pull him off. Masque had several wounds from the battle. One eye was black and swollen, he had slashes on both legs and arms. The one cut he had already bandaged needed the bandage replaced. But time for that when they were back at Fresmon.

Leaana managed to find a way to climb down from the ledge where she had shot so effectively during the fight. She and Masque worked with Fataso to get the prisoners from the cells and load them onto one of the wagons that had been used to transport the prisoners here. They found a couple of horses, hooked them to the wagon, and then set off with everyone to Fresmon.

While they were dealing with the prisoners, Sagan and Togan searched the rest of the temple complex. In a private chamber behind what appeared to be a throne room, Sagan found a series of maps. The maps outlined where the goblin forces were primarily located. Most were on a peninsula on the southernmost part of the Dwarfgon mountains. But a small force had been sent to take the Remis Plateau and patrol up and down the Animas River, looking for converts. Sagan took the maps, thinking that this information might be useful later.

Leaana and Sagan both took a black stone from the altar to take back with them to Romin. That would complete their rite of passage, even though that minor achievement seemed so small and unimportant after everything that had happened during the past few weeks.

They drove the cart to Fresmon with Scrill scouting ahead to avoid any goblin patrols that might be in the passes. Once in Fresmon, they used their time to work on nursing the prisoners back to health. Some recovered quickly, after some water and a large meal or two. Others were still weak, but all were at least able to walk and move on their own. Two of the three who had survived the attack on the goblins helped care for the others with Leaana and Sagan. The third man had been a healer for a small farming encampment down the Animas River from Larin. He tended to Masque's wounds. Several of the cuts needed stitching, but none were life threatening.

While the freed prisoners were recovering with water and food, the four friends discussed their next steps. Sagan and Leaana needed to return home to complete their rites. They would try to avoid goblin patrols by taking the centipede pass out of the mountains and then avoid the Animas river by taking the major route back home. It was a longer journey, but safer. Then Sagan would return with volunteers from Romin to start rebuilding Larin.

Masque and Fataso would take the Arctana pass through the mountains and enter Arctana, the northern elf kingdom. The entrance to that pass was guarded by Elvish soldiers, so once they were in Arctana, they would be relatively safe. From there, they would proceed to Encalla, the capital city. Fataso would take part in the festival and he and Masque would take the maps showing the goblin movements, and would try to get an audience with the king. Fataso was pleased when Leaana offered to bring Scrill to the festival for the final night in three weeks' time.

So now Leaana watched as Fataso and Masque left Fresmon to travel to the Arctana pass, and from there into Arctana. The weakest of the freed prisoners rode in the cart. Not only was the cart carrying people, but it also had food for the journey and weapons from Masque's warehouse for them to use to defend themselves if they came upon a goblin scouting party. The twins watched until the wagon was around the bend, and then they turned to leave as well.

"Wait a moment sis, there is something I have to do that I promised Masque. I don't agree with it, but he made me promise." With that Sagan entered the house where Spinel was still tied up. Leaana followed curious what he had promised Masque. Sagan went over to Spinel, using the blunt end of the brield he hit Spinel across the side of the head. Spinel's eyes rolled back into his head, and he collapsed unconscious to the floor.

Sagan then untied the rope around Spinel's neck and turned to walk out of the house.

"What you're just going to leave him like that?" Leaana asked.

"Yes, he is still Masque's son even though he looks different. Masque made me promise to free him. Masque still loves him, no matter how he has changed. He knows his son, and is convinced that he needs to be spared. I knocked him out, so he would not be able to follow us immediately." Sagan replied, "I didn't mention knocking him out to Masque, but surely, he will understand. Now let's go. We can head out through the Centipede pass and then take the main trade routes back home. With all the goblins prowling through the woods along the Animas, it is probably the safest way to go."

Sagan and Leaana mounted their horses. Togan gave a quick bark and Skanar and Valonic took off down the pass before them. Scrill who had been perched on a tree near by took flight and flew up and into the pass ahead of them. Leaana could see through their shared vision that the way was clear. She and Sagan rode into the pass beginning the long trip home.

They rode through the Centipede pass and camped the first night beside the lake close to lost encampment of Larin. The next day they turned southeast and soon found the major trade route that would eventually take them back to Romin. They would pass through two other encampments, first Shetin and Duatin. Now that they were on the trade route they rode at a steady canter. They talked, enjoying each other's company. As twins they had always been close, now they were perhaps even closer. Each had someone they could talk to about the unique connection they had with their animal guides.

After reaching the trade route Valonic and Skanar left them, Scrill and Togan each took turns scouting ahead. Sagan marveled at Leaana's ability to see through Scrill's eyes. Leaana, was impressed with the skills Sagan had learned with the sword, and how acute his sense of smell and hearing had become.

When they arrived in Shetin it was close to dusk on the third day of their journey. They were received as honored guests. Familiars were people of honor, two familiars were a double honor to the town. They were given a tent to rest in close to the sacred fire and given plenty to eat. They met with the tribal elders after their meal. Sagan and Leaana each told their story to the elders and talked about the continued threat by the goblin army that Spinel had described. Sagan mentioned his resolve to restore the encampment at Larin and asked the elders to send any of their people they could to help. Sagan planned to be there in a month and would accept any who wanted to start a new life. The Elders listened and promised to do what they could to help. They knew of a few hunters that would gladly accept the challenge and they would speak with the rest of the people.

Leaana and Sagan both slept soundly that night. For the first time in many weeks, they were in a place where they both felt totally safe, the tent they were given was warm and had soft blankets and mats of straw on the floor. After weeks of sleeping on the ground the straw mats were almost a luxury. Togan slept on the floor at Sagan's feet and Scrill perched on a small table beside Leaana's sleeping space. The two animals had been the talk of the encampment and all the children had strained to get a look at them.

The next morning, they were brought breakfast and given gifts to honor them. The leather workers had taken Leaana's saddle and built an arm coming up out of the back of the saddle. It would not interfere with her ability to tie on her saddle bags, not that she had any saddle bags or belongings. She had a few sets of borrowed clothes she carried in the pack from Fresmon everything else had been lost when she was captured. The arm would give Scrill a place to perch when she rode and the eagle was not flying.

Sagan was given a new quiver for his arrows. The quiver was covered with extensive bead work that depicted a running wolf. It was a beautiful item and would be well used.

They left the encampment and continued on their way. Two days later they arrived in Duatin. The night here was very similar to what happened in Shetin. Leaana and Sagan again dined with the encampment elders and told them the story of their journey. Sagan again, spoke of his commitment to restore Larin and asked for the Elders to send any that were willing to join him in rebuilding Larin in a month's time. The next morning, they were again given gifts. This time they were woolen cloaks dyed in their family colors of brown and green. The main body of the cloak was brown, and they had a green hood. Leaana's cloak had an eagle pin to close it at the top and Sagan's had a pin in the shape of a wolf. The wool was oiled and treated to make it water proof. They were like so many things in their culture, beautiful and practical at the same time. Once they had their new cloaks, they continued on the ride home.

They rode for two more days camping each night well after the sun had sunk below the horizon and moving on just as the sun would start to climb into the rising sky. At the middle of the seventh day after departing Fresmon they both drew rein and stopped as they topped a small hill and looked down on their home encampment of Romin. They looked at each other and laughed, relief showing on each of their faces. Scrill took off from where she was riding on her perch on Leaana's saddle, Togan barked and ran toward the encampment. Leaana and Sagan both kicked their heels into the sides of Kada and Karr and began galloping the last distance until they were home. A cheer rose in the distance as one of the farmers noticed their approach and spread the word of their return.

Chapter 56

Spinel moved through the bodies of the dead goblins in the temple. His father and friends had been thorough. It did not appear that anyone was left alive. He would go to his chambers, collect the few things that he needed and go to join the rest of the Goblin army. It would probably take him a few days to make his way through the mountains to the peninsula where the army was training but he did not know where else to go.

Suddenly he stopped. He had heard something. A soft moan. He heard it again. He moved in the direction of the sound. Soon he found the source. Basara lay on the ground beside the decapitated body of Darmot. She had the broken shaft of an arrow in her upper arm. A large gash in her side from what looked like a sword stroke, and her leg appeared to be bent at an unnatural angle at the ankle. A large pool of blood spread on the floor beside her but she was breathing and had her good right arm raised to get his attention. The arm dropped after a few seconds the effort using her last ounces of strength.

Spinel realized he had an opportunity here. He could leave her here and she would most likely die from her wounds. Then she would not be around to punish him for his failure. Then again Carnell probably knew of his mission and would most likely punish him and that probably meant losing a limb or possibly his life. But if he could help Basara, save her life, she would owe him a debt and might, just might be willing to forgive the minor failure of not managing to kill the boy Sagan and his wolf. She had not fared much better during their attack and had more than twenty guards to help her.

Helping her probably meant his best chance for survival. He knelt beside her and looked at her wounds more closely. She had somehow managed to bind the wound in her side at some point, so the worst of the bleeding was stopped. That was good. The broken off arrow in her arm while painful was not life threatening, the same with her ankle. The broken ankle would make it impossible for her to walk, and the arrow wound would make using a crutch also next to impossible. He would need another way to move her. He looked around and found a couple of the discarded spears lying where they had been dropped by the humans as they had died.

He went to his chambers and found what he needed. He stripped the blankets from his bed and got some rope. He tied the blankets in place at the base of the spears to make a litter. then tied the rope to the top of the spears to use as a make shift harness for himself. He then moved Basara onto the litter. She groaned in pain as the movement stretched the wounds in her arm and side. He then tore several strips of cloth from another blanket to keep with him for when the bandage on her side needed to be changed. He searched the temple complex for any food he could find and wrapped it in another blanket. Then stepping between the spears he picked them up, put the rope harness across his chest and began to drag Basara out of the temple. It would be a hard trip, but he should still be able to get to the southern peninsula. He just had to keep her alive until he did.

Chapter 57

Leaana was glad to be home, but also impatient. She had promised Fataso she would be at the last day of the festival and that was now just over a week away and she still had to travel to Arctana and the city of Encalla. She would most likely now have to fly there. She really did not know if she could fly there. She had never tried to fly that far. All of her flights in her joined form to this point had been short flights of maybe an hour at most. She had no idea if she could keep form long enough to fly all the way there, but she would have to try if she was going to keep her promise. At least she would be able to leave tomorrow.

When she and Sagan had arrived back home, they had been welcomed as heroes. They were more than a week overdue to be back, and everyone was concerned that something had happened to them. The entire encampment seemed thrilled that Leaana had found her spirit guide and was a familiar. The encampment was doubly blessed now to have two familiars at once. People would nod and say that they had always known Leaana was a familiar even though some of those same people had treated her differently before she left.

Sagan and Leaana had told their entire stories now more times than she could count. Everyone wanted to hear of their adventure and about the horrible goblin, orc, and ogre creatures they had faced. Sagan and Leaana had met with the encampment elders several times to discuss things and clear up details when they had questions.

Both of them had received several gifts from different craft masters. Leaana had a new wardrobe now. All of her clothes had an area reinforced to allow Scrill to perch. Most of the time it was on her shoulder, but she also had a few pairs of gloves so he could perch on her hand.

All the Hunters had been fascinated by Sagan's sword Carameth, and he had showed fighting techniques to different groups over the last few days. He had been given new clothes as well as blankets, and a new tent that had been designed by Tarn, the chief builder. The tent had small springy wooden poles connected by small sections of bamboo. The poles could be disassembled, and the tent rolled into a bundle about the length of Sagan's arm. When the poles were assembled, the tent was tall enough for Sagan to kneel in comfortably. It was a great item for traveling and could serve as a shelter for many weeks if needed.

Leaana had been given a new pack as well. This one had been crafted by the chief leather worker and had been designed for her to wear around her leg in her new eagle form. She could stand with one leg in the pack, transform, and her eagle leg would be inside the pack. She could then use her beak to reach around and pull a wooden knob to tighten the straps. The pack was divided into sections for food and clothing and was larger than normal packs since her eagle form was so large. She could also use the pack as a saddle pack if she was riding.

All this had taken close to a week. She was anxious to be on her way, but she knew she had to give the community time to celebrate them. Tonight, they would have a celebration of their return. Sagan and Leaana would place their sacred stones in the fire ring and then the celebrating would be over, and she would be able to head to the Elven festival.

All the members of the encampment gathered around the sacred fire. Each of the elders wore their ceremonial robes. The drummers struck up a beat and the Elders danced around the sacred flames. Once they had completed three circuits they stopped, and the drums fell silent. Each elder called upon the spirit he represented to watch over and bless the ceremony. Then Pargo spoke:

"Friends we are gathered here this evening to witness the completion of Sagan and Leaana Moongrower's rite of passage. Sagan Moongrower, step forward. Weeks ago, you were tasked with traveling to the Dwarfgon mountains and retrieving a sacred stone for our fire ring. Leaana Moongrower was to go with you as a pack mate. Have you returned with your stone?"

Sagan stepped forward and shouted "Pargo Servant of the Eagle, I have returned with my stone." With that Sagan lifted the black stone above his head and showed it to all assembled.

Pargo Continued, "Then place it at the sacred fire and rise to receive the name you will be known as in adult hood."

Sagan stepped forward, Togan walking beside him, and placed his stone in the ring around the sacred fire. He then stood and turned to face Mayan.

Mayan stepped forward and spoke, "As keeper of the records it is my duty to give Sagan his adult name by which he can start his own line. Sagan you will now be known as Sagan Wolfrunner. You run with the speed and strength of the wolf."

The assembled crowd cheered and then chanted his new name. Sagan left the center of the circle and returned to his place beside Leaana.

Pargo held up his hand and the crowd quieted down. "Leaana Moongrower," he began, "You were tasked to journey with your twin brother Sagan as his pack mate as he learned to be a leader. You instead went your own way and in doing so found your true self. You found and freed your animal guide and took up your mantle as familiar. I hear you also have brought back something from your journey."

"Yes Pargo, servant of the Eagle, I have also brought my tribute to the animal guides. I have brought a sacred stone as well." With those words Leaana held up her black sacred stone above her head for the community to see.

"Place your stone and then rise to learn your name that you will be known by in adult hood." Pargo commanded.

Leaana walked forward, Scrill perched on her shoulder and placed her stone next to Sagan's on the sacred fire ring. She stood then turned to face Mayan.

Mayan spoke, "Leaana, this community has not always honored you as it should but that ends now. Everyone will know your name and of your deeds. You are now to be known as Leaana Clouddancer. You alone can dance among the clouds." The crowd cheered and again chanted her name as she took her place next to Sagan.

Manel, servant of the Wolf now spoke. "Sagan and Leaana, the members of this council have a gift for you. As familiars you will one day lead the people. You will need ceremonial robes for this. We gift you with your first set of ceremonial robes now. You may now join us as we dance and conduct the business of the encampment. May your spirit guides advise you."

As he finished speaking two items were brought forth. Sagan received his set of robes. It was an extremely light and expertly carved wooden wolf head that would fit over him like a mask. From the back of the head flowed gray rabbit fur stitched together so tightly it appeared to be a single piece of fur. The robe had arm and leg strap affixed at his wrists and ankles. The finished piece look like a grey wolf standing on its hind legs. It was a beautiful and masterfully crafted costume.

Leaana's robe was even more stunning. Intricate bead work formed an eagles beak and eyes on a hood that draped over her to just above her eyes. The bead work gave way into cotton fabric that had been teased and frayed to mimic feathers. The entire robe had been dyed a rich golden brown to match Scrill's feathers. Her robe also had cuffed sleeves, so when she raised her arms they looked like a pair of wings. She relished her new costume. She had not expected this she did not expect to be honored in such a way.

Pargo was speaking again, "Now let us hear from our newest leaders in the encampment of how they plan to start their new lives, Leaana Clouddancer speak and be heard by all."

Leaana spoke, "I am leaving tomorrow at first rising. I head to Arctana to keep a promise to an elven friend. I will then try to meet with the elven King and Queen and ask for their aid in dealing with the violence of the new races that I am sure is about to come. Once that is completed, I will go to join my twin Sagan Wolfrunner."

"And you Sagan what is your plan for your new life" Pargo asked keeping with the formality of the occasion.

"I leave in two weeks to begin to rebuild the encampment of Larin. The goblins Leaana and I met are violent. They completely destroyed Larin. The sacred fire there burns no more. I will ask the elders to send a messenger to Arinin to ask for a piece of the sacred fire to be brought to the new Larin location to rekindle the fire. I ask any here who wishes to join me to prepare to leave as well. Once we are settled, I will begin preparing our hunters to fight the goblins, orcs and ogres to protect our families and the Sacred fire"

"You have heard the words of our familiars. Take them to heart. Trials await us tomorrow, but for tonight, let us honor our newest adults and leaders." Pargo said. He pointed at the drummers, who began a slow beat, "Sagan, Leaana, Scrill and Togan dance with us." The elders began to dance around the circle as the drummers picked up the beat. Sagan and Leaana joined in and took their place in the community. Scrill launched herself from Leaana's shoulder and flew swooping in and out of the dancers. Togan barked and howled as he jumped and twirled right behind Sagan.

Chapter 58

Leaana stood with one leg in her new pack and one leg outside the pack. She was in her tent before her transformation, hoping she could squeeze out the door in eagle form. She was inside because she wasn't wearing any clothing. All her clothes were packed in the pack, along with food. Tied to the outside of the pack was the new style tent that Tarn had designed, a bow and a quiver of arrows, and her bedroll. Scrill stood on the ground next to her. She reached for Scrill's mind and called her consciousness to her. She saw the light of transformation and felt Scrill's mind almost take over their body. "During Flight Scrill, I'm going to let you take the lead." She bent her head down to look at her leg with the pack. It was in place and almost tight enough. She grabbed the wooden ball in her beak and tugged. It felt weird to be using her mouth this way, but Scrill's familiarity with the action helped calm her.

They stepped out of her room into the family area, ducking low to get below the entrance. They managed this fairly easily. Leaana let Scrill's mind control the body here. It was an interesting sensation to almost be a passenger in her own body. Crossing the main room, they ducked low again and exited the tent. She could feel the feathers on the back of their neck brush the top of the doorway.

Once outside, she found a crowd surrounding her. Apparently, most of the encampment had wanted to see this new impressive form. Some may not have even believed it was possible. Now Leaana controlled the body for a moment as Scrill instinctively wanted to take flight surrounded by so many people that they were not expecting. Leaana stretched their wings and turned a circle, letting the members of the encampment get a good look. Then she closed the wings, looked at her family, who were all standing at the front of the crowd, and nodded once.

Ready Scrill, Let's go, she thought

READY

Leaana felt the muscles gather, the wings open, and the powerful legs leap into the air. A flap of the wings, they went higher, another flap, another flap and soon they were flying above the encampment. They turned and circled once watching their friends and family wave good bye then they turned north and began to fly towards her friend Fataso and the promise she had to keep.

The journey was not as physically exhausting as Leaana had expected as they spent a large amount of the time gliding on the winds. Conserving energy when they could. The miles went by below them. They would land and drink from streams, along the way but otherwise they soared above the tree tops. Leaana loved the feeling of flying. She wished she could share this experience with Sagan, but he got to run with the speed and strength of a wolf so perhaps it was a similar feeling. They landed the first day just before full dark in a grove of trees where Leaana would be hidden from anyone passing by. They had not seen any one in the area with their eagle sight, but it was a good idea to be cautious.

They landed and Leaana could feel the push of the separation. She staggered for a moment as she had to refamiliarize herself with her own body. That was the longest she had been joined and had started to become accustomed to the eagle form. She reached into her pack which was right beside her and took a tunic and a pair of pants from the top where she had them waiting. She dressed and strapped her beak knife to her arm. She then took a moment to set up the new tent. It went up quickly and formed a small dome. There were twelve short pieces of thin flexible wood, which were connected with small pieces of bamboo. The assembled poles threaded through slots of fabric in an X shape from corner to corner. Each pole tucked into a small pocket on each corner, they bent and lifted the middle of the tent. That done she placed her bed roll in the tent and then ate a meal of smoked salmon, cheese and flat bread. Scrill had caught a squirrel and was happily feeding on it. She could feel the eagles contentment and felt happy.

The next few days were very similar as she made her way to Encalla. When she was just outside the city on the sixth day of travel she landed in a grove of trees, dressed, put her pack on her back and walked into the city. She asked a few of the elves where to find the falconry exhibit and soon found her way to Fataso's wagon.

Fataso was overjoyed to see her and planned to have Scrill perform the next night for the festival finale. Masque was staying with Fataso, his wounds from the battle healing nicely. The three companions talked and caught up over a meal of lamb in a spicy tomato cream sauce served over a steamed rice. The dish was a bit hotter than Leaana was used too but she really enjoyed the strong flavors so different from the meals of her homeland.

Fataso told her that he and Masque had already met with the King and Queen and the King was working out details on what he would do. They were supposed to meet with them again the morning after the festival ended.

Leaana spent the following day exploring Encalla the buildings were tall and seemed to be made mostly of arches. Arches seemed to be everywhere. She watched many performances for the festival and ate her fill of sweet treats that were rare in her encampment.

That night Scrill performed her falconry routine. They even added a part to the act using Leaana as an assistant. Leaana would fire arrows at a target that had been set up and Scrill would swoop down and catch the arrows in midflight. The crowd roared and applauded. Fataso was given the highest honors possible for the festival and brought great honor to the Falconry guild.

The next morning Leaana put on her ceremonial robes to meet with the king and queen. She, Fataso, and Masque were led to the palace by member of the royal guard. Once there they were led into the great hall where king Aalan and his wife Queen Cassata sat on their thrones. The thrones were carved out of a green stone that looked like Jade. They sat in front of a series of arches the ended in an arched ceiling. The arches served to amplify the Kings words so they could be heard throughout the hall.

"Fataso, Masque, we appreciate you returning this morning to hear our plans. You told us quite a tale and we needed time to decide our best action. Who is this young girl that is dressed like an eagle that is with you." King Aalan asked.

Fataso spoke. Being the lone elf in the party it was his place to speak unless a question was asked specifically of one of the others. "My lord, this is Leaana Clouddancer, the girl familiar we told you about. The one who can now actually join with her animal guide and become an eagle.

"If she is a familiar where is her animal guide now." Queen Cassata asked.

"We were unsure of the protocol for animals my lord she is waiting outside." Fataso explained.

"We can wait while you go and fetch her. We would like to see this eagle." Queen Cassata again spoke.

Fataso turned to leave but Leaana placed her hand on his arm and stopped him. A moment later there was an eagle's screech as Scrill flew in from where she was waiting in a nearby tree. Scrill flew in and perched on Leaana's shoulder.

"As soon as you asked about her, I called her my lord." Leaana explained.

"Fascinating I will want to study more of this at a later time." Queen Cassata said.

"It is not often we have a Natarin before us. This one is definitely special. Now that we have seen a bit of the connection between Leaana and her eagle. Let us talk plainly. I plan on sending a force to help stop this goblin army. A small force of 200 members of the Elven guard will be leaving in the next few days to drive the goblins from the bridge at the Remis plateau and help restore safe travel on the trade routes." The king explained.

"Then once I have had time to assemble them, a larger force of 800 members of the elven guard will join them outside the Moose Herd pass where we will await the goblin army and defeat them there." King Aalan finished.

"My lord." Leaana started, then stopped as she remembered only Fataso should speak.

"Go ahead Leaana, you apparently have the ear of the spirits so you might as well have mine as well." King Aalan smiled and laughed slightly as he spoke.

"My lord, my brother Sagan Wolfrunner and his animal guide Togan, are going to be rebuilding our Encampment of Larin. It is not far from the Moose Herd pass. We have no army, but Sagan will be training some of our hunters to fight. He will create a warrior class for us until this threat is ended. I offer whatever help we can to you and your army."

"Wonderful. Our army will camp close to Larin, and we will be happy to work with you any way we can. Now Leaana Clouddancer, my wife has always been a student of your Natarin legends and familiars especially. Would you mind spending the day visiting with her and answering any questions she may have?

"Of course, my lord, I would be happy to. My brother Sagan knows more of our history than I do, but I will be happy to answer any questions I can."

"Fataso, I am preparing messages for you to take to King Mannard in Subarta as you return with the festival representatives. I want you to be my emissary, requesting he also send troops to help defeat this threat. Masque, would you travel with the initial force of 200 as their blacksmith and quarter master? My main army quarter master and blacksmiths will be working to prepare the larger force.

"We will both be honored to serve as needed." Fataso replied, speaking for Masque as well.

"Then you are dismissed. Begin your duties." King Aalan said, and with that, the audience was over.

Members of the Royal guard came in and escorted Fataso and Masque off to await their messages and orders from the King. Leaana was led off with the queen and spent the day answering questions and satisfying the queen's curiosity.

The next few days were spent preparing to leave. Leaana was going on to meet up with her brother on the way to Larin. Fataso would leave with the Subartan caravan soon on their trip back south. Masque was being given a crash course in Elven military policy so he could serve as quartermaster for the upcoming mission.

The day came for Leaana to depart. She again walked out of the city and found a secluded place. Removed her clothes, placed them into her pack, transformed, and almost instantly leapt into the air. Flying to meet her brother and help him begin their next story.

Chapter 59

Sagan sat mounted on Karr. He looked at the group before him. Eleven hunters and fifteen other families had agreed to join him as he rebuilt Larin. He had his saddlebags full, his bow tied to his saddle, Carameth across his back. A lead rope was tied from his saddle to Kada. He was taking Leaana her horse and Kada was serving as a pack horse. She was laden with food, clothes, and building materials. Several of the families brought their dwellings with them, just like the people did in the past when they were nomads. They had never stopped building homes that could be moved easily. It was a part of their culture.

All total there were about fifty men, women and children set to depart. He could smell their fear. By now they had all heard of the goblins, orcs, and ogres that had originally destroyed Larin, and they were all afraid of what awaited them. They were also excited about the opportunity of travel and being able to build a new encampment. Sagan understood their fear, and their excitement. He did not know what awaited them. How would they deal with the goblin threat, how would they establish a thriving encampment? He wished he was better with words so he could assure them or even say something meaningful at this moment.

As he sat making sure everyone was ready Mayan rode up beside him. His horse laden with belongings and his dwelling.

"What are you doing Mayan? The encampment needs you." Sagan asked.

"I am going with you at least for a while until another healer arrives. With the threat you described from the Goblins you may need my skills. Besides I could use a bit of an adventure." Mayan grinned and shook Sagan's hand.

"Now why don't you say a few words and get us moving."

Sagan thought but still didn't know what to say but as he had to say something he just started talking, "Thank you. I can smell that you are scared and excited. I am too. Togan and I will do our best to lead you and keep you safe. We have a long way to go so let's get started." Sagan turned his horse and began to ride off. Togan started running out in front, taking up his normal position of scout. Mayan kicked his horse up and caught up with Sagan.

"Well done. I don't know if I would have talked about smelling everyone, but it was short and to the point. Which gives them confidence that is the type of leader you will be. And that is a very good thing. I am proud to be going with you." Mayan said. He then dropped back slightly behind Sagan, and they listened to the sounds of the settlers behind them talking excitedly as they all began their journey.

The End.

Epilogue

Carnell stood on the platform looking over the army below. Parts of the army were practicing marching and group attack maneuvers. Other groups were practicing combat and fighting. The entire ground below him was covered in activity. Spinel approached.

"It's Time Sir," Spinel said.

Carnell stepped off the platform and followed Spinel back to a white tent. There lying just inside the shade of the tent was Basara. Her arm bandaged from where the arrow had been removed. Her ankle and been straightened and set and the wound in her side stitched closed. She was pale, her green orc skin nearly white. Her features were sunken, and she was weak, but she lived. Carmel knelt beside his love and took her hand.

"Rest Basara. Rest and recover. Once you are healed and ready, we will act. I swear to you the Goblin Birth is nearly over. Soon the Goblin War will begin."